I0584268

Second Edition published June 2021
Published by Indies United Publishing House, LLC
Cover art designed by Damonza

Hardback: 978-1-64456-310-6
Paperback: 978-1-64456-311-3
Mobi: 978-1-64456-312-0
ePub: 978-1-64456-313-7
AudioBook: 978-1-64456-314-4

Library of Congress Control Number: 2021937933

INDIES UNITED PUBLISHING HOUSE, LLC
P.O. BOX 3071
QUINCY, IL 62305-3071
www.indiesunited.net

To the ones who got away. Don't go back. Ever.

Thanks, Jayne! You made it better. As usual.

And if you want to make *your* books better, go here:
https://www.bookaholiceditor.com/

SOUTHERN GOTHIC

D. KRAUSS

INDIES UNITED PUBLISHING HOUSE, LLC

Chapter 1

Friday at noon

Butch's voice crackled over the phone line. "I bought the house."

Art didn't have to ask which one.

"Hello? Did you hear me?"

Art did. Too clearly, despite the line noise. "Are you on a cell phone?" he asked.

"No. Payphone. In Enterprise."

"Payphone? You found a payphone?"

Art could almost see Butch's shrug. "In Enterprise."

Of course. "Why aren't you on your cell?"

"No service. Why are you asking me stupid questions?"

"Seems appropriate," Art said, "given your news. So, here's another- why the eff did you buy the house?"

Now Butch was silent. "I don't know," he finally said, "Just something I had to do."

"Does Cindy know?"

"No."

"She's going to kill you."

"I know." A pause. "Don't tell her."

"Think I have a death wish?"

Butch chuckled, then silence, pregnant with obvious and stark truths, such as purchasing a house in these bad times in an especially bad location, let's say, for example, anywhere within five hundred miles of Enterprise, Alabama, wasn't all that smart, Butchie boy. And preachers don't make all that much money, so now you're carrying an extra, unnecessary debt, brother o'mine, but that's neither here nor there. Butch's eyes had drifted south for thirty, forty years now and stark truths had never deterred him from doing other stupid things. Becoming a preacher, for instance. No need, then, for Art to voice the obvious, that Butch had made an emotional and quite idiotic investment. Maybe if he had bought the house to live in it... but that would be insane.

"I'm going to live in it," Butch said.

Anyone in the dispatch office looking at Art right then might think a sledgehammer had just reached out of the phone and stroked him. "What?"

"It's in pretty bad shape," Butch continued, as though this was a normal conversation. "The windows are gone and I think there's some foundation issues, so I want you to come down and help me."

Second sledgehammer stroke. "What?"

Butch hesitated. "I'll pay you."

Suuure he would. The eagle screamed whenever Butch let go of a quarter.

Art absorbed all this and then rendered judgment. "Are you out of your fucking mind?"

"No." But even Butch didn't sound convinced.

Art mentally scanned the infinite number of proper objections to this most hare-brained of Butch's hare-brained ideas and summarized them in one inescapable fact. "The place is haunted, Butch."

"I know." A pause. "So when are you coming down?"

"I have to go to Alabama," Art said.

Linda didn't miss a beat. "You don't have to. You want to."

"Entirely wrong," he said, "Just the opposite."

At the stove, she put the last trimmings on his pot roast; the savory steam flooded the room and made Art's stomach rumble. His pot roast. His. He ate that or meatloaf or hamburger steak with mashed potatoes for dinner every day, no variation. Well, sometimes he varied, pork roast or potato pancakes, but the variants did not stray far from the original. Linda insisted on adding superfluous vegetables and he humored her by taking a spoonful or two of whatever it was, Brussels sprouts or corn, but usually it ended up scraped into Pace's dog dish.

Surety. After six hundred miles or so each day over roads sometimes dry, sometimes wet, the trailer overloaded with stone for the out trip and empty on the return, his unvaried dinner was something to count on. It had been an evolution. Adventurous when they first married some twenty years before, he'd accepted the dishes Linda pushed, salmon steak, and pastas with elaborate sauces and mixed meats and vegetables, of which she had been justifiably proud. Art had liked them, but as time dulled into a daily routine of early morning truck prep and load after wearying load, his adventures diminished, his horizons shrank, and the rest of him followed suit. He bowed to inevitabilities... more accurately, was crushed under the weight of them... and his only solace grew into an assurance of what awaited every day for every coming year for the rest of his life, including meals.

Linda didn't get it. She insisted, even now, that he try southwest chicken or fajitas or trout almondine, all of which she prepared expertly, but he just looked at it, pushed away from the table and went to Burger King. Nothing to do with her cooking because her cooking was excellent; it was the diminishing of Art's prospects, but there were no English words to properly convey the concept. Maybe the Germans had one, since they seemed to have a marvelous ability to explain whole philosophies in a single term, like *schadenfreude*, but Art didn't know anyone who spoke German.

So she made the southwest chicken or fajitas for herself and Rich and the pot roast for Art and always, always expressed the silliness of two different meals as she chalked up one more disappointment in him, which was okay. He always, always let her know how good the pot roast was, how much he appreciated her extra effort, and privately agreed with her that it was a strange thing, as he chalked up his own disappointments.

"No." She shook an agitated spoon at him. "Just the opposite of opposite. You're just like your brother."

"I am in no way like my brother."

There must have been warning in his tone because she got off that right away. "How long?"

He shrugged. "Couple of weeks. Want to go?"

She looked at him as if he were crazy and dished out dinner and set it before him, enveloping him in a savory fog and he smiled. Umm, good. "Rich!" she shouted, "dinner!" and immediately there was a "Coming!" from somewhere in the back without a concomitant thundering of feet to lend it validity. Linda would make two more calls before Art had to intervene so he took those moments to admire her handiwork: the dark brown slightly overdone slices of meat, just the way he liked them, the crater of gravy held back by walls of mashed potatoes, a pile of string beans he could tolerate. Not a fajita or almondine for miles. Mom, in his head, forty years ago: "Eat!"

"Rich!" Second warning as Linda futzed about the stove. "What about work?" she asked with her back turned.

"I can suspend my deliveries for two weeks."

"Will the quarries drop you?"

"No. I'm too good." Said with a bit more hubris than she liked and she turned and pinned him to the seat with her fear-of-poverty eye lasers.

Art inwardly shook his head because everything was always about money, wasn't it? If he were a good husband, he would work eighteen hours a day, every day of the year, never taking time off (except to drive her someplace she wanted to go, but even then, he would have to make up the hours somehow), and spend the remaining six hours left in the day doing home repairs and chores, thereby saving her the expense and time so she could blow his paychecks on more jewelry and clothes and he would never, ever buy something foolish for himself like a tool, unless it could be used directly for one of the home repairs she demanded, like installing gold and ivory marble shower tiles. If he were a good husband.

He wasn't.

"Don't worry, it'll be fine," he dismissed.

She frowned murder at him, reared back and yelled, "Rich!"

That was it, the final warning before missiles launched and Art, glad for the distraction, added his own, "Boy, get in here now!"

"All right, all right!" dopplered from the back of the house to the kitchen as big, clumsy, human feet tromped towards them, followed by four even bigger and clumsier dog feet as Pace trundled behind, a big dumb happy look on his face. Art had to smile even as he rumbled, "Boy, why do you make your mom call like that?"

"I was doing stuff." And he plopped down, staring at Art's plate. "You eatin' that again?"

Art didn't hear that last part because Rich had said exactly the same words in exactly the same tone of incredulity ever since the kid had turned eight about, what, five years ago? It was white noise by now. "Stop doing stuff when your mom calls." Art patted Pace's big dumb head. "Hello, you big dumb dog." And got a big dumb smile in return.

"Pace, outside," Linda ordered and Rich, groaning about the injustice, herded the Lab out to the porch where the dog immediately turned and pressed his big dumb face into the screen, aggrieved.

Art smiled. "Sorry, dude."

"What am I having?" Rich asked, and Linda dished chicken Florentine with great satisfaction. "Thanks, Mom, really looks good." Said with great satisfaction. Dig at Art.

"So when are you leaving?" Linda asked.

"Saturday."

"Leaving?" Rich blinked. "Where you going, Dad?"

"To see my brother."

"Uncle Butch?" Rich's eyebrows rose in hope. "Can I come?" Butch and Rich got along great, always roughhousing and reading comics to each other, at least on Butch's infrequent visits. Art never understood how his brother had a better relationship with Rich than he did.

"You have school," Linda reminded.

"Ah, Mom!" Teenager's standard objection, which had some merit. Art had realized, somewhere near the end of 7th grade, that further schooling was a waste of time. Most people could read and cipher at a fairly expert level by that point; if you can't, you're pretty much a lost cause. He didn't act on that conviction until the middle of tenth grade, because, well, habit. And Mom. And her husband, Ridge. But having already mastered math and history and English – at least, all that he considered necessary for average social functioning – through casual reading, Art no longer saw the point.

"But, but..." Mr. Ragu, Art's counselor (why do people with weird names go into education? Do they enjoy the torment?), spluttered in complete astonishment as Art signed himself out, forever, "You have a genius-level IQ!"

"So what?" Art said and walked out, forever.

Rich did not have a genius-level IQ. Or maybe he did and was simply bored. But he did not spend time casually reading math, history, and English; he spent it parked in front of the television. He was what the experts called a "visual" learner but how much larnin' can you get from *SpongeBob SquarePants*? Rich approached schooling with an air of indifference, so if there was someone who needed all the larnin' that could be squeezed out of public education, it was him. Take a look at Butch, who had attended school with an air of befuddlement but who liked going and got good grades, even though he was about as far from genius-level IQ as Rich. Proof that persistence rewards.

"You're staying here," Art gruffed around a forkful of roast. Rich glowered but said nothing. The old gunfighter had spoken.

But, uh-oh, Rich suddenly brightened, a strong indicator of a very bad idea. "Uncle Butch is still in Arizona, right?"

Art saw through this gambit immediately. Rich was angling for location as a pretext to go, since the trip would be "Educational, Dad! I could write a paper about it!" Like that would ever happen.

"Not at the moment."

"Then where is he?"

Art considered. "Hell."

Chapter 2

Monday at noon

Enterprise. Good Gawd Awlmighty.

Art stared at the Boll Weevil Monument smack in the middle of the intersection, a gleaming marble fountain supporting a coy, long-gowned Greek goddess lofting what looked like a tick on a dish. The goddess looked different from how he remembered: all white now. She used to be silver and Art wondered if local junkies had scraped it off to sell for dime bags. The goddess had often been the target of local pranksters, including Art, who must have thrown about a thousand boxes of Tide detergent into the fountain and then stood by to watch the entire intersection turn into a bubble bath. He chuckled. What else was there to do here on a Saturday night?

Everything else looked different, too. Updated. They'd put pavers down the main street and modernized some of the building facades. Progress comes to Coffee County. Art glanced over. Same crappy stores, though.

The light changed and Art gunned the Ram, the growl of the Hemi a mating call 'round these parts, and he watched a few blondie gals appraise the truck and then him as he headed down the New Brockton Road.

Still got it.

He gave himself a rearview mirror once-over: graying hair cut bullet-head short, piercing green eyes, thin eyebrows, tight, small mouth and well, yes, a bit of poundage collecting about the middle, but what do you expect for the late forties... er, early fifties? Plaid work shirt and jeans, Timberlakes. If it weren't for the New Jersey plates, he'd look like he lived here.

Lived here.

His breath stopped, just stopped, as though someone had thrown a cork down his throat. Spots swam before his eyes and

Art gasped, pulling for air while wrenching the truck over to an empty spot past a corner street, getting a few horns and "Damn Yankee!" hoots. He put the truck in park and slumped forward, massaging his neck, settling, then the mantra: "*Tranquilo, jefe. Calmate, paz, paz,*" as he slowed and breathed, slowed and breathed, the hand around his throat relaxing, the bands around his chest loosening.

Damn asthma.

Art watched the spots in front of his eyes dissolve. Not supposed to have these attacks anymore. Supposed to have outgrown them. He blinked. Well, hadn't he just driven back forty years? Wasn't he ten again?

...Art wheezes and gasps, writhing on the couch. Dad stands over him:

"Ain't nothing wrong with that boy a little hard work won't fix, so get your ass out there and start pulling them weeds!"

"Owen! He can die from this!"

"Well, he can die from this, too!" The sound of a belt being pulled. "Git!"

He'd been in the hospital a week that time; a couple of months later, week-and-a-half. Before the year ended, almost three weeks. Almost died.

Almost.

He took in the long, sweet breaths. Oxygen. His whole life had been a pursuit of oxygen. Cool the lungs, calm the blood, mountain air blowing off some glacier easing the ache in his chest, his heart, his head. It had taken years after they'd left here for his lungs to untie and his asthma to dissipate. And now he was back. And now, it was back.

Co-inkidink?

Perhaps there was a perimeter, a no-go zone, a black-gated wall circling an all-seeing eye rising from the center of a haunted house twenty or so miles from here, three or four miles outside the crapass town of Yoman. Crossing the border triggered dragons and demons and moribund asthma and the closer to the house, the more intense the attacks. Perhaps he should turn around, right now, and go back to New Jersey, the increasing distance easing the cotton in his lungs and throat until he breathed freely again.

"What the hell am I doing here?" he whispered. Indeed, what the hell?

The last time he had been here was what, ninth grade? Thereabouts. Art, tired of New Jersey and Pemberton and Mom and her new boyfriend (later husband), Ridge, and Butch and Butch's whackassed friends, had asked Dad if he could c'mon down. Dad, always game to prove to Mom how wrong she had been to leave His Wonderfulness said, "Wa'al shooore! C'mon down!" Art had lasted until Christmas and then got the hell out and vowed never, ever, upon pain of scourging with cactus whips and scorpion paddles, to cross the Alabama line ever again, much less Enterprise city limits.

And here I am.

Art braced, expecting cactus whips and scorpion paddles to fly through the windshield and scourge him but all that happened was a stiffening of his throat. He frowned. This will be a problem, so let's go home right now before the asthma wakes completely the fuck up. We'll pass this off as a mere lark, simply a couple of wasted days.

He checked the road behind him, ready to pull a U-ey, and then studied the road before him, the one to New Brockton. New Brockton. Hmm. A better town than Enterprise, that's 'fer sher,' even without a bug fountain. It was farther from Yoman, too, perhaps outside the asthma barrier. He'd had a good time there in third or fourth grade, or whatever the years were he'd attended before transferring to godawful Yoman. Be a shame to get this close and not have a look-see. Perhaps he should ease into the danger zone, find an oasis first, a cabin in the cool mountain air to rest his ravaged lungs then probe the border a bit and see if the orcs stir. It's not like anyone important was expecting him...

Gonna have to wait a bit longer, Butchie boy.

Art dropped it in first and headed straight, glancing briefly at the left turn under the bridge which would carry him to the house and Butchie and the all-seeing eye. "The power of Christ compels you," he muttered as the turn disappeared in the mirror.

Twenty minutes later, on the outskirts of New Brockton, he slowed down and cruised at a snail's pace while he stared at the neat little brick ranchers with the box hedges and backyard gardens of tomatoes and snap beans and string beans and beans beans beans because these southrons, they do love them some beans, uhm uhm uhm. Art had frequently measured a man's intelligence by how much said man waxed enthusiastic over beans, no sort of a pun intended by that.

"Yeah, boy! These about the best pinto beans I ever tasted!"

"Dad, they're just beans."

"Ain't just beans, them's food, boy! Grown yourself! You didn't have nothin' else you'd be eating them up!"

"But we do." Art unwraps a Pop-Tart, completely bored with the conversation.

"That's why you're so fat, boy!"

That stung. That really stung and Art gritted his teeth. Okay, gonna have to endure a lot of such memories over the next few days. Deal with it.

Art had reached the middle of the town and there, on the left, New Brockton School. "Well, well." Art pulled into the drive and stopped in front of the double doors. "Well, well," he repeated and peered around for a visitor parking spot. None. And no one about so, stay here.

Art pulled out his Nokia, rather surprised to see two bars. From what Butch had said, he figured he'd need to find a payphone, a dimmer prospect here than in Enterprise. He hit the button and heard it ringing, again rather surprised. Figured the two bars were spoofs. "Would you believe," he said to the person who answered, "that I'm now parked in front of my old elementary school?"

She giggled. "Really? I didn't know they had schools in Alabama."

"That's funny, that's funny. Know what else they have? Monuments to bugs."

"What?"

So he told her about the local cotton farmers getting wiped out by the boll weevil, so they switched to peanuts and got rich and one day, sitting around scratching themselves, said, 'Ya know, Hiram, if tweren't for that there boll weevil, we's be poor!' and the monument was born and she laughed out loud but then had to hang up because people were looking at her suspiciously. "Call me back when you can. Goodbye." And Art clicked off in a better mood.

"He'p ya?"

Startled, Art looked to the passenger window. A blond, thin-haired, squinty-eyed guy of about sixty or seventy leaned in, his Resource Officer badge clacking against the sill.

Art held up a placating palm. "Uh, no, sorry. I was just driving by. Used to go here."

Squinty blinked, a barely discernible motion. "Was a while ago, right?"

Thanks, asshole. "Yeah, quite a while."

"All the way from New Jersey to pay us all a visit, huh?"

"Well, no, not really."

"So watcha doin' here?" Said kindly, with promised violence if Officer Squinty didn't like the answer.

Good question, Oshifer. I'm avoiding demons, avoiding memories, trying to get my breath back. But those probably wouldn't suffice as legit answers. "Like I said, just riding by." Art gestured at the school. "Do they allow visitors?"

"Only if you got some business." Officer Squinty eyed him, as best as possible. "You got some business?"

Art considered. "Yes. Unfinished." He nodded and gently pulled away. A couple of wrong turns later, he parked behind the school with a fairly decent view of the back field. Art took out a forbidden cigarette and lit it, blowing a smoke stream out of the window. A Raleigh, Dad's favorite brand, not because they were any good but because he got coupons off every pack. Collected enough to get a set of patio furniture. Way he and Mom smoked, they should have gotten a house, a car, and a world cruise. Art bought a carton when he gassed up in Virginia, just for the memory, and had already smoked half of it, just because he could. No Linda and Rich to give him crap about it. His renewed asthma did give him crap about it, but go screw yourself.

He blew a smoke ring at the field. Good times there playing soldier and tag and football and baseball with his buddies Crawford and Lang and Stick and... who was that guy, the short little punk who played probably the best game of basketball ever? Tony. Yeah, that's it. His best friend in third grade here. Odd how you forget things like that.

Forget things.

Art frowned around the cigarette. Now he remembered: he'd gone to New Brockton for just one year, not two, third grade only and then on to Yoman School for some reason or other involving district lines; he rarely ever saw New Brockton after that because Dad and Mom had no reason to come here. Mom shopped on Ft. Rucker and Dad preferred the stores in Enterprise. Yet Art remembered this town with greater fondness than the others.

Because things hadn't happened then.

...A cloud slipped over the sun and it was midnight and cold and maybe rainy and Art was at a wavy glass window squinting through the water and bad optics and there were some kind of lights back there at the pool. What were they doing?

What were they doing?

"Ouch!" Art flapped his hand in reaction to burning ash reaching his finger and sparks flew everywhere around the cab and he stomped and slapped and cursed at them, because damnation, he didn't want to burn a hole in the upholstery. Again. A woman came out of a house and stood, arms akimbo, staring at him; if the sheriff came along and snagged him and then talked to Officer Squinty... well, he'd just disappear down some dark hole, wouldn't he?

Art slapped at other possible smolders, started the truck, waved at the woman, and drove off.

Chapter 3

Monday afternoon

Art stared through the windshield at the Damascus School, amazed. It looked exactly as it did in 1969: a godawful eyesore brooding in the middle of a parking lot made of weeds and dust and broken concrete – hardly a parking lot at all – shimmering in the heat waves like a desert mirage, a paint-peeled disaster of sun-bleached clapboard walls underscoring busted-out windows and rusted-metal roof, its giant gaping double-door entrance looming over broken concrete steps, acres and acres of meandering unplanned structure. All falling down.

But not fallen.

By now, someone should have (a) knocked it down (b) burned it down or (c) replaced it with something more serviceable. Like a peanut warehouse. But, no. Still here. Still crap.

Art got out, the sledgehammer of boiling air making him gasp. Man, this place. It's not even May yet and already the world melts. He wiped his brow with the back of his hand and did a slow three-sixty. Fields, crap, distant collapsed barn, more fields, more crap, and then Damascus School.

That's why no one's done anything to this place. How else would you know where you are?

Art hadn't as he felt his way out of New Brockton, the unremembered roads triggering no familiarity, only knowing that the house and Yoman were Off Thataways somewhere, so he'd headed Off Thataways, certain he would end up in Mordor and then he spotted the blurry abandoned hulk and headed towards it. The Damascus School oriented him. He now knew that Butch, the house, the black gates, and retriggered asthma were about a mile Over Yonder, as the carrion crow flies from rytch hyeah.

Right here.

Unhurried, Art walked towards the steps, shading his eyes at the shadowed entrance. No orcs; at least, none that he could see. He tested the bottom step with a boot heel; some dangerous softness to it, but it seemed like it would hold. Hold? Why? You seriously thinking of going in there?

Art shook out a Raleigh and lit it to help him decide. Judging by the visible rot, entering was a life-threatening prospect. Roof could come down or floor collapse, and Gawd knows how many noxious and evil critters made the place home.

But he'd lost something in there, not sure exactly what, and he'd like to get it back. Whatever it was. Whatever the danger.

He took in a big puff and swirled a cloud of cancer overhead as he carefully selected those steps promising solidity and mounted. He stood at the gap, gingerly tested the floor and, when it didn't break, planted his feet on the other side. He blinked in the sudden darkness, letting his eyes adjust.

Man.

As empty now as it was back then. No lockers, no wall hangings, no trophy cases, none of the standard school fare. A big blank. Dust and dirt and occasional graffiti of the 'Mary Loves John' type, dating it to a more innocent age, way back when white men were white men and everyone else was nervous.

Art drifted along the hall. The boards groaned but held. Good workmanship way back in them thar twenties. They built Damascus back then as a School for Colored People, a genteel way for the Coffee County Public School system to ensure its white chilluns were never sullied by black ones, everything going along reasonably well and innocuous and see no evil until the fifties and court orders and new ways of thinking brought everyone together... he shuddered, remembering the brutal integration of Yoman School... then sat empty, until Dad got a 'holt' of it.

It grew darker the farther inside he went and Art pulled out his cell phone. Two bars still... wow, Butch, your phone sucks... and he scrolled through an updated listing of missed calls, voicemails, and texts, mostly from Rich. Later for those and Art turned the ghostly phone light down the hall, the auditorium entrance glowing faintly in the distance.

Art walked down to it and stood. The double doors, off their hinges, lay dumped to the side. Someone must have been pissed off. Or pissed drunk. He swept the ghost light around, the glow barely reaching the far side and made worse by the screen dimming every few moments until Art tapped it back to brightness, creating an eerily strobed floor-scape of indistinct piles of crap, maybe old school desks, or old amplifiers and guitars, tossed away in fits of rockgasmic rage, dissolving over the years into sawdust and metal.

"DOO DOO DUT! DO DUT! DOO DOO DUT! DO DUT!" Art bellowed the wondrous guitar riff from 'Louie Louie', satisfied when a little dust fell from the ceiling. Every band that ever played here either led with that or reached it within five songs, making it the most-covered Top Forty hit within a fifty-mile radius.

"Each night, at ten, I see her again. I FUCK HER, oh yeah! All by myself!" Art sang the illegal lyrics, the ones denied by every music publisher but which every kid growing up in the sixties knew by heart. He expected, any moment, for hordes of Baptist preachers to burst through the door and rend him for his blasphemy, in the same manner they rent the Friday night dances held here. But, silence. Of course. No need to re-burn scorched earth.

Art reached the stage and rolled over the edge, stood, dusted off, and marveled that still nothing collapsed. C'mon, how much stress is necessary before the abandoned and neglected succumbs? A lesson in this, perhaps. He shone the cell light around then closed his eyes and became ten years old. No, eleven...

...

Standing here while some peanut-farmer band with homemade gee-tars, slapped-together amps and three-piece drums set up behind him, "Watch it, kid!" Watching Dad at a fold-up table half blocking the entrance waaaay over there, taking dollar bills and issuing tickets. "Why's he doing this?"

Butch, trying to help with the instruments but proving more nuisance than roadie, shrugged. "Money."

...

Which, for Dad, neutralized all convictions. Not more than a week prior, Butch had cranked up WBAM as the Kinks wailed about who's got who and to what degree and he and Art and Cindy danced up and down the living room lip-synching at ear-shattering volumes and Dad came in screaming like an Alabama thunderstorm, "Turn that hippie shit off!" But look at this: Dad, waaay over there, about to make fifty bucks off that hippie shit.

How he got into it, Art had no idea, but somehow Dad acquired rights to the tumble-down school and rewired it and put up advertisements and signed some bands and here, in the middle of godawful nowhere Alabama, live rock music and dancing, every Friday night, courtesy of Turn-that-hippie-shit-off Dad. Sitting over there in his suit, smiling as if he liked kids and rock and dancing, as if he were cool and with-it and the little girls, the pre-teen girls flocked around him and then, and then...

The band, despite Butch's assistance, got everything plugged in and looked at each other and hit the first notes of 'Wipe Out' and the floor jumped and girls screamed and Butch was in the middle of it all in his stupid Nehru shirt and love beads and crew cut and horn-rimmed glasses having the epileptic fit he called dancing in front of some very surprised older girl and Art was pushed off the stage and into the crush and somehow dancing too and it was loud and crazy and fun and wonderful and 'Louie! Louie! Do you really have to go?'

Every Friday night.

And then...

...The Baptists raged against the Damascus School Friday Night Devil Music and scheduled mandatory Friday night services, you youngin's attend or else; the church ladies with the pointy glasses and gingham sack dresses and dried-up cunts, their eyes narrowed, sneered and clucked and cold-shouldered Mom and Art in the Piggly Wiggly. Art was worried but no one else cared; they laughed at the Holy Rollers, the Devil Music Friday Nights continued with defiant kids ranged across the dance floor while the peanut-farmer front men roared words of sin and abomination, the guitars twangy and drums too loud and they all danced and sang and it wasn't the Baptists and their dried-up cunt legions that killed it, not at all...

Art stopped breathing. Fearfully, he spun about, sure the ghost of some outrage would rise through the floor to exact a terrible revenge. Art settled on the auditorium entrance where Dad's desk and suit were. The dark shifted. Not a ghost. A demon. Art watched it move against the back shadows and lean in his direction and grin Dad's grin of rot and fire and death. Then it was gone.

Blood thumped in his temples but it wasn't 'Mony Mony'; it

was the risen beast, the constrictor around his chest squeezing, squeezing... spots in front of his eyes and Art gasped. "Dammit. Dammit all," he squeaked and went down to one knee. Air, please God, air. Calmate, tranquilo... The spots browned and faded and his lungs opened and the pounding thinned and Art took in the long sweet breaths. After a while, he stood and clumsily dismounted the stage, concerned when a board gave partial way but held. Hadn't reached breaking point yet.

He went back to the truck, not looking at the school. He considered a cigarette but, no. Things long thought dead had reasserted themselves.

Butch, what have you done?

Silly question. He's re-opened Dracula's tomb.

Chapter 4

Monday afternoon, still

Up ahead, the intersection of Hell Street and Hades Avenue.

Art headed towards the distant stop sign marking the midnight crossroads where souls were bought, lives bargained, and the devil man's dog howled in the ditch. Go straight across the intersection, end up in Yoman, town of the soulless and lost. Turn left and before you know it, back at Enterprise, town of... bug monuments. Turn around for the Damascus School and peanut-farmer bands. Turn right...

Turn right.

Art coasted to the stop sign as slowly as possible, not worried about impeding traffic because there was none. Afternoon of a workday, all the locals were in the fields. People 'round hyeah worked hyeah, not in offices or factories, because the people hyeah owned their land generation to generation and pulled their livelihood out of the red dirt generation after generation, proud sons of the soil and the south, centuries of inbreeding evident in stunted limbs and harelips and albino-red eyes good only for squinting at dirt clods while sniffing manure and staring at their hogs with bad intent. Art chuckled grimly as he eased to a stop.

He fished out a cigarette and lit it and regarded Bark's Store across the road, or what was left of Bark's Store: remnants of cement walls sagging off a concrete foundation but still upright due to a couple of strategically connected roof beams; two rusty halves of old gas pumps in front, the ruined legs of Ozymandias.

"Look upon my works and despair," he whispered. Now what the heck happened here? Bark's had been a good little country store, an add-on to the Bark's ramshackle house, best place to get candy and soda pop on a hot spring day like this one. It was a waypoint, like the Damascus School; everyone knew Bark's Store.

Now? Bark's ruins.

Art's eyes drifted to the right... No, don't look! the devil man will take your soul. But he couldn't help it, because every Saturday morning he, Butch and Cindy, weekly allowance in hand, trotted up the shoulder from the bottom of the hill all the way up here, dodging pickups until they reached the devil man's crossroads and then scurried over and piled inside Bark's, the *sproooing* of the screen door announcing them.

The store itself was about two feet by three, an Escher print of seemingly endless treats piled on top and around and sideways, jars of penny candy lined up like a firing squad on the counter in front of a 400-pound cash register from the turn of the 19th century, cascading displays of Hershey bars and Paydays intermingled with chewing tobacco and gum and bread and peanut butter, freezers and shelves all crammed together in the space of a phone booth.

Wispy haired Mr. Bark, wizened and tobacco-brown and wrinkled like a fielder's glove, perched behind the register on a metal stool held together more by prayer than engineering, gold pince-nez balanced on his nose, presiding over the chaos with nods and smiles. While Art stuffed his pockets with Mary Janes and Fireballs, Butch and Cindy gathered Push-ups and Fudgsicles and Yoohoos and RC Cola. Coins exchanged and commerce completed, Mr. Bark smiled and nodded and clattered nickels and *sproooing,* they were outside.

Jammed together on the stone garden bench tilted dangerously in the shade of the mimosa tree in the Bark's front yard, they slurped and chewed and fussed at each other. The Bark's had a big Chow dog that stood bear-like in front of them seeking his chances, black tongue at the ready, Art delightfully disgusted whenever the dog licked his hands with that obscene looking thing. "Ewww!" but nonetheless kept his Fudgsicle within dog-tongue range. Perversity was a hallmark of kid-ness.

Mrs. Bark, as wide as her husband was lean, stood on her porch wearing a sunbonnet five times too big for her head, her chicken-feed-sack print gingham dress unable to cover her old-lady slip, arms akimbo and frowning at them, probably convinced chilluns should be doing better things on hot days than eating sweets and rotting their teeth and turning into butterballs.

"That's why you're so fat, boy!"

Art brushed that away. He'd never understood Mrs. Bark's

attitude because the Deats kids augmented her livelihood. Maybe that's why the mimosa and the bench were now gone; her judgments had driven off the customers. The wreck of the store was her cautionary tale. Which made no sense because the devil man's crossroads was a primo location and there should be some kind of store here. Some kind. Where else could the field hands 'round hyeah go for a bag of peanuts and a chaw when they finished plowing the cows or planting the chickens? Yoman had a store – at least, it used to. Maybe that's gone, too – but Yoman was off yonder and Enterprise was thisaway and Damascus and its Friday night dances thataway and here was...

Here was.

Art watched ghost clouds suddenly cover the world and ghost rain fall on three blurry figures struggling with suitcases up the side of the road heading for Bark's, but not for candy or soda, oh no, for safety, while the fat one on the end cried tears more obvious than the rain and screamed at the other two, "Why? Why?"

Why?

A car horn behind almost blew Art through the windshield and he jerked around to see a pickup truck and for a second, just a second, it was a yellow Ford with a demon driving... but no, no it's a Silverado with some guy wearing a white shirt and tie impatiently tapping the horn at him and damn, damn what is happening? He reeled and unconsciously yanked the wheel to the right and tapped the pedal, and headed down the hill.

Into the devil man's arms.

The Silverado followed him, right off his bumper the whole time, and the driveway was only a few hundred yards away and Art was on it before he recovered his breath. What do I do? What do I do? Race down the road towards Elba, then make the big country-square-block turn back towards New Brockton then Enterprise and then New Jersey and never, ever come back, that's what you do. Instead, he slammed the brakes, grinning when the white-shirt guy blanched and braked hard, and Art heeled the Ram and pulled in. The Silverado kept going; the guy glared as he passed but Art had forgotten about him because he was here.

Here.

"Abandon hope," he muttered then stared.

My God.

The once-smooth driveway was a mess of rock and clay, two ruts of bare raw ground clearing a path through it. Good thing he brought the truck. To his right was a barren wiregrass field covered with maypops and briars and poke salad, haven of quail and snakes.

What the hell?

The thousand or more slash pines that used to cover the field so thickly it was almost impossible to get a lawnmower through there were gone. Finito. Vanished. Some previous owner must have sold the trees for lumber. Art felt an odd pang in his chest for the games of hide-and-seek that used to take place in there.

To his left, the Leyland cypress trees screening the house had grown wild and insane and grappled with each other in a chorus line of bum fights. Spanish moss and kudzu draped over and through them and across the driveway, even into the ruts, a solid green-and-gray wall of anarchy. Art couldn't catch even a glimpse of the house through it. He'd have to continue up the driveway to do so. He didn't move.

Art sucked in as much of the cigarette as he could and then pitched the butt out of the window right into a blocking cypress and waited for it to catch fire. No such luck. He sat back and gazed up the rise at a pile of cement-block-and-roof-shingle rubble where a two-story garage should be. Vine-covered and washed out, it had been a pile of rubble for quite some time. Art pulled out another cigarette but didn't light it.

Your handiwork, Daddy.

Dad had erected the monstrosity of a garage on weekends and afternoons, with an incredible amount of screaming and hitting and beating of his two assistants, Art and Butch. Took about a year. As a result, Art developed impressive construction skills. Butch didn't. Years later, driving cranes and cement trucks and erecting two-story garages for pay instead of under threat, Art realized Dad was shoddy, a corner cutter, a cheap-ass motivated to improve property for minimum cost. Hence, the current state of rubble.

The upstairs of the garage became Art and Butch's bedroom, which was a vast improvement over their previous bedroom, the den. Up here they had their unbunked bunk beds set as far apart from each other as possible, with a nightstand and several decrepit chests of drawers filled with sweaters and crap Mom didn't want

21

to throw away set between them as a buffer. And Dad's extensive Playboy collection, started in the early 'fifties, which Dad made no effort to hide. Perhaps he thought they'd be educational, and he was right. The magazines made the nightly dangerous trek from the house to the garage room worth it. Art remembered bedtimes on cold and rainy winter nights when Butch and he ran from the house to the precariously built back stairs, both heedlessly pounding up the shaking and wet and swaying too-wide steps, both terrified, sure vampires converged on them from the miasmic woods, Butch urging him on as Art's lungs closed. They'd slam the door and lean against it, gasping, knowing full well it was no proof against werewolves. Jump under the magic covers with the comfort of Miss January 1956, safe from the undead, locked in, isolated.

Just the way Dad wanted it.

Art took his foot off the brake and slowly drifted up the ruts. A nondescript Ford sedan with Arizona plates sat catty-corner to the garage rubble. So, Butch was here, somewhere. The cypresses petered out the closer he got to the end and the cement block washhouse in the backyard materialized, roofless but still standing. Of course. Dad hadn't built it; it was there when they moved in. Dad did replace the roof, though, so there you go.

And then Art was at the top of the driveway. No hiding anymore: he turned full in his seat and stared at the house.

My God.

It was more or less intact. The roof was still on, shingles missing here and there but serviceable, which was a surprise because about the second year they lived here, Dad had, with an incredible amount of screaming and hitting and beating of his two assistants, Art and Butch, replaced the existing roof. Some subsequent owner must have replaced Dad's replacement. The landscaping had run wild but in an odd direction, away from the house. Fleeing evil. The screened-in porch enclosing the back door was still there, minus the screens. And the ceiling fan. And the steps. But still there. The back door was not. Instead, a gaping portal, black and corrupt, hung there. The portal rippled and extended and grew teeth. And smiled.

Art goosed the truck and was on the Ford before he knew it. His breath trembled and he gripped the wheel far too hard. Fearfully, he glanced over his left shoulder expecting dead things to shamble towards him, but only the back of the house glowed in the afternoon sun, most of the asbestos tiles still attached, holes where the back windows used to be. Skull eyes.

An odd motion behind the washhouse caused Art to brace for zombies but it remained in one place, rhythmic flashes of shadow and sun. He shut down the truck and got out.

Wow. Hot.

Should get back in the truck and run for the border with the a/c cranked rather than go see what zombies are doing behind the washhouse, but then he would have wasted a three-day drive. He walked around the far side, keeping the washhouse between him and the main house.

Butch, shirtless, badly sunburned, not even wearing a hat, the idiot, was in a waist-deep hole with a too-short shovel in both hands, a pile of red clay and rock next to him. He straightened and did an exaggerated back bend then gawked at Art. "There you are."

"Yeah. Here I am." Art made a big show of lighting the cigarette; he knew how much that irritated Butchie. "What are you doing?"

Butch shovel-pointed at the washhouse. "I'm trying to restart the well."

"At the risk of being repetitive, what are you doing?" Art punctuated that last with an enormous cloud of Raleigh blown right at Hatless Boy. "Specifically, what does digging a random hole in the yard have to do with restarting the well?"

Butch frowned at the smoke cloud enveloping him but said nothing, looked at the hole and then the blockhouse and then helpless. A slight shake of the head.

"Get out of the hole," Art ordered and took an end of the proffered shovel, pulled Butch out and then pitched the shovel contemptuously away and went into the blockhouse, Butch at his shoulders. "You have to do it in here."

"Dig?"

"No, you idiot, reprime the pump." Art examined the rusted piece of junk tilted precariously in the center of the slab. "That's the pump?"

"What's left of it."

"Good God." Art was momentarily speechless. "Do you even know if there's water down there?"

"I'm assuming."

"Ass out of you and me, ya know?" Art briefly wondered how all the common-sense genes had managed to bypass his brother. "All right, this is a non-starter. You'll need to get someone out here to plumb the well and see if it's viable. If it is, we have to replace the pump. Probably have to clean out the well first. Gonna cost a fortune."

"I thought you could do it."

"I could, but I'd go to jail. Lots of rules on water. Is there water in the house?"

"Just bottled."

"Great." Art stepped outside, losing the shade offered by the one or two ceiling beams stretching across the washhouse. He took a long drag, savoring the smoke, and cast a sideways look at the house. The missing-window skull eyes glared back at him. Why are you here, they asked.

Decent question.

"I'm thirsty," Butch said, pushing past and Art followed because a drink would be great. Something about 110 proof. Butch stepped onto the remains of the screened-in porch, picking his way carefully. Art saw why. Loose concrete chunks mined the dangerously cracked pad. Easy to turn an ankle here, so he picked his way just as carefully. Butch tromped right on through the doorway teeth, apparently blind to the slobber running down the sides. Art did not want to be eaten, so he stayed just out of bite range. From there, he saw that the kitchen flooring had buckled. Not a long fall to the ground, but breaking through might trap him for God-knows-what living under there. Zombies.

So ya gonna stand here all night playing switch?

Art put a hesitant toe across the doorway and stopped dead. A pulse under the ruined floor throbbed under his foot. Something ugly and detestable licked its lips. Come closer, boy...

"You all right?"

Art opened his eyes. Butch leaned against the remnants of their old kitchen counter, a sweating water bottle in his hand. Art looked down at his feet. He still hadn't cleared the threshold. He didn't want to lose his soul. Butch raised eyebrows, poking the bottle at him.

"Yeah," Art said, stepped across and lost his soul.

Odd sensation, that, like vertigo, as he slipped moorings and

24

balance and certainty. The floors solidified, the kitchen swirled bright and yellow with sanded pine cabinets and a humming refrigerator and blinky overhead neon lights. Little Art stood at the chrome sink, the faucet running, the glass forgotten in his hand as he furrowed a brow because outside through the window, back beyond the washhouse, at the above-ground pool, something moved. What was that?

Time whirled again and he put out a hand to steady himself on the door frame, felt noxious substances there and hastily pulled away, swaying. Butch, alarmed, urged the bottle on him but Art shook his head, took the last drag on the cigarette, then deliberately threw it down on the crap floor.

Butch goggled. "You'll burn the place down!"

"Good."

Butch *tsk*ed then spilled a little water on the sparks, stamping on them with his heel. Art pushed past him to the center of the kitchen and did a three-sixty.

Man, the place's trashed.

Half of what was once the kitchen door leaned across what was once a floor-to-ceiling pantry, its own folding fan door hanging precariously by one hinge.

Looks like somebody had kicked their way in with little concern for getting caught. Well, yeah, who would notice? The zombies? The door kickers did a good job ransacking the place.

The sink was gone, the pantry shelves, most of the old counter and anything that even remotely looked like it had wiring. Everything was gone, taken for the scrap value. The whole house was nothing but scrap value.

He stepped past the splintered half counter into what had been the den. The floor groaned and bent and Art stopped, letting it settle. A couple of rusted pipes stuck out of the floor where the gas heater used to be. Mold rendered the walls streaky black, broken sheetrock here and there trying to hide behind torn wallpaper draping over it. The skull eyes stared back at him from where the double windows used to be. No doubt those followed the sink to the scrapyard.

Piles of plastic sheets lay wadded up underneath the empty window frames. Art didn't know if the vandals had left them or Butch intended to jury-rig substitutes. Didn't want to know. Didn't care.

Art looked down at the floor. Right about here there'd been a fold-out couch that had served as Butch's and his bed until Dad finished the garage and banished them both to its upstairs room bunk beds and Playboy collection. Every night they'd fought for what little sleeping space a double-sized one-inch-deep crappy fold-up mattress offered, a fight Art generally lost because Butch was bigger and stronger. Back then.

Could take him now. Easily.

Folded up, the couch became a place of GI Joes and soldiers and early morning wrestling matches until Dad or Mom yelled, "Knock it off! You'll be late for school!" They grabbed lunch pails (Art's was Batman and Robin), ran out of the porch and down the driveway, still dark, the red bus lights flashing on the Damascus Highway. Nighttime, they did homework at the little built-in desk and shelves set against the wall opposite the couch. Butch and he sat side-by-side sneering at each other because Butch was two grades ahead and supposed to be smarter. Art tested him on dates and facts and crowed when Butch got them wrong, once crossing out Butch's math homework with a pen and forcing him to do it again because Butch was supposed to be smarter and wasn't, just wasn't, so there, jackass.

And then, bedtime. Fold out the couch, drop the mattress without catching fingers in the metal frame, turn off the lights, the attic fan pulling in cool air through the window...

...then the noises.

Art gazed towards the bathroom at the end of the hall. No door. No bathroom fixtures, either, layers of cracked tile the only clue to its former function. Two bedrooms flanked it: the one on the left was Mom and Dad's, the right, Cindy's, their doors gone, too. The noises came from those rooms. Sometimes it was Mom and Dad groaning and grunting and one night, Art called out, "What's that?"

"Dog under the house," Dad snarled back, "Now go to sleep!"

Funny now. Not then.

Sometimes other noises: Mom weeping. Cindy, in her bedroom, weeping.

Lots of weeping in this house.

Butch appeared next to him, still holding out a water bottle. "Messy, I know." Art grasped it with trembly fingers and took a big swig. He gasped at the cold and settled, settled.

"Bit of an understatement."

Butch laughed. "Yeah, I know. Gonna take some work."

Art's turn to laugh, but with no humor. "There's no amount of work will set this place right. It should be condemned. Leveled. Buried." He took another swig. "Forgotten."

Butch said nothing. Art tipped the bottle, finished it, then pitched it contemptuously towards the bathroom. It rolled around with a startling amount of noise and Art braced for a zombie to come screaming out of the floor, red-veined eyes fixed on him.

"Just gonna have to pick that up later," Butch observed.

"Be my guest," Art said, pushed past and went outside to his truck.

Butch hovered at his shoulder. "Are you leaving?" He was worried.

"No." Although he should. "I'm just getting my tools."

"What are we working on?"

Art paused. "Everything."

Chapter 5

Monday evening

By almost sunset, Art had the porch and its steps re-formed and re-set, using a couple of leftover bags of Quikrete he happened to have in the back of the truck. He'd have finished earlier, but Butch had helped. Art smoothed off the last corner, exasperated. "Did you seriously believe you could do all this by yourself?"

"Nooo," Butch sang while dusting far more 'krete off his arms than he got into the wheelbarrow. "I know I suck. I was banking on you helping me, and, really, thanks. Thanks so much."

Art snorted, "Dude, this is just a porch. This is just grunt work. If you're stymied by this, how in the hell did you plan to get the pump running?"

Butch threw 'I don't know' hands.

"Well, that has to be next." Art grabbed one of the last water bottles left in the cooler, poured it on a hand towel and wiped his face. "You can't use bottled water for all this work. That will make this one of the most expensive repair jobs in history."

Butch smiled. "And the toniest."

"*Phfft.*" Art grimaced. "Right. But then you'll have to change brands, not this generic crap out of the Pig Wig." Art gestured at the small mountain of plastic bottles off to the side.

"Schweppes?"

Art chuckled and didn't want to. Butch was the Funny Guy again, easing all the fear and worry through jokes: hey, things are bad, I know, but we can have a laugh.

Always had a laugh ready, didn't you, Mr. Saturday Night, got-a-millyun-ub-em, hey'd'ja hear the one about...?

Butch frowned at him. "What's wrong?"

Art said nothing, threw the towel on the ground and pointed at the porch. "Don't touch that. I'm going to find a well drilling company." He marched over to his truck, got in and rummaged around until he found the Nokia, flipped it like a stiletto and admired it for a second.

Only the best for our boys.

..."*What do you need that for?*" *Linda screeched just as she did every single time Art bought something he needed, like a brand new Ram truck and a brand new table saw.*

"*Because I need it.*" *His stock response and she should be glad...*

Because this thing was 3G and he could now sit here and look for a phone number instead of wasting gas driving around looking for a phone book. At least, he *should* be able to. One bar, and barely that.

Jeez! We in Bumfuckistan or something? Christ on a crutch, this is the Yew Ess of Aay! Allegedly. Maybe he should delete all of Rich's annoying texts that were crowding memory. Keep the other texts. The not-annoying ones.

Some 2G pages loaded, which took freakin' forever, but they dropped a few times and he hastily wrote down phone numbers during the few minutes he was in contact with the civilized world then made calls and an appointment when he had enough bars to do so. Took freakin' forever. By the time he emerged from the truck, the sun was down on the ground. He fished for a cigarette. "They'll be here day after tomorrow."

Butch sat on a stump located on the shade side of the washhouse playing swordfight with some Johnson grass, two coolers next to him: the one they'd used for the job open and upside down on the ground, the other open and right-side up and filled with slush and water bottles. Apparently, he'd pulled the slush one out of the house while Art was on the phone, which meant the idiot had done exactly what Art said not to do.

Good Lord.

Shaking his head, Art walked over and examined the porch – all intact – which meant Butch must have executed some rather extraordinary gyrations over the steps and around the cement repair while balancing the cooler. Would love to have seen that.

"So what do we do now?" Butch asked

"We knock off." Art lit the cigarette and blew a satisfying cloud at the sunset. Had to admit, there was something about the end of a good day's work, even when spent on a nightmare project.

The guys building Auschwitz probably had similar wrap-ups.

Butch's feet spasmed in the direction of the house. "You sure?"

Art regarded him flatly. "I'm not twenty-five anymore, ya know. Neither are you."

Butch looked between the house and Art, made 'oh well' hands then fished out a bottle of water. He raised an eyebrow and Art cocked one in response. "Got anything stronger?"

"I thought you quit drinking."

"I did." Pause. "Well?"

"No," Butch muttered. His face closed and he dropped his head, studied the ground.

Art wondered at the odd response. "Have you?"

"More or less."

"More or less," Art echoed him, which meant more. Old habits are hard to break, ain't they, Butchie Boy? Even with the Lord's help. Art fished his own water out of the cooler, eating a few halfway-melted ice chips in the process. He drank half the bottle in one motion, actually enjoying the brain freeze. "Man!" He smacked his lips. "How much better if that was wrapped around some Jack."

Butch made a disgusted sound, launched off the stump and stalked towards the porch, looking as if he intended to mount it. Again.

"Don't push your luck," Art warned.

"I wasn't," Butch said and stopped right before the first step and then stood, undecided.

Art watched for a moment to ensure his stupid brother wasn't about to do something stupid, then turned west. The sun had dipped halfway below the horizon, something he surmised from the light diffusion because the woods obscured sight lines. "What are you doing here, anyway?"

Butch made his way back to the stump. "I told you, restoring the house."

"You on vacation or something?"

"Vacation?" Butch looked puzzled. "You think this is fun?"

Eh, hey, maybe. Sometimes stuff like this was. "I mean, are you using vacation days, sick days, days off without pay, what? And how much time have we got if that's the case?"

"Oh," Butch said softly as he – finally – understood. "No.

Nothing like that." A pause. "We've got all the time we need."

Art blinked. "Why? You on a leave of absence? A sabbatical? You preachers even get sabbaticals?" Art took a puff. "Preacher on a sabbatical. I think that's an appropriate use of the concept."

"I'm not on sabbatical."

"Then, what?" A long, long pause without response and Art stirred, uneasy. "What's going on, Butch?"

Butch carefully put the water bottle back in the cooler. "I no longer have that congregation."

Really? "You mean, you gave up that cakewalk church in Flagstaff, with all them college babes running around it thinking you were the shit, to take one out here? Here?" Art waved an unbelieving hand at the miasmic woods. "Here in bumfuck Alalejuah-bama, with slope-headed, one-eyed, humps-on-their-back crapheads filling the pews? Got a call for snake-handling or something?" Art took a disgusted drag. "And, on top of it, you buy the house." He shook his head. "Unbelievable."

"I don't have a congregation out here, either."

Really. "To repeat, what's going on, Butch?"

Butch sighed, eyes still on the ground. "I'm on administrative leave."

"For...?"

An even longer pause. "I seem to have lost my faith."

Art couldn't help it: he burst out laughing. The only reason he didn't fall, helpless with mirth to his knees and roll around, was the look of utter shock on Butch's face. "About fucking time," Art said after he caught his breath,

"It's not funny, Art." Genuine sorrow in Butch's voice.

"Yes, it is. Welcome to the real world, asshole. Now." Art took a last *schadenfreude* puff and watched the sunlight disappear. "Where are we staying? And don't tell me, 'In the house.'"

Butch pointed wordlessly at the garage rubble. Art squinted at it and then, wide-eyed, back at Butch. "What, supposed to burrow in there?" But all Butch did was stab an emphatic finger. Art, puzzled, walked to the side and then he saw, partially hidden by the undergrowth, a tent pitched near the woods.

"Great," he muttered.

Art strolled over and pulled back a tent flap. Butch had set up an air mattress on a folding metal frame, but it only slept one, and barely that. There was a little space between the frame and a military-style footlocker Butch had for a table, but Art was damned if he was going to sleep on tick-ridden ground. He stepped back and pointed at Butch's nondescript Ford thing (it's a Ford. That's all he needed to know) and announced, "That's your bed," and then pointed at the tent. "This is mine."

Butch fussed with a newly-lit campfire (Man, the guy was fast) wedged in the garage rubble and waved an 'okay, okay' hand at him.

Art squatted his way into the tent and tested the mattress. Firm, just the way he liked it. There was a battery-run Vornado on the footlocker and Art turned it on, immediately mollified by the volume it threw. That should take care of the gnats and steamy night air. Had to admit, Butch knew a thing or two about comfortable camping.

Art backed out of the tent and went over to the campfire and watched Butch juggle flat-bottomed iron pots and pans while maintaining the fire and necessary temperatures in a masterful display of camp craft. He turned out a fairly extraordinary meal – chili, cornbread, Swiss chard, and even peach cobbler. Impressive. He figured they'd have hot dogs on a stick. "If the world ends," Art said, "I'm living with you."

Butch chuckled and spooned a gigantic portion of chili into Art's bowl. "Gonna have to eat it all. Raccoons will be all over us unless we empty the pans."

Don't have to tell me twice.

Art ate to the point of serious injury, ninety percent chili and cornbread, thank you very much, and shove that chard crap right where the sun don't shine, but he did sample the cobbler. Purty good. He said as much as Butch bustled about trying to scrub burned chili out of the Dutch oven. "Don't tell Linda," Art said, "or she'll hit me with a baking dish."

"Maybe she should," Butch said as he started a generator he'd set up on the other side of the rubble. A series of lights strung about the pines glowed to life, illuminating the area. It was full-on dark now, but you'd never know it. Also impressive. Art settled deeper into a rather comfortable camp chair and forced a series of belches to get even more comfortable.

"Nice," Butch called from the dark past the edge of the lighted area.

"Better than farts."

"True."

Butch stepped into the light, juggling dishes and buckets and paper towels, and somehow put it all away without mishap. Art watched with amusement. "Sure you threw the leftovers far enough out?"

"Yep." Butch settled into another comfortable-looking camp chair across the fire. "Got a spot off towards the trees. Haven't been bothered by critters yet."

"Just how long have you been here, anyway?"

"About a week."

"What have you been doing all this time?"

Butch made 'whatever' hands. "Setting up camp."

In that amount of time, Art could have built a house. Well, at least framed it. He shook his head and amused himself with a crossword puzzle book as Butch attempted to replicate Art's previous belches, managing one or two halfway decent ones.

Amateur.

Art dropped the book and dug deep, producing a set of sonorous, gut-wrenching burps that had both of them convulsed. The ensuing contest (with a couple of inadvertent farts) kept them both occupied until bedtime. Butch shut off the generator, the sudden darkness relieved by some strategically placed solar lights. Art helped Butch slope another air mattress across the various consoles and illogical backseat configurations that Ford insisted upon, which would no doubt result in Butch twisting his spine out of position sometime before morning, then went into the tent and flipped on the Vornado and flopped onto the bed and was dead asleep in about three seconds. Good day's work.

A noise woke him. "Great," he said, immediately aware of his surroundings: woods on the edge of a swamp filled with evil creatures like the Cryman, a long-clawed, long-haired, red-eyed demi-human that stole children out of their homes. It stalked hyeah 'bouts, emerging nightly from a gully way back in Stuart's Woods. One summer afternoon, Butch and Art and Cindy and two farmer kids, Daniel and Kevin, all filled with bravado and the courage of daylight, hiked to the gully's entrance, a little doorway carved by wind and rain into the side of a sheer, red clay wall draped under several feet of Spanish moss. Witch hair, Cindy called it, and they squeezed through, one at a time, onto a ledge overlooking a series of red clay alleys and switchbacks and other

33

walls running off into the darkness. Then something had moved in one of those alleys and they had almost killed themselves squeezing back out, Art screaming in terror.

And now, after all these years, the Cryman had come for him.

Art chuckled and rolled off the mattress and slipped on his flip-flops. He affectionately patted the Vornado, which had lost some of its power as the battery drained, then stepped through the tent flaps.

"Good Gawd!" he breathed. Felt as though a wet, boney, on-fire hand was slapping him upside the head. Hey, Jesus, it's spring (late spring granted but still), and it's nighttime. Think you could lower the temperature to, oh say, ninety-eight?

He squinted in the half-glow provided by a couple of the solar lights, spotted an appropriately-sized hickory at an appropriate distance, lumbered over and relieved himself against the base.

Ah.

More and more, he was up at odd hours draining the weasel. Should get that prostate checked, but he wasn't going to let some doctor finger him. Unless she was cute.

He stepped away and looked up. Stars falling on Alabama in late spring patterns, a bit obscured by the heat haze but the same damn stars he used to glimpse on his terror-fueled runs to the garage stairs. Butch loved them, outside every other night or so around dusk with his stupid toy telescope pointed at them. "Here!" he'd crow, "Arcturus!" Art gawped through the sweat-drenched eyepiece but all he saw was a bright point of unfocused light with a red glow dancing around it and then Butch yelled at him for moving the telescope and Art would slap it and run.

Good times, good times.

Art gave the stars a glare and then carefully stepped towards the back of the rubble.

All right, let's go see if the Cryman is running around eating tossed-out chili. Hope it's him and not something deadly like a snake.

He scrutinized the ground as he walked. As if he could actually see something. At least a rattler would give warning. A copperhead wouldn't, though.

He made slow progress, snake concern and inadequate flip-flops impeding him.

After what felt like an hour but could only be five minutes, he found himself between the rubble of the garage and the rubble of an old clapboard shed that used to front the chicken coop. The chicken coop... oh, jeez he'd forgotten about that.

Dad had put it up about the same time as the garage, splitting Art and Butch's efforts between both projects with an equal splitting of screams and slaps. This had been the easier project of the two because there'd already been a sort of coop attached to the shed, so it had been a matter of moving that and nailing this and then fencing the whole mess in. Dad threw about ten chickens inside and Butch took right to them, spending a lot of time feeding and watering and gathering eggs and screwing hens behind the coop, Art supposed. Art had no interest, only assisting when Dad threatened him with death, a slightly more heinous consequence than messing with chickens.

Stupid, smelly things. And dangerous.

One of the roosters weighed about twenty-five pounds and had three-inch spurs and really, really didn't like Art, chasing after him any time he showed up in the yard. Dad shot it one day when the damn thing went after Mom.

Good.

One summer, Dad forced them all, including Cindy, out into the yard as he set up tables and boiling pots of water and an axe and a stump and it was chicken Armageddon. Conflicted, Art had approved the wholesale beheading of the stupid, smelly things, while thoroughly repulsed by the subsequent feather-plucking and eviscerations. Almost gave up chicken after that, especially when one of the beheaded jumped off the stump and pursued Art around the yard, turning as he turned, on his heels closer and closer as he frantically tried to escape, screaming in terror as the bloody thing stayed on him. Dad and Butch and everyone laughed and laughed.

Assholes.

Ever since, chickens chasing him was one of Art's recurring nightmares and he scanned the remnants of the shed. Ghosts of massacred chickens, bent on revenge, might be massing back there, having enlisted the Cryman to cut off his retreat, ready to swarm him and peck him to death with their ghost beaks. In the morning, Butch would find Art's body, his face frozen in a rictus of terror, thousands of little beak holes all over him.

Chuckling, Art turned towards the tent... wait a minute... over there where the pool used to be, did something move? Art stopped.

Darkness and haze shrouded everything, but he swore part of the dark had shifted...

...little Art standing at the kitchen window and what were they doing back there?

He closed his eyes tightly, then blinked them wide open.

Yes. Something definitely moved.

Art held his breath, not sure if the Cryman and his ghost chicken army had infrared vision. Something pulsed deep in his lungs, the stone reborn.

Get ahold of yourself.

Angrily, Art shook his head like Wile E. Coyote and deliberately drew in an oversized gulp of hazy air, breaking the stone and forcing it back.

You will not get me. You will not take over my life.

Again.

Art pushed forward ready for combat. All right, Cryman, here I am. Let's see what you got.

There. Dark on dark, two figures on the other side of the long-gone pool; silent, regarding him. Not Crymen but humans, small, half-grown kids or maybe the stunted in-bred adults that populated this area.

"What the hell are you doing here?" Art snarled. Goddamn rednecks, about to rifle the camp.

Startlingly loud, from right behind him, "Art?"

"Ack!" Art whirled, fists up, heart revving, to confront Butch's starlit figure. "Jesus, man! You scared the shit outta me!"

Butch, apparently thinking that was hilarious, blew out Art's night vision with a sudden flashlight.

"Dammit!" Art threw an angry palm before his eyes. "Not at me, you idiot!" He threw his other hand towards the shadow figures. "Them!"

The beam whipped over and Art, blinking, followed it.

Nothing.

"Where?" Butch played the beam around, but nobody.

Disgusted, Art said, "Ah, they run off." Would have enjoyed a good fight.

"Who?"

"Couple of goobers. Think they were checking out the camp."

"Really?" Butch probed with the beam, all the way out to the woods. "I didn't see anybody."

"Well, duh," Art snorted, "You drove 'em off."

"Hmph," Butch snorted back, "I wasn't the one stomping around out here like an elephant."

"Oh, bat crap. I wasn't making any noise at all."

"You kidding?" Butch was incredulous. "I thought a tree had fallen over or something. Woke me up."

"Bat. Crap."

"Not bat crap. Maybe you were sleepwalking again."

"I haven't sleepwalked in decades," Art snarled. Haven't had an asthma flare-up in decades, either.

"Well... there isn't anybody out here."

"There was."

"No, there wasn't."

Art steamed, debating whether to clock Butch, pack up, and peel out. The stone in his lung chose that moment to reappear and he concentrated on it, taking slow breaths while thinking of cool waters in tranquil streams.

Haven't sleepwalked in decades, either.

Butch focused on the ground, tracing the pool's old location with the flashlight. "What are you doing?" Art asked between breaths.

Butch snapped off the flashlight. "Nothing." A pause. "Let's go back to bed." With no further word, Butch slid towards the camp.

Art watched as Butch's diminishing shadow took on the same shape and size of the two goobers. Nobody out here, huh? He considered a cigarette but rejected it in consideration of the stone, and headed back to the tent.

Chapter 6

Tuesday morning

About sunrise, goddamn blue jays woke him. Art stepped outside and snake-eyed a pair of them flitting in and out of the pines edging the yard. Egg-stealing fucks. Art tripped his way to the same hickory tree (might as well mark my territory) and relieved himself. Butch, already up, fussed around the fire, and Art moseyed over and saw Swiss-cheese-and-onion omelets in the making. "No," Art said, and made him cook scrambled eggs and bacon, instead.

"You'd make someone a good wife," Art said as he finished off the last bacon bit, smacked his lips and swilled the remaining third of a water bottle.

"Shut up."

Art tossed the paper plate into the fire and Butch cleaned up while Art considered then rejected a cigarette and okay, enough fooling around, time to get going. He inspected the porch steps, mentally slapping himself on the back for a job well done, same for the pad, and then up and to the door and over the threshold, braced to lose his soul again but no replay (once lost, always lost) to renew the attack.

"So what are we doing?" Butch, behind him.

Art pointed. "We're replacing the floors. All of them. Starting here." He stomped in emphasis. "Get a couple of pry bars out of my truck."

Butch, surprise, knew what those were and brought them back in moments and proved really good at tearing things up, really good, and they had the floor off in about an hour.

"Christ," Art said, staring down between the joists.

"Pretty ugly," Butch agreed.

They stared through the crawl space to the ground, all dirt and debris. Art expected snakes and zombie 'possums to come flowing up and around their feet any second like a B-horror movie. "Got a flashlight?"

Handy, he meant, since Butch had damn near blinded him with one last night. Butch whipped probably the same one out of his back pocket and handed it over. Mr. Be Prepared. Carefully, Art lowered his head between the joists and examined the dark space beneath. "Christ," he repeated.

"What?"

"Smells like something died down here."

At Butch's sudden jump, Art pulled back out, ready for combat. "What?"

"Ah... nothing." Butch's hands flew around in agitation.

Bit of an overreaction. "Jesus, bud, relax, critters die all the time in crawl spaces. Especially in abandoned houses."

"Yeah, I know. Yeah. In the crawl space. Right."

"Well, yeah. What'd you think I meant?"

"Like, you know, something was buried under there."

"What, like a body?" Art sat back, fished around in his pocket for a Raleigh. Found it, lit it. Ah. "Doubtful. Woods are better. Little chance it'd be found. This." He cigarette-pointed at the hole. "is probably a dog."

"A dog?"

"Yeah, a dog." He took in a long, luxurious puff. "Remember when one got in down there and had puppies?"

Butch screwed up his face. "Yeah," he said softly. "Yeah, I remember that."

They both sat on exposed joists, sharing the memory. One autumn, a skinny ill-treated Bluetick coonhound had forced its way through the crawlspace door on the far side of the house and decided to live under there, growling at them whenever they peeked inside. Wouldn't let them near the puppies, either, and Art wanted one. Neither the dog nor its puppies were there when they got home from school one day and Dad wouldn't answer any questions. Dad's shotgun was slightly askew in the cabinet.

Dogs meeting uncertain fates. That happened around here a lot. After Cha Cha took on an 18-wheeler about six months after they'd moved in and lost, subsequent dogs appeared and disappeared, most of them arriving in the back of Dad's truck, jumping out waggy and wriggly and happy to roam yards and woods with a bunch of kids, then gone. "Dun rund off," Dad snarled at their tearful questions, his shotgun slightly askew in the cabinet. Art learned not to get attached, a tough proposition for a kid faced with a brand new German Shephard-mixed puppy excited to see him while Dad eyed it with flat eyes. The upside, Art learned about the impermanence of things. Especially things he loved.

Art took the cigarette down to the filter. De-e-lightful. "Listen." He threw the smoldering butt through the joists, ignoring Butch's frown. "These floors are a disaster. Gonna have to rebuild them, subfloor and all. So, we need to get a bunch of stuff."

"Like what?"

"Boards, plywood, anchors, barrier, flooring nails and screws... and tile. If that's what you want."

"Sounds expensive."

Art laughed. "Well, yeah. Didja think it wouldn't be?"

"No, I mean..." Butch flopped a helpless hand. "I'm between jobs right now."

"Oh, right." Art stood. "That whole loss-of-faith thing. So we'll make it linoleum instead of tile. Where's the nearest Lowe's?"

Butch made an 'I don't know' face. Art *tsk*ed and walked outside, retrieved his phone from the truck charger. After a few minutes acquiring a signal (thanks, Verizon) and a few more minutes searching, he walked back inside. Butch hadn't moved. "Amazingly enough, there's one in Enterprise," he said, waving the Nokia at him, "Figured I'd have to go to Dothan."

"It's not so backward here anymore, ya know."

"Yeah, right," Art dismissed. "I think we might as well do the floors all the way from here to there." He pointed back to the bedrooms. "Those can't be any better so, in for a penny..." and he waggled a hand. Your penny, Butch, not mine.

Butch blanched. "Really? You haven't even looked at those floors yet. They could be fine."

Art gave him a 'you're joking, right?' look, pulled out his tape measure and pad and, with Butch in tow, spent the next half hour getting the measurements for the kitchen. Would have been quicker, but Butch helped. Keeping his temper in check, Art moved on to the den, impatiently directing Butch around the perimeter with the end of the tape. Art ended the struggle in front of the bathroom, bouncing up and down on the floor like a trampoline. So, yeah, Butch, this is all crap, too. He considered the bathroom next but, screw it – that was a project in itself. Without a word, he eased to the right, past the wreckage that was once a door and into Cindy's bedroom.

A bedroom for a princess.

That's what Dad had said, smiling with no humor as he stood in the middle of it, putting the finishing touches on the pink-canopy bed he'd put together next to the pink throw rug, pink overstuffed pillows on the pink bedspread, big blue teddy bear nestled between them, Barbies everywhere, David Cassidy and Bobby Sherman posters leering from the walls. Cindy jumped up and down, all excited, and Mom smiled, too, a real smile, but her eyes were dead.

The princess did not live happily ever after.

Art frowned at the room. All the sheetrock was broken, as though someone had deliberately smashed it; which maybe they had. Both windows gaped like those in the den but were plastic-wrapped, courtesy of Butch earlier in the week, obviously; vandals were rarely so conscientious.

A line of ants crawled up one corner and disappeared through a hole into the ceiling. Here and there sheetrock drooped over, held in place by flowery wallpaper some previous owner must have put up. Sheetrock dust and the usual crap that gathered in abandoned houses covered the floors but, surprisingly, no water damage, which made no sense because good ole 'bama thunderstorms should have blasted through the open windows with impunity. Perhaps the princess's wards were still intact. Hadn't kept the room from turning into Frankenstein's dungeon, though.

Shaking his head, Art flipped the end of the measuring tape to make that funny *waaadDAAP!* sound of flexing metal and called "Hey!" Hey, Butch, get your butt in here and hold the end of the tape, this time without effing it up.

Silence.

"Hey! Let's go, man!" Art called again, but no answer and Art grew annoyed. More annoyed, that is. "You want to get this done, or what?"

Silence.

Art stepped into the hallway. Empty. "What the hell?" and escalated into full-on pissed. So that's how it is, huh, Butch? You buy the House of Usher and leave the work to me? "Asshole!" he called and, muttering far more poetic insults, measured the princess's floor, adding the numbers to the pad, then pressed the tape button to get that equally satisfying *waadaadaadaadaa* sound, and flipped the pad closed. If the numbers are a bit off, too effin' bad. Butchie. You can always fix it later. By yourself.

He stepped into the intersection of hallway and bedrooms and bathroom and there, right there, the opening to the living room, which connected to the far dining room in one very long open sweep. The center of all existence back then and he stepped through and surveyed.

Actually, not bad.

The double bow window overlooking the front yard was still in place, surprise, surprise, glass intact and everything. Imagine that. Apparently, it was too sophistimacated for the vandal hordes. He bounced to test the floor and, yep, in the same condition as the rest of the house. So were the smashed-and-drooping sheetrock walls. Art pulled out another cigarette and slowly walked to the middle of the living room and time traveled.

Over there, against the south wall, the console stereo. Think it was a Magnavox, but it could have been a Curtis Mathes. Big TV tube in the middle – well, big by the standards of the day – a radio on one side and a turntable on the other. Butch would throw on the Shondells, crank it up, and they were 'Mony Mony'-ing all over the living room until Dad screamed at them to "Turn that hippie shit off!" Dad wouldn't let them touch the radio because he had it tuned to some shitkicker station and, apparently, it took an electrical engineering degree to get the frequency right, so he got them a good-sized portable (definitely a Magnavox. 'Murican knowhow), what them crazy kids back in the eighties would call a 'boom box,' and they set it on the floor between the two rocking chairs and tuned it to that hippie shit on WBAM (the Big Bam!) and they'd just rock and rock to the rock, Creedence and Airplane and the Association and 'Pappa's Got a Brand New Bag' *doodoodledoodledoo!* ...Art air-guitared the transition chords before James Brown swung into the horns.

Good times, good times.

Art remembered when Bobby Kennedy got shot. Butch and he had been rocking in the rocking chairs to the Big Bam when the announcement came on, the DJ terse and unemotional.

Butch had bust out laughing, "Good! Now Wallace will win!" Art had looked at him like he was crazy. "Somebody just got killed, Butch."

"So?" Butch snorted and went back to the rock.

A little on the cold-blooded side, hey, Butchie boy?

Art slowly pivoted on his heels and drifted past the phantom couch and coffee table and into the dining room, the ghost of Dad's overstuffed chair marking the border. A dining room table and a hutch at this end, Mom bringing in platters of meatloaf and fried chicken and mashed potatoes as Dad scrutinized the kids for any violation of his ever-changing rules, which gave him the opportunity to play his favorite dinnertime game: Beat and Maim.

You minded your dinner Ps and Qs; that is, if you wanted to keep all your teeth.

Sometimes they had visitors – Dad's friends (never Mom's because she wasn't allowed any) or Dad's relatives (never Mom's because they weren't allowed to visit) – the kids banished to the kitchen to eat alone and out of sight-and-hearing where they had a blast. Bean fights, plopping potatoes in each other's tea, smearing seats with gravy whenever someone got up to get something...

Good times, good times.

Smiling, Art tested the floor. Yep, same crappy condition, so out with the tape measure and pad and, before you knew it, he had all the measurements he needed to buy all the materials necessary to convert the floors from deathtraps to viable structures. With one last look around, he stepped into the empty kitchen, heard a shuffling noise on the porch and popped his head out to find Butch shadowed against the light.

"Thanks for the help," Art said.

Butch didn't move, didn't say anything, a mannequin, blank-faced and plastic, facing the kitchen, a distance in his eyes. Art turned to where he was looking, but it was just dreary dust beams wavering in the half-light of a wrecked and forlorn house. "What's with you?" he asked.

Butch shook as if suddenly awakened. "Nothing. So?"

"So?"

"Well, what do we do?"

"We?" Art gave him a mild look. "You've decided to help?"

Butch made an exasperated sound. "What do you want me to do?"

"Not sneak off. And give me your Lowe's card."

"Lowe's card?"

Of course, he didn't have one. Only men did. "Yes. For going to Lowe's and buying all the materials we need to rebuild all the floors. Which needs a lot more material than you think, so give me a card, any card." He held out a hand.

"Uh..." Butch hesitated and stared at the hand; the moment extended and Art got mad.

"Jackass," Art said. "I am not paying for this. Not one effin' penny. So GIVE ME A CARD!" and he turned the hand into a threatening fist.

Hastily, Butch reached into a wallet and dropped an American Express into Art's insistent palm. Art gave him a hard look, walked out and got into his truck and backed out, slinging a little gravel at Butch standing helplessly near the porch, arms flapping helplessly.

Jackass.

Chapter 7

Tuesday

Lowe's. The adult toy store. Not *that* kind of adult toy, although the smell of fresh lumber was a bit arousing.

Art stood in the middle of the aisle, head thrown back, savoring. Ahhhh. Sawdust, overheated blades, freshly delivered cement bags, newly made bricks... these were his perfumes. In the middle of a project, Art would stop and take it all in: mixer trucks with their mortars idling, house frames silhouetted against the noon sky, cement blocks piled next to mounds of dirt... his sculpture, his paintings, the fashioning of beauty from disparate materials, a palette, and Art was the painter. Sadness overcame him when the finished house or garage or patio glowed in the sunset because, now what? Even though perfect, a masterpiece, the customer next to him astonished and spouting praise, Art felt an odd sense of loss as he modestly lowered his eyes under the effusion because, yes, of course it's great, of course it looks wonderful and will last two hundred years, well past your great-grandchildren, what do you expect? Art wielded magic.

But now, he needed to find another dragon to slay.

Like this one.

He had two carts piled high with woods and stains and nails and brackets and plans, plans. Dust of bat, eye of newt, a pinch from one, a handful of another and swirl the demon winds into new floors, new foundations, new structures.

Wizardry.

"S'great, idn't it?" said a jovial voice next to him.

Art opened his eyes. A fat, jovial guy, decked in a Lowe's vest and carrying a laser measure, grinned at him.

"It is," Art said.

"Putting in floors?" the guy, identified by name tag as 'Dave,' threw a critical eye at the carts.

Art warmed. A fellow wizard. "You know your stuff."

Dave flashed a good 'ole boy set of yellowed and missing teeth. "Yep. And I can tell you do, too." They beamed at each other.

"So," Dave smacked eager hands together, "looks like you're doing a house. Building?"

"No. Restoring."

"Oh." Dave nodded sagely. "So you're going to do the walls, next, if I miss my guess." All said in the honeyed accents of the Deep South, where "I" became "ah" and "my," "muh," and more syllables were added than English called for: "gay-yes."

"Nope, you lose," Art laughed as Dave snapped 'durn it!' fingers. "This is a total reconstruction. The systems next, then the walls."

"So you're going to be cleaning out our electrical and plumbing supplies, too, huh?" Dave admired the carts again.

"Looks that way."

Dave's eyes took on a retailer's gleam. "You know, we have free delivery."

"I thought that was out only twenty-five miles," Art said, calculating. If he could talk Dave into it, could save Butch a couple of bucks. "I'm way out on Damascus Road."

"Is that a fact? Well," – W'aal – "a mite bit outta our area, but we might make an exception." Conspiratorial grin. "How way out?"

"Just past the Yoman intersection."

Dave's grin vanished. He blinked. "Just past?"

Probably six feet beyond their drop-dead limit, Art figured. Dammit. "Bottom of the hill?"

"The Deats' place?"

Now, Art blinked. "You know it? By that name?"

"Yes. Yes, I (ah) do." Dave stared at him, as if Art'd grown a second head. "You bought the Deats' place?" Tone of incredulity.

"No." Do I look stupid or something? "My... someone else did. I'm just helping." Pause. "So how do you know it?"

"Everyone knows it. It's haunted." Dave regarded him. "And I'm afraid it's outside our delivery zone. Sorry." And Dave hustled away. Art watched him go.

Haunted.

Got that right, Dave.

Art shook his head and did quick calculations of loads and balances. He could get the two carts into the Ram without much trouble, but he needed at least two more to make a dent in this job. Try loading all four carts? Hmm. Even with his usual dexterity and brilliant loading skills, best he could do is a little less than three. Maybe if he stacked it up and took it easy on the curves and prayed... no way, just no way. So, whether you like it or not, Butchie boy, you're paying for delivery. If he could find someone to deliver. Maybe if you hadn't bought a haunted house, brother o' mine, the locals would be a little more helpful.

Grabbing the end of one cart, Art positioned himself in front of the other and crabbed his way to the registers, the carts weaving back and forth and threatening to amputate the feet of unwary shoppers. "'Scuze me, "'Scuze me," he apologized. He left the carts off to the side of the big contractor register and went back and got two more loads. He now had a train of materials and maneuvered a representative one up to the register.

"Oh, my goodness!" The cute happy checkout girl (name tag 'Allison'), quite reminiscent of Velma from *Scooby Doo*, flashed her overly thick round glasses at his carts. "You are going to be busy!"

"That I am," Art agreed and waited as Allison went through the piles of booty with her laser gun while babbling on about weather and boiled peanuts, Art unable to follow how one subject segued into another. "Oh, my goodness!" she couldn't help saying as the total appeared. Oh, my goodness, indeed. Let's escalate it. "Need about half of this," he waved at the carts, "delivered."

"All right." The location figured out, Allison's eyebrows went up. "The Deats' place?"

"You know it too?"

"Everyone knows it. It's—"

"Haunted, right, I know. So what's the charge?"

She furrowed a cute little brow. "Well, nothing! It's in our delivery area."

"Really," Art said and made a mental note to have a later conversation with Dave. No increase to the current heart-stopping total, then, which was small comfort. Thank God he wasn't paying for it. "Here you go," he said, flourishing the American Express.

Allison took it, now going on about the merits of living in a haunted house ("It's so interesting!"...of course, Velma would think that), and then onto the merits of the Enterprise High School baseball team; Art glanced away to relieve the endless stream of nonsense as she swiped the card... and swiped it... and swiped it again. "Hmm," she said, eyes now in Velma-suspicion mode.

"What's going on?" Art asked, knowing full well what was going on.

"It's refused. Says I have to confiscate it." Velma-suspicion turned full on him.

An impatient movement behind made Art glance back at the redneck hick hillbilly shitkicking goatfucker with a cart overloaded with lumber threatening to push into Art's calves. Art glared him back and then turned into Velma's glare.

Goddamn Butch all to hell.

"Here," he said, savagely, whipping out his wallet and practically throwing his contractor card at her. She took it, frowning even deeper as she now actually read both cards. "Deats." Her eyes took on a strange cast. "The Deats are coming back?" Said like someone inquiring about the Mongol horde.

"No," he raged, "only my idiot brother."

She held the cards out as though they were radioactive. "How come the names are different?"

So, the resemblance to Velma was only physical, huh, bright girl? "Because the bad one's my idiot brother's." He could barely get the words through his clenched teeth.

"Oh," she said, gave him a sympathetic look, and swiped Art's card. Which worked. Of course. At least there was no delivery charge.

Hesitantly, Allison held out Butch's card. "Do you want to give it back to him?"

"No," Art said, taking his own card and crabbing out the door.

Chapter 8

Tuesday

"This is a lot," Butch said, eying the precarious load of lumber shifting and threatening to spill on top of his head as Art untied it. Art considered an 'accidental' bump off-center but then he'd never get paid.

"It's only half. The other's being delivered," Art said, brushing past him.

Butch blanched. "How much did it cost?"

"It cost *me* a lot." Art yanked the top boards off the pile and pitched them towards the porch.

"Huh?" Took Butch a moment. "Oh. Crap. So where's my card, then?"

"Velma has it. Ya wanna lend a hand here?"

"Velma?"

Art grabbed an armful of boards and swung them viciously through the air, dangerously close to Butch's head, who stumbled back. "Watch it!"

"Fuck off." Art snatched tools off the truck and stomped towards the porch. Moments later, a wary Butch followed him.

The next half hour or so enhanced Art's chances for felony murder charges, but there was a tranquility in the work that eventually soothed his overpowering urge to shove a hammer sideways up Butch's butt, and he remained in full tranquility while explaining to Butch, *ad infinitum*, *ad nauseam*, why identifying the load-bearing walls was important. "You want the house to collapse around us?" seemed to make the point.

Then Art had to break it down: step one, cut the new floor joist and pre-position it down there in the crawl space. Step two: install it quick. Don't want to leave that part of the wall unsupported for too long, Butchie boy. That aforementioned house collapse, ya know. See how it all relates?

"You mean," Butch said as it came clear, "you want me to go down there?" He was pointing at the monster-ridden ground visible between the open floor joists.

"Well, yeah."

"Why?"

Art sighed. "This is a two-man job, Butch. I don't see anyone else here."

After dropping way too many tarps on the ground (like that would protect him from radon and quicksand and rabid Bluetick coonhounds), in he jumped. Butch held the replacement joist at-the-ready stance while Art cut out the old one, removed a couple of pieces of bridging, yanked out some unused wire (there's always unused wire to yank out), tore out the band board and the mudsill then bolted the new one in place. He and Butch then went topside to prepare the next joist. "That's one," Art said.

"Of how many?" Butch asked, pulling cobwebs out of his hair.

Art grabbed a board. "Too many."

Slow going. Especially with Butch helping.

A couple of hours into it, the Lowe's truck showed up, further delaying what Butch's incompetence had already delayed. Not that the Lowe's guys took their time; the two yahoos had the truck unloaded and the boards stacked in what had to be record time, at least, for Alabama goobers, their eyes wild and rolling. Art was tempted to yell "Boo!" but didn't want both of them collapsing in terror.

By dark, they were only a third of the way done. Granted, Art had blown the whole morning getting materials and there was the lumber delivery but, c'mon. If he'd done the work himself, it'd be finished by now, two-man job or no.

In the washhouse cleaning up, he eyed Butch. "How do you manage to get through life being all thumbs?"

Butch wasn't offended. "Hire people who aren't."

"That could get awful expensive. Speaking of which..." Art raised eyebrows.

Butch dried his hands and, without looking at him, said, "I'm good for it."

"Really?" The eyebrows went higher. "Not the impression I have, given the rejection and confiscation of your card."

"I said I'm good for it."

"Zat a fact?" Art filled another bucket with bottled water, deliberately spilling one of the bottles on the cement pad. "By chance, do you happen to have another card onto which I could transfer the newly inflated balances of *my* card?"

Butch said nothing, which Art took as a 'no.' Butch pushed out of the washhouse and headed to the tent, Art on his heels. "'Cause, you know," Art continued the subject, "it'd be real nice to be able to tell Linda there's no need to worry about that in-o-o-o-o-ordinately large Lowe's bill because you're," Art made air quotes, " 'good for it,' especially since she knows this isn't exactly, you know, a *paying* project." He paused. "Ya know?"

"I said I was good for it." Butch reached for pans, slamming them around.

"Could you be a little more specific? For Linda's sake, I mean. How, pray tell, are you good for it?"

The slamming increased. Art didn't press it, merely stayed somewhat in the way, eyebrows raised. Butch did his best to ignore him, but at last let out a long breath as he settled a pot of water on the camp stove. "I'm waiting for a payout."

"From what?"

"My... termination."

Hello. "Termination? You mean, you were fired?"

Butch was silent and Art felt as if he'd just walked into a soap opera. "How do you fire a preacher?"

"Pastor," Butch corrected, "and it's done all the time."

"For what? Improper snake-handling, insufficient pillars of salt, ratio of fire and brimstone?" Art was thoroughly enjoying himself.

Butch, obviously, wasn't. He leaned heavily on the table. "Improper conduct," he said.

Hello hello. "Like, what? Sexual harassment?"

"I don't want to talk about it." Butch moved away, irritable, and pawed through the half-melted ice in a chest.

Art *did* want to talk about it. "So, is that it? You were boinking the organ player or something, and she didn't like it? She is a 'she,' right?" Art was still thoroughly enjoying himself.

Butch glared at him. "I said I don't want to talk about it!"

"Well, Butchie Boy, I think you need to let me know the par-tick-elers, 'cause, you know..." Art waggled eyebrows, "if you wuz doing the dirty in violation of your Lord's concepts, then I'm thinking there ain't gonna be much of a termination payout." He paused, dropped his eyebrows and stared hard. "And that means, my Lowe's card remains unacceptably high."

Butch pulled out some plastic-wrapped hunk of unidentifiable meat, brought it back to the stove and dropped it, sizzling, into the pan. "There will be a payout."

Art kept his belligerent stance. "Why? Did the bishop or Pope or whatever come on to you?"

"We're pastors, ministers, elders, senior pastors. No bishops. No Popes."

"Whatever." Art dismissed that. "But izzat it? Some Crystal Palace guy wanted you to go down on him?"

"Man, you're offensive!" Butch banged down the pan and spun on Art, eyes blazing, fists white. Art took a wary step back. Butch was generally passive, wimpy, willing to take a lot of guff. Up to a point. Then he went nuts. Bruce Banner nuts. You wouldn't like him when he was angry.

"Dude!" Art held up a defensive hand. "Calm down. Just answer the question."

Butch breathed hard, a nerve jumping on the side of his head.

This was about to get ugly. Art located a tree branch out of the corner of his eye. Might need it.

"I..." Butch stopped, going inward, turning back into the wimp Art knew so well. "I... look. Just take my word for it. There's a settlement coming and you'll get reimbursed."

"When?"

"When it comes."

Art threw up exasperated hands. "Well, gee, right after the Apocalypse or the Rapture or whatever it is you guys believe in? Is that what I tell the collection agency?"

"It'll be soon." Butch was back at the sizzling pan. "They want it done quick." An aroma of fried hamburger rose in the air.

"Do they?" Art's eyes narrowed. "Now, why is that?"

Butch turned and looked at him, something unfathomable in his eyes, an off-light, a confession. "Because they do." Monotone. The voice of the funeral director, the judge passing sentence.

Art felt something very, very wrong in the air. "What did you do, Butch?" Art spoke quietly as shadows, blood-tinged and grinning, rose on the edge of the camp.

A car pulled into the driveway.

They both blinked at it. The headlights dazzled, so Art couldn't tell what kind of car or how many people inside. Given where they were, probably a 1979 rusted-out Buick filled to the brim with gape-jawed hicks, all coming over to see wot the hayl y'all Yankees a doin' hyeah? Art re-located the branch. Definitely going to need it.

The car pulled up opposite the house, bathing them both in high beams. The engine roared a bit as it shifted into park, then cut off with a bit of run-on. The headlights went last. Art rubbed the dazzle out of his eyes. A 2005 Hyundai Something-or-other. With New Jersey plates. He knew that car.

"Ruh-roh," he said.

The driver's door opened and Cindy stepped out. The remains of the day lit her in orange and gold and white, a Piney queen...

(princess)

...in tight jeans and chambray shirt tied at the bottom, her long, wild auburn hair Medusa-ing about her head, sharp cats' eyes, yellow and pale, lasering everything. She stared at the house, frowning, unreadable. Then she turned and looked at them.

A stunningly beautiful woman, even if she was his sister, even if she was well north of fifty. She had a smokiness about her, an ephemeral sense that she was everything any man would want, but they would never, ever have her. Not completely. Art did a quick inventory of all her past boyfriends: the dumbest of them were the ones she held onto the longest; the others, the smart ones to a man, eventually said to him, "Dude, what's the deal with your sister?"

What, indeed, was the deal?

The decent boyfriends (because they had jobs and some kind of future plans) didn't last long. Initially, Cindy would be enthusiastic and gushing and there was talk of marriage and she had, indeed, married two or three of them. But, in relatively short weeks or months, she was staying out all night and then coming home drunk and screaming and throwing things and accusing the decents of heinous crimes like screaming and staying out all night and throwing things and then she was gone, running off with a biker or meth head or gang member of some kind, a relationship that lasted far longer than with the decent ones.

And a lot of that, Art believed, had to do with this house.

"Cindy," Butch said, a helpless tone in his voice, an apology. She blinked once, walked over and punched Butch hard in the face.

"Aap!" Butch yelped as he spun, holding his nose.

Cindy looked at Art. He held up two placating hands. She gave him a hard eye, slowly turned and went back to her car. Moments later, she was gone.

Art watched her taillights disappear, then said, "I think she's pissed."

Chapter 9

Wednesday morning

Damn blue jays again. Art rolled out of the tent and wished he had a BB gun. A Daisy, just like the one he'd used to shoot Dad in the shoulder back, what, in 1963 or 64? Butch and Art and Dad had been out in the deep woods somewhere on Fort Sill making some approximation of hunting. Dad stood right in front of Art, saying, "Keep the barrel pointed at the ground, you idiot," and Art, the BB gun up and aimed straight at Dad, grinned and pulled the trigger.

Who knew a BB could hurt like that?

Dad yelped and rolled back and then rolled on top of him.

Who knew a beating could hurt like that?

Butch stood there open-mouthed and watched as Dad wrenched the gun from Art's hands and slapped him around with it. Didn't intervene, even though he held a nice .22 single-shot rifle that would do considerably more than sting Dad but, really, why should he? He wasn't getting the beating. Besides, that would simply intensify Dad's rage and one or both of them would end up dead; so Art did what these occasions called for and cried and screamed and begged for forgiveness but with a certain sense of satisfaction: call me an idiot, and see what happens.

See what happens.

Butch had a gourmet breakfast going already. Art strolled over. Blueberry pancakes, if you can believe it, something actually tolerable and Art almost went for the 'make a good wife' comment again, but thought it a bit stale. Let's try a different tack. "How's your nose?"

Butch said nothing, but his ears flamed. Art made exaggerated movements around Butch's shoulder to get a look at his normally rather prominent nose. Made a good target. "Swollen, but okay," he reassured Butch and placed a consoling hand on the shoulder which Butch promptly knocked off. Art chortled and reached for a plate.

A truck pulled into the driveway.

"Not again!" Art feigned great drama, clutching at his heart and throwing an expressive arm but, no, not Cindy.

Caleb's Well Drilling and Repair. At least, that's what the amateurish letters on the side said. The guy Art had made the appointment with. In the recent excitement, he'd kinda forgotten about it.

The old hippie redneck who clambered out of the driver's side had to be Caleb. He looked like a Caleb, sporting half-gray, half-mulleted long hair as proof that he had lost all recent interest in grooming, his half-stubbled face reiterating that lack of interest, while his sleepy eyes and mountainous stomach betrayed heightened interest in beer, the ensemble completed by a stained T-shirt and jeans.

But he was a runway model compared with the two jokers who spilled out of the passenger side. *Real* rednecks, real oxy'-snortin', wife-beater wearin', ponytailed, too many tattoos on pipe-stem-meth-ravaged arms and the intense look of hate and murder in too-intense eyes that a lifetime of ignorance and bad luck and drug addiction caused.

"Mornin' Mr. Deats!" Caleb belched with a cigarette-ravaged voice as he looked between Butch and Art to identify his caller, waved a beefy, dewlapped arm, then rolled over to them at the stove, hand extended. "You got some well problems?"

"Good morning to you, sir!" Art employed his best Yankee accent while vigorously pumping Caleb's languid hand, "and indeed, we do! Isn't that right, Mr. Deats?" He raised waggish eyebrows at Butch.

Butch stared at the two rednecks, who hadn't moved an inch from the side of the truck, but already hostile. Art grinned and elbowed Butch out of it. "Yes, the well," Butch said and waved a vague hand at the pump house, maintaining his contact with the rednecks.

"Man, that smells good!" Caleb ambled over and positioned next to the sizzling griddle a little too close for hygiene's sake. "Blueberry pancakes, umm umm. Why," he said to Butch, "you'd make someone a good wife!"

Art laughed so hard he almost fell to the ground. Caleb

sported an ear-to-ear grin and the rednecks traded their hostility for guffaws. Butch looked at all of them, saying nothing, his face working.

Art led a grinning Caleb and his two mutants over to the pump house. "I knew some Deats some years ago, but that was over in Dothan." Caleb said as they hit the doorway.

"Doubt were related," Art replied, since all his Deats cousins were Texas crapheads, not Alabama ones, then gestured at the pump. "Here's the problem."

"Wooeee!" Caleb did his best Enos impression, although Art suspected it was inherent. "That is one ancient piece of shit. Doubt I can get parts for it."

Well, no kidding. It'd be like repairing a Sopwith Camel. "Is the well viable?"

"Well," – 'W'aal – "dunno until we get the water tested. One good thing, the cap's in place." Caleb tapped the bottom seal of the old pump with his boot. "Shouldn't be no contamination. At least, from the surface." He peered at the open roof, saying nothing.

"Okay." Art kept his tone neutral. Best to let Caleb think Art was 'ignunt' about these kinds of things and see what kind of scam this hayseed would try. "So, what do we do?"

Caleb chewed his lip. "I think we should pull this old thing." He patted the pump. "Plumb for depth and take a sample off to the lab. We'll seal the top of it while we're waiting, but, tell ya, there's really not a lot else I can tell ya until all that's done."

Reasonable. And professional. Art shrugged. "Okay."

Caleb nodded, looked at the mutants and said, "Let's get to it."

They all stepped outside, the mutants straight for Caleb's truck, Caleb and Art staying in front of the washhouse. Butch was still at the grill, stacks of pancakes next to him. He stopped and stared at the mutants, who glared at him as they collected crap off the truck.

"Want some pancakes?" Art asked.

"Naw," Caleb laughed, "Done et. Don't let me stop you, though." Caleb pushed back his ball cap (Deere) and looked at the house. "Did you buy this place?"

"Not me. Him." Art pointed at Butch, still engaged with the mutants.

"Are you like the original Deats people?"

"Distant relatives. From out west." Neutral tone.

"Hmm." Caleb chewed a lip. "And ya took the place." A studied pause that made Art wary. "Did he do any checking before he bought it?"

Art gave Caleb the bad eye. "Dunno. Why?"

Caleb shrugged. "Place is haunted."

"I've heard that. In what way?"

"The usual. Lights, ghosts, scary stuff."

"Seen it yourself?"

"Nah," Caleb said, "Hurd it from udders."

"All the way over there in Dothan. My, how news travels," Art observed. "And what's supposed to be the reason?"

"Huh?"

Art kept his temper. "For the haunts."

"All I heard" – hyerd – "was someone got kilt here and the family disappeared and the place been haunted ever since."

Well, at least half of that was right. "Who got killed?"

"Some kid."

Hmm. If you speak metaphorically, then Caleb was entirely right. "No one got kilt here. At least, before we disappeared." He grinned at Caleb's confused look and said, "Gonna get me some pancakes." Art pushed off, deliberately forgetting to extend another breakfast invitation to Caleb which, if Art remembered his southern protocol, required three requests before the recipient was allowed to say yes. He grabbed a tin plate and some 'cakes and poured Mrs. Butterworth's all over it. "Say," he said to Butch around a forkful, "did you know this place is haunted?"

Butch didn't respond, remained fixed on the mutants grabbing things off the truck. "What's with you?" Art asked.

"I don't like those kind of people."

"What kind of people would that be?"

Butch paused. "Redneck assholes," he said, gaze never wavering from the mutants, one of whom had paused in his tool-gathering and equally intent on Butch.

Art was amazed. "You actually said 'assholes.' Gonna get the vapors, I am." Art waved at the mutants. "What's your problem with them?"

Butch was silent for a moment. "They remind me of Dad," he toned.

Art almost dropped his plate. "How the hell do they do that?"

Butch looked at him, eyes deep and murderous. "The hate," he said, then walked away.

It was surprisingly difficult to get the pump off the wellhead. Caleb and the mutants had quite the go at it, and all three of them seemed to know what they were doing but still, a bitch.

"Rusted in as good as a weld," Caleb said, wiping his forehead with the ball cap.

The mutants sat back on haunches and stared at the half-removed pump. Art stood quietly. He had come to respect Caleb and his pals, so reserved comment.

Caleb shook his head, raised an eyebrow at mutant number one, and said, "Torch."

They all, including Art, strolled back to the truck, Art curious about Caleb's inventory. Caleb pulled up the truck's side panels and Art whistled: state of the art plumbs and bits and lengths. "Do you have a well rig, too?"

Caleb raised an appraising eyebrow. "Yes, a Schramm. You know what a well rig is?"

Art was non-committal and Caleb grinned knowingly. "I was thinkin' you knew a bit more than you was lettin' on."

They had an arc welder strapped against the back of the cab, and the mutants pushed and unbuckled and gathered while Caleb kept a careful eye on them. Butch came over, holding the last plate he was cleaning, to see what the ruckus was about and stayed to observe. Work is fascinating. Butch could watch it all day.

A car pulled into the driveway. Art didn't have to look at it to know it was Cindy, but he looked anyway. Needed to see what side she got out of so he could run to the other.

She drove up halfway and stopped, frowning out of the windshield with her dark look, the one that usually preceded a pounding of poor little Art when he'd done something like bury her Barbies in the sandbox, or when a judge gave her a little more of a fine or time in jail than she felt she deserved and then she let the judge know what she thought of his (or her) heritage, which resulted in a little more time and fine. Fortunately, the look immediately switched to Butch.

Butch didn't look back, stayed on the mutants, although he

knew very well she was there. His jaw tightened, though. Caleb glanced over then back at the mutants, who stayed on task.

Cindy got out, stood behind the open car door, and surveyed the house and front yard, at least what she could see through the cedars lining the driveway which shouldn't be anything since they were too damn thick. Still, her eyes narrowed, the dark look withering all life, and she scrutinized the scene. Art wondered what she saw. Maybe the endless games of freeze tag they used to play there on the front lawn, or pitch, or... something else entirely.

She took in a small breath and slowly shook her head, hair flowing about her face, alive, all her power in the auburn locks. She stepped out, the Medusa eyes fixed on Butch and initiated a slow, violent, seductive walk towards him.

"Cindy!" Caleb blurted.

They were all slapped into tableau by that: the mutants' startled expressions turning quickly to leers as they spotted her; Butch, baffled, because he expected to meet his demise at Cindy's hands; Caleb, jaw dropped, eyes bugged, and a look of pleasure and dread; and Art, equally jaw-dropped, but able to say, "You know my sister?"

Caleb glanced an affirmative. Cindy turned from her intended victim, Butch, and dropped her cobra stare on him, instead. A slight smile formed. "Caleb."

It was a word of ice, a caress from the hangman, an acknowledgment of his existence with absolutely no indication of anything else. No joy, no promise, no regard, and Caleb's stunned face fell in a bit.

You're not the first one, bucko. "So how do you know my sister?" Art leveled up, noticing a bit of threat in his voice that he really hadn't intended.

Caleb repeated the glance at him and then went back to Cindy, and could he be blamed? She stood there, a north wind, cold and beautiful. Deadly.

"How've you been?" she asked.

"I..." and Caleb trailed off because there was nothing he could say, nothing at all. Just look at him. Just look at her. It was Golem and Galadriel.

After a moment more of the tableau, Cindy said, softly, "Good to see you again," blasting Caleb once more with her dark magic, turned, walked over to Butch and then towed him by the elbow towards the stove.

Caleb visibly shrank, as if a part of his soul he'd long protected had just dissolved. Art was familiar with the effect, having seen Cindy cast this spell on a few previous occasions. "Why don't you tell me how you know my sister?"

Caleb, sorrowful, diminished, flicked an eye at him. "Everyone knows your sister." He turned back to the mutants, who stared at Cindy's threatening walk. "Hey!" he said and they jumped and went back at it, still tossing leers her way.

Art grabbed Caleb's T-shirt sleeve. "What do you mean by that?"

Caleb frowned at him and something ugly stirred in his eyes. He wrenched his arm away and stalked after the mutants, who dragged pipes and tanks and hoses over to the pump. Moments later, Caleb, goggled and gloved, applied a hot blue flame to the well base.

Maybe Cindy had applied a hot blue flame to his heart.

Art stayed with the well workers to avoid Cindy and Butch over by the tents. There'd been some rather heated exchanges between those two; the rising voices carried over the torch and the hammers that eventually freed the well cap, but the words were unintelligible. Art imagined their content: Cindy inquiring mildly if Butch had lost his effin' mind, followed by his feeble attempts to refute that. It finally quieted down over there and Art stepped outside and glimpsed them both sitting in camp chairs in front of the tent. Cindy was smoking, probably a Camel Light, her favorite. Such a girl cigarette.

Caleb came out with a sample jar of water, which he held up to the sun. "That'll do it."

Sediment and things roiled inside. "Doesn't look good from here," Art said.

Caleb shrugged. "Water's always fulla junk. Still could be potable." He placed the jar inside a small box, sealed it and put his initials on the tape. "I'll get this over to the lab. Should have a yes or no by this afternoon." He paused and looked across the way to the tent and the smoking Cindy. "Say the sample's okay," he said, still on Cindy, "wot you want us to do?"

"Get it running."

"Awright," Caleb nodded, broke his contact with Cindy and whatever the hell was between them, and looked back at the mutants to check on their hose-rolling and tank-breakdown progress. Satisfied, he went back to Cindy, then to Art.

Art took him on. "So she's the Deats you knew from Dothan."

Caleb said nothing.

"Uh-huh. And she never mentioned us." More nothing. "Or this place." Even more nothing. "And you never made the connection." It was a one-sided conversation and Art grew tired of carrying it. "So you want to ask me something?"

"Just..." Caleb hesitated, going back to Cindy, who either didn't see him or chose not to. "Just... are all y'all coming back to live here?"

"One of us. Why?"

"Well..." he stopped. Frowned. Looked frustrated and moved to the mutants to help them arrange equipment for transport back to the truck. The three of them, with great efficiency, stored everything, secured loose things, closed panels. The two mutants got in and Caleb pulled out a clipboard and leaned it against the hood.

Art walked over. "Well... what?"

Caleb ignored that and handed him an invoice. Art looked it over. Reasonable. "Take plastic?"

"Visa or MasterCard. No American Express. They charge too much."

"Do they ever," Art agreed and handed over a card and Caleb ran it through a portable card machine and Art, mentally, added the total to Butch's bill.

"I'll give you a call," Caleb said, getting in and starting the truck.

Art walked over to the window. "So, again, just what?"

Caleb stared at Cindy, put the truck in gear, repeated, "I'll give you a call," then backed down the driveway. The mutants stared at Art, hostile, all the way out of sight. "Great," Art said and then walked over to the campsite.

Cindy and Butch sat quietly, Cindy's cigarette still glowed, Butch's coffee cup half full, the two of them gazing in different directions. Neither of them looked up when Art pulled open a folding chair and plopped across from them. "So where do you know that guy Caleb from?" he asked her.

Her eyes predatory, evaluating, rested on him. "From around."

"Was he a boyfriend or something?"

She blinked. "Or something."

"Did you know him from Yoman?"

Slow, luxurious draw of smoke. "No. Dothan."

"Dothan. You met that guy in Dothan. When was this?"

The eyes turned bright yellow, a prelude to attack. "You sure ask a lot of questions."

"Yeah." He scootched the chair closer. "Yeah, I do. F'rinstance, how many other guys from Dothan do you know, and when the fuck did you ever get the time or opportunity to do so? And what the fuck are you doing here?"

Butch leaned forward, anger on his brow. "Language!"

"I'll fucking use whatever fucking language I fucking damn fuck shit hell and bastard I fucking want to." He glared Butch back. "Well?" That at Cindy.

She looked amused. "I could ask you the same question."

"I'm here to help. You're not. So?"

She took another long puff, put on her contented cat look, and said, "I'm helping, too." Pause. "In my way."

"In your way." Art stared at her for a moment, then stood up fast, driving the camp chair back. Butch jumped but Cindy remained still, amused. Art spun and stalked towards the house. "Coming?" he barked over his shoulder at Butch.

Chapter 10

Wednesday afternoon

Art had discovered fairly early in his career that teeth-grittin', stomach-boilin', eye-bulgin' anger made a hard day's work easier. It let him drive nails and burn steel almost without the benefit of tools. He'd also discovered how easy it was to reach that state. With baseline anger and a trigger halfway pulled most of the time, it didn't take much. At least once or twice a week Art stormed out of the house in the wake of some silly fight with Linda and turned in one of the most amazingly productive days he or Conrad, that twat, had ever seen.

This had drawbacks, such as he and Linda were barely on speaking terms anymore but, hey, she benefited from the bigger paychecks. And if she didn't take the bullet, then he'd vent on someone else. Like Rich.

Or Cindy.

So he started on the floors in the perfect mood to finish them, and finish, he did. By about four o'clock. And pretty much by himself. All Butch did was get in the way, which had the added benefit of fueling Art's anger and improving the workflow. After he had driven the last nail across the joist, Art threw the hammer with an almost savage joy up through the opening, little caring where it landed, and spat, "Done!" With the joists, anyway.

Butch was, by this time, huddled in a far corner of the crawlspace, eyeing him warily. "We are?"

"What do you mean 'we,' paleface?" Art snarled and pulled himself through and balanced on the kitchen joists. He had half a mind to kick Butch right in his stupid, useless, dumbfuck head when it popped up, but he didn't want to ruin his boots. Instead, he bounced up and down to get a feel for the repair. "Good," he announced, and stalked out, ignoring Butch's hand flapping weakly around the opening.

Art stopped on the porch, still chewing nails. If he were at work, he'd launch straight into another project like repacking the truck's wheel bearings, but he wasn't at work, wasn't at home, was here. Maybe he could go ahead and start laying the floorboards and he cast a bloodshot eye at the pile stacked against the garage rubble, but no. Repacking wheel bearings benefitted him (and that twat, Conrad); rebuilding this place did not.

So why was he here?

An excellent question. Did he have an excellent answer?

Yes. Because Butch had asked him.

And Butch was a blithering incompetent and this gave Art a chance to rub that in Butch's over-educated face. And because he was curious. So, weren't those benefits? Of a negative kind, ones that wounded more than elevated, tore at old scars. And that made him even madder, but it was generalized rage without the concreteness of specificity, such as Linda's frivolous spending or lax oversight of the boy. He'd fueled this work fest by getting non-specifically mad at Cindy. No, that's not accurate. He's not mad at her; he's frustrated, which was enervating, not empowering. And *that* made him specifically mad.

It all works out somehow.

He yanked a cigarette out of his shirt pocket, lit it and puffed angrily... no, puffed in frustration. No one was telling him what was going on, just like when they were kids. Cindy and Butch and their secrets, always cutting him out. Even now. He glanced at the driveway but Cindy's car was gone. Figures. She never answered any of his questions, anyway. Heck, he couldn't answer his own.

"So... now what?" Butch had crept up behind him.

Art took a puff. "I don't know," he said.

"I mean, are we going to do more floor work?"

"I don't know."

"You said we have to replace all of the floors."

Sucking in more smoke, Art turned. "I. Don't. Know." He puffed all three words right in Butch's face.

Butch waved the smoke away, stepped back and coughed. "You didn't have to do that." In answer, Art took in a giant lungful and blew a stream of Raleigh right at him. Butch retreated through the other side of the porch and stepped down to the kudzu-covered patio. "What's wrong with you?"

"What's wrong with all of us?" Art said, more to himself, and stepped down the other side, heading towards his truck.

"Where you going?" Butch called.

Art ignored him, got inside and backed down the driveway. Butch watched, open-mouthed as Art yanked onto the road, pointed towards Enterprise, and roared away. He took out his cell phone and laid it on the seat next to him, keeping an eye on the bars. About ten miles later, just past the bridge over a small nameless creek, he had a decent signal. He pulled onto a gravel hump and punched a button.

She answered on about the fourth ring. "Are you all right?"

"No," he said. No "hello"; they never said hello.

There was a pause. "Tell me," she said.

"I'd love to, but I don't think I really can." Another pause. "I'm working on a haunted house."

Intake of breath. "Really? Have you seen some ghosts?"

He thought about the pool. "No. Maybe. I think some local yokels are messing around. But I did see them back when I was a kid."

"What kind of ghosts?"

"What kind are there? Shades of something wrong. I saw them around the old pool."

"You had a pool? I'm jealous." Her laugh tinkled like crystal, so different from Linda's. No judgment in it.

"Not that kind of pool. Above-ground. Big one, but still plastic. We used to jump in there at night, when it was hot."

"So it was a happy place. Then why the ghosts?"

"That's a good question." Art drew as much of the Raleigh as was left, pitched it out of the window, pulled out another and lit it. "I guess because it wasn't really a happy place. There may have been moments when we laughed our asses off splashing each other and stuff, but those were just moments. I don't think there were enough of those to offset the rest."

She absorbed that. "I'm so sorry," she whispered and there, right there, the warmth. A little tingle in his stomach arose. "Thank you," he whispered back.

"When will you be home?" There was an answering tingle in her voice and Art couldn't help it, he stirred, hardened. He couldn't with Linda anymore because, because, well, Linda was Judgment.

This one wasn't. He thought of her, strawberry and red, a little overweight, but offering... everything. In her bed, her eyes on him, hungry, and he'd enter and she always gasped right at that moment and for all the moments until he came so hard he was dead, completely dead, for a moment; everything, all of life, his entire soul reduced to that one eternal, timeless explosion. And she was so grateful. And wanted more. And was the only woman who could coax him to it.

"Soon," he said.

"Okay." Accepting, but a promise in it. "Better be. Conrad's being a real bitch."

"Conrad," he snorted, "that twat. Is he threatening to fire me?"

She laughed. "Every day! He's storming around the office talking about how you're ungrateful and he made you and you have no loyalty and he's going to get rid of you. The usual."

"Yeah." Art wasn't bothered. Conrad knew damn well he'd never get a combination truck/heavy equipment driver /mechanic and all around Jack-of-all-heavy-trades who owned all his own gear (including the tractor) like Art for the cheap rates he paid. Imagine if Art had a degree, how much more he'd command.

Except he'd be just another idiot. Like Butch.

The conversation ended at some point, Art wasn't sure, and he sat in the truck for a few minutes, post-coital. He took a puff. Life was long moments of darkness and suffering, punctuated by a comma or two of relief, of actual joy. Most people wanted it to be the other way around, but, no. Never appreciate the commas, then; you'd stop working for them. And the long moments would eat you.

Art tossed the cigarette out of the window, started the truck and turned it around. Guess it's time for another series of long moments. Go back to the house, get into an argument with Cindy, get into an argument with Butch, punch Butch in the mouth. Butch would either fall down bawling or turn into the Hulk and end up breaking Art's back or something.

Talk about rage.

The Hulk's appearances depended on how Butch was approached. If someone made him feel the issue under examination was his fault, then he'd stand there and take it, apologize the whole time while someone kicked his ass. Once, back in New Jersey, some guy slapped Butch around because he'd taken the guy's laundry out of a washing machine.

"Why'd you let him do that?" Art asked as Butch nursed a

black eye.

"I shouldn't have touched his stuff."

No, Butch, the guy shouldn't have hogged the machines but, hey, that's you.

But if attacked personally, then the unholy green beast emerged.

Art'd personally seen the beast only twice. The last time was about twenty-five years ago in a Piney bar somewhere out past Chatsworth, where Butch told him he was getting out of the Air Force to be a preacher. Art laughed, calling out to a couple of nearby lumberjacks that Butchy boy here was seekin' the Lord, Hallelujah! and the lumberjacks thought this great sport and came over and, well... by the time it was over, Art had backed against the wall, the jukebox between him and the Hulk, as ambulances and police converged and Butch beat feet through the back door, but not before he'd head-kicked one already unconscious lumberjack and tossed the other one through the window and given Art the most hateful, murderous glare humanly possible.

Butch paid the damages and the hospital bills. Charges were dropped. And Art did not see Butch again until five years later, at Art's front door, sporting a reversed collar.

That was bad, and he'd heard stories from awed witnesses of other Butch/Hulk incarnations just as bad, but not as bad as the first time Art had seen the beast.

In Yoman.

Yoman.

Art slowed as he approached Bark's Store, hesitated, then yanked the truck to the left and headed down the road.

Let's see about Yoman.

Wow. How time rots all.

Art leaned against the fence, his fingers entwined in the chain link separating the collapsed mass of what was once the Yoman School from the rest of civilization. What the heck happened here, an earthquake? The Damascus School had fared better than this. He studied the mass of bricks and mortar trying to figure out where formerly recognizable architectural features once stood.

Okay, the stairs that swept up to a porch flanked by white plantation columns should be about there. The two brick wings extended right and left, a big front yard the middle of which was more or less where Art now gawked, so behind him would be the school's original chain-link fence and gate sited to keep the kids in (or the locals out).

Hmm. Wonder if this chain-link fence is the same one, now repurposed?

Art, still attached to the fence, looked over his shoulder at where the gate used to be and through which all the kids poured during the ten-minute morning recess and raced down the block to Atco's, a combination store/gas station/barber shop/whittlin' place and lair-of-layabouts, to buy honey buns and moon pies and RC Colas with peanuts poured inside and then race back before the bell rang and Principal Harvey met them with a belt in his hand.

He turned back and went on tiptoes to get a view behind the brick pile. The lunchroom, connected by a covered walkway to the main building, had been back there, staffed by peanut-farmer wives who cooked up greens and harsh cornbread and lots of unrecognizable fatty meats rendered edible by layers of pepper juice. Nutritious and delicious, especially on top of moon pies and peanutted RC Cola. Then, out of the side door to hot, dusty, red fields interspersed with swing sets and teeter-totters and baseball and schoolyard cruelty.

All of it now a pile of fenced-off brick junk.

Art wandered around the fence, trying to recognize something. Anything. But no, the decay was complete. He stopped at the west side and glanced at the neighboring house, a gabled three-story Victorian, brooding behind willows and magnolias. At least that's still there, and well kept; painted, yard trimmed, strong indicators of ongoing habitation. He doubted it was Old Lady Dunfrie, a withdrawn, grayed husk who'd lived there alone the entire time Art attended Yoman. She was nice, though, and let Butch and him stash their bikes in her yard because parking them at school was a guarantee of getting the spokes kicked out. Peanut-farmer kids didn't have nice bikes; only outsider quasi-Yankee kids whose father flew helicopters for a living did.

And, boy, did Butch and Art have nice bikes. Heck, they had nice everything. Dad always acted as if they were on the verge of bankruptcy, shrieking about bills and food and waste and lights left on and the damn kids tearing up their damn clothes, but he bought a new car for Mom every year and poured millions into his damn boat and one Christmas got the kids nice bikes, even though he acted as if it broke him and we better be grateful because Dad must now forgo eating and gasoline just so you spoiled brats can have some play toys.

God, what an asshole.

Butch loved his bike, a five-speed Schwinn blue beauty with handlebar brakes, quite the novelty in 1968. Butch was on that thing every available moment, taking a Grit Newspaper route that took him sometimes twenty miles on a Saturday over the side and dirt roads of Yoman, as far afield as Ino and occasionally the outskirts of Elba, collecting fifteen cents an issue, five of which Butch got to keep while racking up gift points. Just as the Saturday sun broke the horizon, there'd Butch go, a big stack of Grits perched on the back as he pedaled like mad down the road, pedaling back anywhere between noon and five, sunburned, soaked through with sweat, but most, if not all, of his Grits gone. He recruited Art into the enterprise, but Art was good for about two miles before the Alabama sun drove him into the confines of Bark's Store. Butch ended up doing most of the work himself.

Guy was crazy.

Art re-eyed the fence and the mess it contained and then made his way around until he was on Old Lady Dunfrie's porch. He knocked. Something stirred inside the house, and he waited patiently until a young guy, maybe thirty, but with rapidly thinning sandy hair and a face shaped like a hatchet, peered suspiciously at him through the jalousie. "Hep ya?"

"Sorry to bother you," Art said, immediately wondering what the guy was doing home before five o'clock. Unemployed? Drug dealer? "I'm interested in the property next door." Art pointed back at the school.

"Y'ar?" said with incredulity. Hatchet Face opened the door to look, with even more astonishment, at Art's dust-covered, sweat-stained person. "You are?" he repeated, but with different emphasis, as if Art didn't look as though he could afford a canvas tent, much less a piece of property.

"Yes." Art gestured at himself. "And sorry for my appearance. I was restoring floors in an old house. Drove by and saw that and, well, was wondering." Sounded plausible, even to him.

Hatchet's eyes narrowed. "Y'ain't from around here, are ya?"

What gave it away, Chief? That I speak grammatically correct English? Art put on his disarming smile. "I used to be, but I've spent quite a few years up north."

Hatchet nodded. "Yeah, you sound like a Yankee. So what, you thinking of buying it?" Hatchet gestured towards the school.

"Do you own it?"

"Nah." Hatchet shook his head. "District took it in receivership. Think all they want is the taxes paid." He looked at Art expectantly.

"Um." Non-committal. "Used to be a school, right?"

"It was. I went there, most of the people around here did."

Art peered at Hatchet but, no, the guy was too young to be a classmate. "So what happened to it?"

Hatchet shrugged. "Everyone went off to the consolidated schools in Enterprise. District didn't want to pay for the upkeep, so they sold it some developer in Florida, but he let it all run to hell. There it is." Hatchet threw out a regretful palm.

"Hm. Didn't Mrs. Dunfrie live here in this house?" Art nodded at the door.

Hatchet's eyebrows rose. "She sure did. She died some years ago, left no one, so Daddy bought it. So you did live here before."

What, think I was lying about that? Art narrowed. "Like I said, I went here, too, up through fifth grade. Long before your time. So," – quick change of subject – "you think anyone would get mad if I look around it some?"

Hatchet considered. "No, probably not. Kids get in there and mess around and the constable chases 'em off, but if you're interested in the property, don't think anyone'd mind."

No doubt, Art thought. Didn't look like anything else was going on 'round hyeah anymore. I mean, look at this guy. "Your dad lived here his whole life?"

"Yep. Owns an insurance company in Dothan. He's there now."

You should be, too, Junior. "I might know him. What's his name?"

"David Jones."

Art blinked. "David Jones? Davey Jones? Everyone called him Locker?"

"Yeah!" Hatchet smiled, revealing a sore need for dental

work. "That's him! What's your name so I can tell him?"

Art snorted. "Locker," he said more to himself. He stared at the puzzled Hatchet. "Tell your dad it's Art Deats."

"Deats?" Hatchet blinked, startled. "You're a Deats?" He blinked again as Art nodded confirmation, then backed through the door and rapidly closed it in Art's face.

Art chuckled. What a small world.

He walked off the porch and made his way around the back of the site, picking his way carefully among jutting timbers and piles of metal that had escaped the fence. It took a bit of maneuvering, but he centered himself in what had to be the play yard, the swings to his right, the back fence and back gate leading to Atco's on his left, all spotlighted by the falling sun. So that meant he was facing the outdoor basketball court... where he had seen Butch turn into the Beast for the first time.

Against Locker.

Chapter 11

Forty, fifty years ago

Nineteen sixty-eight. Thereabouts. Maybe 1969, one or the other of those bloody, frightening years in American history, when bullets felled politicians and cities burned and Dad screamed at the television almost nightly. Art wasn't into time or events then, so he could not tie it to a specific date. Just a zeitgeist.

Definitely spring, though. Late spring, when summer winds showed up to give a taste of what was coming... you know, sort of like now? The hallways boiled, the classrooms more so, and the only respite came here in the play yard, where hardy spring coolness made a valiant last-ditch effort.

Art and a couple of his pals loafed at the fence behind the swings while watching the little peanut-farmer girls' dresses fly up and show their underwear. The little girls shrieked, "Get away! Get away!" but with a teasing smile, because they knew their future depended on showing underwear to some peanut-farmer boy, their protests a nod towards Jesus of a modesty their own experience told them was nonsense. Art and his pals roared approval, especially for the poorer girls who had rips in their underwear and showed a bit more than Jesus would like, and they were set for an afternoon of this when the clarion call of schoolyard action sounded, "Fight! Fight!"

Like iron filings to a magnet, the entire populace of Yoman School flowed from their various schoolyard pursuits to a point just outside the covered cafeteria walkway where flurries of dust and concentrated shouting pinpointed the fight's epicenter. Art was too short to see over the eighth and ninth graders who, by rights, had taken the front row but, in the inexplicable manner of schoolyard communication, he knew that the fighters were Locker and Butch.

Which was astounding. Butch was one of the unlikeliest

fighters in a school renowned for its fighters, peanut-farmer kids who practiced their dad's sense of prickly honor over everything, from what someone thought of black people (although that wasn't the word they used), to whether one backed Auburn or Alabama. Butch had quickly proved willing to stand there and eat humble pie rather than engage (a startlingly similar manner to how he dealt with Dad), and the school fighters were contemptuous of him, tripping him all the time, taking his lunch, not picking him for baseball and basketball (although Butch's spasticism probably counted more), but generally left him alone because he was a Yankee (why did Alabamans think Oklahomans were Yankees?) and odd and harmless and wouldn't fight, so where's the fun in that? They even tolerated his surface friendship with Claude, the one black kid in the region willing to go to Yoman, thereby allowing the school district to say they were complying with the federal mandate.

Art, powered by incredulity, forced his way through the crowd until he could peer between the elbows and ribs of the bigger kids. Tableau: Locker, a hulking slope-browed, black-haired, blue-eyed craphead who was particularly cruel to just about everyone (a birthright because his daddy was an alderman) had the front of Butch's Nehru shirt (Butch was the only one in Yoman who wore Nehru shirts, general ridicule notwithstanding) locked in his two callused fists as he jammed Butch against a supporting pole. "I said," Locker pushed his deeply freckled face almost against Butch's nose, "your sister is a whore!"

Art, at that point, felt an irresistible urge to fly at Locker and rend his calf with raging teeth. The press of bodies made sudden, wild attack near impossible, and Art struggled against the wall of eager, cheering yahoos blocking him...

...until the change in Butch's face stopped him cold.

Butch wore a perpetual expression of confusion and fear. From the moment he got up, heck, even while sleeping, he looked like an abused puppy. It was his normal school face, his home face, his standing-before-the-wrath-of-Dad face. The only time it worked into something else was in moments of delight, buried in a collection of Ray Bradbury stories or his stupid X-Men comics. Or in moments of injustice, like that time Art crossed out Butch's math homework because he didn't like that Butch was in a higher grade than him and, therefore, regarded as smarter.

As previously stated, Butch wasn't smarter, dammit. He's just older.

Butch's abused puppy face had the power of deflection, the same way a whining, crying puppy keeps its neck unwrung. Instead, it gets kicked across the room with a contemptuous snort. And if Butch had maintained puppy face, then all Locker would have done was throw him against the pole once or twice, making Butch's head ring, and then toss him to the ground and walk away, sneering and pointing while his pals sneered and pointed in support. Butch would have dusted himself off, cowardice reconfirmed, and gone back to class.

But Locker had made a very serious mistake. Very serious. He had not just insulted Cindy, he'd done so with the ring of truth.

Cindy and her girlfriend, Shorty, were always hanging out with the boys, always twitching their asses at the boys and doing things like goosing the boys to make them jump. Late at night, the boys pulled their pickups and Camaros up the driveway, lights off, until Dad walked out to see who it was and then they sped off.

Boys boys boys.

They included older, almost-men like Sawyer, the guitar-playing cotton farmer who sometimes hid in the garage late at night and once stole a chainsaw from Dad; or Ike, local thug who prowled the property at odd hours and slipped into the garage bedroom and told Art and Butch very dirty things until Cindy snuck out of the house and the two of them slunk away into the night, and who knows what went on.

Caleb was probably one of those.

And Locker's insult, bolstered by fact, was enough to get most brothers raging, fists clenched and breath shortened because a brother does not brook insults made against a sister, even accurate insults. But it was far more egregious in this case because Butch and Cindy were close. Very close.

Those two were bonded, melded, indivisible, with no liberty or justice for Art. The force field between them blocked all others; he'd lost count of how many times he'd watched them run into the woods with a bunch of toys to play house or army, how many times he'd stumbled upon them in the backyard playing on the tire swing or badminton at the droopy net set up in the far garden or huddled together behind the chicken shed whispering. They always drove him off, screaming to leave them alone, and then conspired to make it look like he broke things or misbehaved and Art endured much undeserved Dad-wrath as a result until he, finally, learned to stay away when they were together.

Outside the house, in school, in the stores, they maintained their separate personas, ran with unmeshed friends, stayed at different sides of the hall. But they always sought each other's eyes and passed winks. Two more-incompatible people didn't exist, but Butch and Cindy were soldiers in foxholes, companions by circumstance, blood brothers.

Survivors.

And Locker had stepped right into the middle of that.

Art saw it before anyone else because he was more familiar with Butch's standard face pattern and knew when it changed, but he had never seen this change before. Oh, sure, crybaby Butch, scaredy-cat Butch, happy Butch, those he knew, but this... was different. The term immediately leaping to Art's mind was 'Beast man,' or whatever that guy in Butch's *X-Men* comics was called. As he became more familiar with the syndrome, he called it the Hulk. Butch's almost invisible lips compressed into complete invisibility, his deep-set eyes (just like Dad's) narrowed even more – if that were possible – and the befuddled light in them burned like the fifth circle of Hell. Locker must have sensed the change because his brow furrowed and he flinched, inadvertently losing his hold on Butch's shirt.

Another very serious mistake.

Butch moved like lightning, with a speed and ferocity everyone thought him incapable of, and that Art had long suspected he could muster, slapping both sides of Locker's head with the palms of both hands, the sound like a thunderclap. Grabbing and wrenching Locker's ears into silly putty, Butch drove his forehead as hard as he could into Locker's nose. They were odd moves, but Art recognized them as techniques Butch had pulled from some Bruce Tegner books and practiced on a duffle bag filled with sand that Butch hung up near the tire swing.

The simultaneous head-slap-and-nose-break just about killed Locker right then, but Butch wasn't finished. As Locker screamed and reeled back, Butch threw a stiffened leg straight into Locker's crotch, essentially driving Locker's balls up through his head, and then pivoted on his support leg and drove the heel of the ball-kicking leg straight into Locker's now-locked knee.

The pop sounded all the way back to the swing set.

That was a bridge too far, because Locker was Destined for Greater Things, a natural-born athlete representing good ole Yoman at Enterprise and Auburn and then Dallas or Pittsburgh. But, not after this. Several surgeries later, Locker's limp was under control, but his star quarterback future was gone and he now ran a back-country insurance office while, apparently, harboring a lifelong hatred of all things Deats.

And, even then, Butch did not stop.

As Locker collapsed screaming against the opposite support pole, his white face already conveying a realization that the Dream was Dead, Butch fell on him and hit and hit and hit. Over and over, blow after blow, Locker's face exploded in blood and bone as Butch, devil-mask eyes blazing red and beast (later Hulk) fangs bared, beat and beat and beat. It took Principal Harvey and the idiot baseball coach... Curran, yeah, that was his name... to pull Butch off and, even then, Harvey had to stroke him a good one to get him under control. And just like that, mealy-mouthed puppy face Uriah Heep Butch re-appeared, slack-jawed, bewildered, looking like that mule in the Bugs Bunny cartoon, "What'd I do, what'd I do?"

Ambulance for Locker. Butch sent home (rode his bike), Cindy in the office for the rest of the day and Art, bewildered, moved through the halls, all his friends staying ten feet away, all of them scared this Deats' madness would incarnate and he'd break their knees, too.

No one did anything. This is Alabama. You don't call someone's sister a whore.

Dad didn't say, or do, anything, either. That was baffling. At the very least, he should have screamed at Butch about pending lawsuits but, no. Such suits would never manifest – this was Alabama – yet Dad rarely needed a pretext to scream and beat one of the kids and... nothing. Art kept his distance from Butch, and Butch and Cindy resumed their secretive ways as if nothing happened. Butch came back to school a week later.

A week after that, Cindy ran away.

Art blinked at the rubble. She had, hadn't she? Her and Shorty, right out of the school, right out of the school day. First Art heard about it, Principle Harvey pulled him out of class and sat him down in the Office of Death, where paddlin's were administered,

Art convinced he was about to meet – again – the infamous three-foot long thin-bladed cricket club with blister-raising holes drilled in it, when Harvey asked if he knew where Cindy was. Well, in class, Principal Harvey sir, and please don't beat me, sir, beat her, instead, but she wasn't in class, wasn't anywhere, and five minutes later the whole school and its environs knew that she and Shorty had decamped sometime after the morning break. Bewildered, Art floated through the rest of the day with his friends resuming their ten-foot distance over this new Deats' madness. Later on, Art glimpsed Butch sitting in the Office of Death, a grim, pre-Hulk look on his face and Art wondered whose knee would turn to kindling next.

Three days later, a State Police car deposited a red-faced and tear-streaked Cindy on the porch, the nine-foot tall-and-wide trooper pulling Dad aside and whispering something and then leaving and Art wanted to pull the trooper aside and suggest he stay for a while to prevent Cindy's upcoming murder. But Dad did... nothing. At all. Said nothing. Screamed nothing. Mom didn't either. Cindy went to her bedroom and stayed there, not returning to school which was about a week away from ending, anyway. Bewildered, Art looked to someone for explanation but no one provided it, not even Butch, who gave him a pre-Hulk face when he asked, promising to turn Art's skull into kindling and leave it alone, shall we? He did. He finished school that Friday, and the summer was on them and everything was gone and forgotten.

Gone and forgotten.

Just like the other Deats girl.

Chapter 12

Wednesday evening

Butch squatted at the camp stove attending to something. Looked like chili again. Art, planted in one of the camping chairs under the shade of a larger-than-usual pine, watched while periodically shifting out of the sunset. "Ever hear from Dale?"

Butch stopped in mid-stir. "Dale?"

"Our other sister."

"I know who Dale is." Butch sounded irritated, as if Art had questioned his intelligence. Which he did. "Why?"

"Just wondering if she's gonna pull up here and punch you in the nose, too." Art took a swig from a warm beer. Need to get more ice.

Butch *tsk*ed his annoyance, resumed obligations to the chili and Art resumed a vegetative state, figured the subject dropped.

"I lived with her for about a year." Butch said

"Who? Dale?"

"Yes. That's who we're talking about."

About twenty minutes ago, chief. But since you re-raised it..."When did you do that?"

"After high school."

"Back in the seventies?"

"Yep."

Art stared at Butch's back. "You never told me that."

"You never asked."

Which was true. Art had no real interest in Dale, a shadowy figure in the background of his childhood, sullen teenager playing Bob Dylan records and waving contemptuously from the back of a car filled with other teenagers, *doo-wop* blasting from the radio as they sped off while Dad screamed at them from the porch and Mom wrung her hands. Give her credit for that, but theirs had been an adversarial relationship, Dale yelling at Art to stay out of her room and Art taking every opportunity to do the opposite and mess with her stuffed animals.

She left Oklahoma for the hippie kingdoms of San Francisco right before the rest of them left for the peanut kingdoms of Alabama. Art had not heard from her since, and experienced only fleeting thoughts about her since, like right now, so no surprise he'd never asked.

"Why'd you go out there?"

"Had to get away from New Jersey."

"Why'd you come back?"

"Had to get away from California."

Art laughed. "And then you joined the Air Force. Man, can't settle down, can ya?"

There was a silence. "No," Butch whispered.

The silence stretched and Art felt it encompass something else, something he did not know about and, frankly, didn't want to. Need a change of subject. "Sooo, how was it?"

"What? Living with Dale?" Butch shrugged. "It was a hippie lifestyle. I stayed in a back room overlooking the beach, slept all day because I was working in a halfway house at night. All kinds of people came and went, all hippies, all stoned. Couldn't have a conversation with any of them that made sense."

Art chuckled. "And what was Dale like?"

"The most hippy of them all," Butch chuckled back.

That was a supremely satisfying answer and Art sat back, smiling. It was a good image of his shadow sister, the one eaten by the sixties, now more figment than real. She had made an excellent escape and took on a contrarian life effectively designed to erase all traces of previous existence. Whatever she was doing now, it was better than what she had left behind.

"Do you remember when she visited here?" Butch stirred the chili.

Art blinked. "Dale was here? I don't remember that."

"Not surprised." Butch tasted the chili and smiled at it. "It was only one night. She came to see Mom and brought her husband."

"Husband?"

"You know." Butch's chili-taste smile remained, which was odd. "The black guy."

Art did know the black guy, but indirectly: Dad freaking out on the phone late one night as Mom stood next to him, hands clasped in agony, and all Art could derive from Dad's ravings was that Dale "married some nigger!" There had been days of gloom afterwards, with Dad on the edge of murdering everyone, warning them all to never, ever speak Dale's shameful name or mention her nigger husband and what would soon be her nigger children to anyone because it was a family horror. At least to Dad. Art didn't think it was a big deal, although he knew better than to say anything anywhere within a five-hundred-mile radius of Yoman.

After that, to mention her became downright dangerous because Dad would slap the crap out of you as he chanted her litany of sins: pariah, defiler of all things Good and Decent, citizen of Mammon, a whore drunk on the decadence of San Francisco. She was wrongness, anathema; add to that Art's lack of contact with her and she faded from memory, becoming a smudge, a mere impression laid over the past in the way a long-forgotten pet will randomly come to mind.

But you'd think he'd remember something as dramatic as her black husband showing up hyeah in Klan Country. You'd think. "So, what happened?"

"Hmm?" Butch absently stirred the pot.

"When Dale showed up with her Zulu warrior and, I'm bettin', a couple of zebra children."

Butch shook his head. "You're pretty crude, you know that? The kids were cool, at least, they were when I was staying there. I don't know what they are now."

"Probably senators."

Butch laughed at that. "Probably."

"So, what happened?"

Butch was silent for a moment. "It wasn't pretty. The husband, Carl, yeah, that was his name, big guy, real nice, stepped out of the car with his hand out to shake Dad's, and Dad leveled a shotgun at him."

"No shit?"

"No shit. Told him to get his damn nigger's ass off his property before he blew him right out of his pimp shoes."

"No shit?"

"I paraphrase. Dale was still in the car, just watching, a couple of babies in the back. She didn't even get out. Carl just stared at Dad a moment, shook his head, got back in, and drove off."

"Wow." Art shook his own head. "That must have been

something. How did I miss it?"

"You didn't. You were standing right there. Crying."

Art concentrated hard but not even a glimmer. Amazing the things he'd forgotten, like Dad almost murdering a brother-in-law. "Don't have it. At all."

"Not surprised." Butch was nonchalant. "It wasn't good."

Butch apparently believed Suppressed Memory Syndrome was an asset, but Art didn't. What other important truths had he purged? "So Mom didn't get to see Dale and the grandbabies."

"Mom snuck out later and visited them in a motel in Enterprise."

"In Enterprise?" Art snorted. "Wooeee. Surprised Carl didn't get lynched."

"Me, too."

Art pitched the empty beer can towards the trash bag, not caring whether he made the opening or not. He considered another one but decided on a cigarette instead, lighting it while musing over the extraordinary gaps in his fond memories. He glanced at the pool. "Ever hear from her? Since your hippie days, I mean."

Butch made an 'eh' shrug while spooning great gobs of chili into plastic bowls without spilling a drop, demonstrating some coordination. "A few times. I even dropped by on my way to Korea. She divorced Carl and was on her third or fourth husband when I was last there. She became a lawyer, too."

"Keeping up the Deats tradition, I see." Art dragged the cigarette out, feeling a stir in his lungs. The stone? He tested, but no. Maybe a ghost of it. He glanced at the pool again.

Butch was looking at him blankly. "Huh?"

"Multiple marriages, not the 'becoming a lawyer' thing."

"*Pfhht*. I never married. And you're still married to Linda."

"In theory," Art observed, "but we are the exception proving the rule. How many times did Dad marry? How many times did Mom?" He puffed deeply. "Cindy?"

"An exception is singular. Two of us among your sample population didn't marry several times."

Art blew an admiring whistle. "Wow, Butch, that almost sounded scientific, but I refute your refutation. The Deats boys," – he waved a finger between them – "obviously regard the institution of marriage with greater respect than do the daughters." He paused. "Even if you, obviously, wanted nothing to do with it.

And even if I remain in it solely out of cussedness."

Butch sat down, gesturing at Art to take the steaming bowl he left on the side shelf of the grill. Art reached as Butch said, "I just never met the right girl."

"Kinda odd, that." Art balanced the hot bowl on his lap as he grabbed another warm beer and simultaneously spat the cigarette onto the ground. Talk about coordinated. "That's a handicap in your chosen line of work. Right?"

Butch frowned. "Not really."

"Not really? Aren't all you Holy Rollers supposed to cleave unto one woman and anytime you lay with her it's in the missionary position with all your clothes on and it better, by God, result in a child nine months later, or you have fornicated for pleasure!" Art raised an emphatic finger.

Butch let out an annoyed breath. "You're such a jerk. You can marry or not, no matter what the congregation thinks. I chose not to."

"All the women in your congregation ugly?"

"No, quite attractive. And, believe me, they were in pursuit. I never ate so many casseroles."

Art laughed. "I'll bet. Slip you a little tit while handing over a dish, hmm? And, nothing?" Art regarded him. "You're not gay, are you? Because you should have been a Catholic priest, then."

Butch laughed back. "No, I'm not gay." He put his empty bowl on the grass beside him and stared off. Towards the pool, Art noted. "Do you know we have other brothers and sisters?"

Completely out of left field, that. "What are you talking about?"

"Brothers and sisters. From Dad."

Art always suspected, but had no confirmation. He looked at Butch suspiciously. "How do you know?"

"Just do." And he lapsed into silence.

Art lapsed into an identical silence. He didn't want to pursue it. One nasty childhood trauma a night – remembered or not – was about his limit.

Chapter 13

Thursday morning

A screeching, annoying sound blew Art out of bed. "Damn bluejays!" he groused, struggling against a blanket that had, somehow, tied itself into Houdini-like knots. What am I doing with a blanket, anyway? It's too blasted hot. The annoying sound resolved into something distinctly not a blue jay as Art extracted himself. A car horn.

By the time Art escaped and fell through the tent opening and scrambled to his feet and squinted at the sunrise lined up almost perfectly with the driveway, the horn had stopped. Art made out Butch's silhouette at the top of the drive, back turned, arms crossed in a stance of pure belligerence as he confronted a rather startled Caleb silhouette which, spotting Art, boomed out, "Morning!"

Art ignored the urge to pee and strode across the grass to put himself between Butch and Caleb and the still-popping truck and the two mutants who had joined forces behind Caleb and glared hatred at Butch and the rest of existence.

"You just get up?" Caleb, pleased with himself, talked past the increasingly hostile Butch straight at Art.

"Yeah, with a little help from you," Art said, still bleary, "What time is it?" He shaded his eyes against the red-stab sun barely clearing the ridge across the street.

"'Bout 6:30," Caleb said, "Tried to call you last night, but the cells don't work right out here. Depends on which way the wind blows, I reckon. I had to get here early 'cause we're ready to install this." Caleb rolled to the back of the truck, grabbed a tarp and with a flourish pulled it off, gesturing at something there.

Art stepped around to see. "Man," was all he could say. A brand new, shiny, water-pressure tank next to a shallow-well submersible pump and various cables and pipes. "Is that a fifty-five gallon?"

"Forty-four," Caleb beamed, "Flint and Walling, about the best you can get. And that" – he pointed at the pump – "is a fifteen-gallon F&W submersible. It's a bit high powered for whatcha got." He thumbed back at the washhouse. "But, you'll have plenty of water, that's fer sure!"

"For sure," Art echoed, "but, gotta say, Caleb, looks expensive. And I don't remember ordering any of this."

"Cindy did," Caleb said.

Surprised, Art looked at the beaming and glad-to-be-of-service, very happy Caleb. Bet he was. "Did she pay for it?"

"She said he would." Caleb nodded at Butch, stock-still and unreadable and locked in glare combat with the mutants arrayed in a line in front of him.

"Hm," Art expressed his doubts, something Caleb missed completely. "You know we don't have any power, right?"

"No problem," Caleb said, "We'll test it with the generator," and he slapped one attached to the side of his truck.

"So I guess that means the water is good?"

"High iron and sulfur content," Caleb replied. As if Art needed to be told that; he remembered the rotten egg smell and rusty taste of the water when he'd taken sips from a hose or sprinkler those many years ago. Caleb continued, "It'll be drinkable, though. You won't even taste it because of the filters." He nodded at some canisters fitted on a couple of the pipes.

"Okay." Art gestured at the pump house. "Have at it." He stepped through the mutants, hooking Butch and his basilisk gaze by the elbow and dragged him back to the tent. "Make breakfast," he ordered, "Blueberry pancakes." That should keep him out of the way.

Art peed against his favorite hickory and then cleaned up in what should be the last water-bottle-filled basin – that is, if Caleb was successful – and made sure Butch stayed on task by threatening him with dismemberment if he as much as glanced at the washhouse.

That made Butch sullen. Apparently, he wanted to play with the mutants. "All right, all right," he pouted. "Why, what are you doing?"

"I'm going to Lowe's. We need more stuff. And you need to stay here and keep an eye on things. But keep an eye on things from within a five-foot radius of your fancy cooking stove. I don't want to find you anywhere outside that radius when I get back. Which should be about two hours. Get me?" And he glowered Butch into submission and then drove to Lowe's and bought several more layers of wood and board and eye of newt. Dave was nowhere around, and Art kept his interactions with Sam or Stan or whoever the hell was helping him to a minimum and made sure to avoid Allison's register. Didn't need any more ghost stories.

Ah, look, Cindy's here. He pulled up behind her car as tight as possible so she couldn't leave unless he agreed. He got out and stared towards the washhouse from which a lot of banging and yelling emanated, catching flickers of motion and shadows in the doorway. A mutant popped out, jumped into a trench on the side of the building, did something, yelled, and went back inside. Okay. Work progressed normally.

Butch and Cindy occupied camp chairs around the grill, not talking, not looking at each other. Art strolled over. "Leave me any?" he asked. Wordlessly, Butch pointed at a covered dish next to the grill and Art helped himself to cold pancakes and coffee. He pulled up another chair – man, Butch came prepared, didn't he? – and ate in their silence; only the background sounds of banging pipes and mutant-yelling broke it.

At the last bite of pancake, Art made an exaggerated swipe at his mouth and belched, "Ah!" ending the meal with an equally exaggerated smack of his lips. "Tolerable, Butch, tolerable. Now," Art noisily slurped his coffee while staring at Cindy, "what are your plans today?"

She turned her cat's eyes on him. "Nothing, really."

"Wanna help finish the floors? You can't be any worse than Mr. Fixit here." He jammed a thumb at Butch.

"No thanks," she said, but there was a hint of a smile on her lips.

Art daintily wiped his fingers. " 'Preciate you getting Caleb out here so fast. Be nice to take a shower tonight."

Butch jerked out of his zombie stare. "How we going to do that?"

"With your generator and a hose. To continue with the original subject." Art turned back to Cindy. "What, exactly, did you do to spur ole Caleb to such high levels of activity?"

Her eyes narrowed. "He's always been a hard worker."

"No doubt." Art put an innocent expression on his face. "We are talking about the same thing, right?"

"Asshole." She made an irritated movement, got up and walked away.

Butch's jaw tightened. "What are you doing?"

"Just asking questions. So." Art was on him. "You given any thought to turning on the power?"

"Can I?"

"Nope." Art pulled out a cigarette. "Whoever took all the fixtures also took the junction boxes. And probably a lot of the wiring."

"So, why'd you ask me?"

"So maybe you'd finally realize how hare-brained this whole idea is," Art said, lighting the cig, "Or, because, after we fix the floors today, we're going to fix the wiring and, by the time that's done, the local yokel power company will have you set up." Art took a long draw and stared languidly at Butch. Exhaling luxuriously, he said, "This is the moment when you call the power company and arrange that."

Butch put on an 'Oh' expression and then pulled a cell phone out of his pocket. He frowned at it. "I can't get a signal."

"The wind must not be blowing right."

A puzzled look, then Butch got up and walked around holding the phone up to the air, testing. Art watched for a moment, amused, then took a final, satisfying puff and flung the cigarette away. Sure hope something catches on fire.

Cindy leaned against Caleb's truck, arms crossed, watching the washhouse. Caleb leaned next to her. The mutants popped in and out, each time stopping dead, staring at her hungrily, then continuing about their business when Caleb glared them back to work.

"Say, Caleb," Art said, walking up, "How are you with electricity?"

"Pretty good." He brow-nodded towards the washhouse. "I do the pump wiring on all these installations."

"How about houses?" Art watched Cindy as he spoke.

"What, like this one?" Caleb, suddenly interested, pointed at the house.

"That one," Art confirmed, still watching Cindy. Her lips tightened.

"What are you looking to do?"

"Get it all up and running, like the water." Art waited two beats. "Think I might want a pool in the back, too."

Cindy cocked an eye at him as Caleb got very interested. "Oh, really? In-ground?"

"No, above-ground." Art, eyes boring into Cindy, pointed vaguely at where the pool used to be. "Right there."

Cindy made a disgusted sound, pushed off and walked through the kudzu-covered patio and around the front of the house and out of sight. Caleb watched her go. "Did I miss something?" he asked.

"I think we both did," Art said.

Butch came up at that moment, annoyed. "I still can't get a signal." Caleb pulled out his own cell phone and the two of them began the signal dance, sashaying back and forth, raising and lowering phones. It was all Art could do not to laugh.

After a while, Caleb said, "Nothin'," confirming Butch's experiments. "If you need to call someone, you'll probably have to head up the road."

Butch sighed, "Looks that way." He frowned around Caleb's truck to where Art's truck had sealed all possibilities of escape. "I don't think I can get around you."

"Don't need to," Art said, "Just go out the other side." A secondary driveway careened north through the property and connected over a culvert back onto Damascus Highway. Or, used to. Barely a track through the wiregrass now and shouldn't even be that, unless yahoos occasionally trespassed on Deats' property to chase ghosts or fuck sheep, whatever. Art wasn't sure the culvert would hold under Butch's POS. Didn't care, either.

Butch turned a wary eye at the track, then wordlessly went to his car parked on the other side of the tent. After some effort, he got it started and gingerly picked his way along the track. Art didn't bother seeing if he made it out or not and walked around the front to where Cindy had gone.

She was over by the goldfish pond, or its remnants, poking at the green scum across the top of the wrecked cement with a long stick, stirring the mess around like a giant soup. Wow, had this taken a beating. There used to be one of those funny boy-peeing statues in the middle of it that served as a fountain. Used to be goldfish in there, too. "Careful," Art said, coming up behind, "you might get a water moccasin out of there."

"There's nothing alive in here," she said, continuing to poke.

Art looked at the house. "You're telling me." A pause. "I keep hearing it's haunted."

"The pond?"

"Now you're just being funny."

She smiled at that and pulled out the stick and regarded the end of it. Art didn't see anything interesting there. "Who's telling you the house is haunted?" she asked.

"Everybody in a fifty-mile-square area. Is it?"

"Of course it is. Look at it."

Art did. It certainly met the minimum criteria: abandoned and brooding and shabby. Backdrop for a Freddy Krueger movie. "Does that have anything to do with the pool?"

She stared at him. "That's a very strange question."

"Well, this is a very strange situation."

"Hmm." Sounded like agreement. "No," she said, after a moment. "Why would you think it did?"

"'Cause the other night, I saw a couple of ghosts hanging around it." He regarded her. "Why would that be?"

Like a thunderstorm popping over the horizon, she darkened and her eyes blazed lightning and she viciously threw down the stick and stomped past him, heading straight for his truck. Probably gonna take a rock to it. He lost her for a moment behind the juniper screen, but an odd twist of the wind parted enough branches that he saw her grasp one of the hangers leaning over the top rail. "We doing this, or what?" she yelled at him.

He shrugged. "Sure," he said and went over to lend a careful hand.

Chapter 14

Thursday

She was better at it than Butch, far better. After a couple of demonstrations, Art didn't have to tell her what to brace, what to nail, and what to hold. They worked in tandem, like a single unit, Art staying surprised at how well this was going. By three-ish, they had done the entire dining and most of the living rooms. "Lunchtime," Art said, wiping his hands.

Cindy was propped against a footing. "Wimp," she said, and grabbed another hanger.

Okay, you're on.

They stayed until almost dark, getting almost all the way to her old bedroom, at least the hallway outside, but were slowed down by a rotting sill plate and a few other obstructions they had to get out of the way. At one point, they abandoned the joist work and installed the plywood flooring. At another point, Butch stuck his head in and asked nervously if they wanted anything. "Pepsi," Art said. "Beer," Cindy upped it and Art laughed and Butch frowned but brought them. "Caleb's done," he said.

"Is he still here?" Art asked.

"No."

"Did you pay him?"

Butch left. Art chuckled, and he and Cindy finished the floor base and went back to the joists. They crawled out from under the far side of the house, which was closer to where they ended up and actually easier to exit because the wooden grate over the foundation entrance had rotted away.

Should be whole colonies of Bluetick hounds living here. Ghosts must have scared them away.

They stood and groaned and popped backs and knees into proper alignments and brushed cobwebs and crap off each other. Art looked around, interested. He hadn't been over to this part of the yard yet. So let's take a gander.

This side of the house faced the southern woods fronting the long drop down to the swamp creek, an area now so tangled with moss and thorn bushes it was impenetrable. Used to be a clear distinction between those woods and the yard but decades of neglect blurred the lines. Too bad; it was a great place for hide-and-seek, but now it was a better place for snakes and Crymen. A giant red oak tree or, at least, the last gasp of it, marked where the halfway point between woods and yard used to be. Only part of the tree had leafed; the rest was dead. Sad. It had been a cool tree, great for climbing and hitting with a stick and running around until he was dizzy. Butch's duffle punching bag and the tire swing used to hang from it. During evenings like this, mosquito-borne and half-saturated with humidity, they would push each other on the swing and, sometimes, to Butch's outrage, he or Cindy would climb on the duffle bag and jump off it and laugh or fall off and cry and then, sweaty and panting and this close to heatstroke, they'd all run and jump in the pool.

The pool.

Art squatted at the corner of the house, eying the back of the washhouse and the old pool area. He shook out a cigarette and offered one to Cindy, who took it wordlessly and squatted down next to him. They lit off each other.

"You do good work," he said.

"Thanks."

"Maybe when we get back to Tabernacle we can get a business going."

She eyed him, half a smile on her lips. "Sure. Start without me."

Art laughed. The chances of Cindy actually showing up to do a day's work were too remote for him to plan a work schedule. She'd definitely show up to get the paycheck, though. He eyed her. "You still haven't told me what you're doing here."

Art expected her to shoot back with, "You haven't either," but she simply took a long puff, exhaled luxuriously, and said, "I don't really know."

"That's the best answer I've heard the last four days," Art said as he stood and stretched, gingerly feeling the spot on his lower back that was imbued with degenerative arthritis and would, eventually, put him in a wheelchair. Please.

Motionless, she stared past the tire tree into the woods. "I just can't believe this place still matters," she said.

Art was a bit surprised by that but recovered quickly, jerking a thumb at the wall. "This crap house," he said, "this crap land," – a scornful cigarette-laden sweep of the palm – "and this crap Alabama doesn't matter at all."

She regarded him coolly. "You don't really remember very much, do you?"

"I remember everything fine. I remember we got treated bad here, that Dad was an asshole and Mom was no help and we were scared all the time, and the way we left here," Art paused to take a frustrated puff, "was bad. Everything was bad. This place is bad. None of us should be here."

"What do you remember about us leaving?"

Flashes. Images. Fear, mostly. And how sudden it was. A day in late December, after Christmas. Mom wasn't there; she'd gone to New Jersey the day after Christmas to take care of Gramma, who was sick. Cindy looming in the garage door. "There's trouble. We gotta go."

He didn't know the specific trouble, only that it involved Dad and that it was very important they get the hell out of there before Dad got home from work. The three of them fleeing up the side of the road in a rainstorm, a hastily packed suitcase over each of their heads, Art crying and terrified that Dad's truck would come over the hill and catch them, a taxi ride from Bark's Store to the Dothan Greyhound station where Mom had wired tickets and then three days and nights to New Jersey, sure Dad would be waiting at every bus stop. There were more details, but he preferred glossing over them.

"How... random it was," he finally answered.

She clucked, annoyed. "Wasn't random." She had turned her attention to the washhouse... or the old pool area... Art couldn't tell which. "Wasn't random at all."

"What was it, then?"

She said nothing, remained fixed on the pool. He moved restlessly. "Why did you run away?" he asked.

"We all ran away."

"No, not that time. Before. Just you."

Her brows furrowed. "Huh?"

"Back when we were at Yoman School. After Butch broke

Locker's knee."

She looked genuinely puzzled, then her face cleared. "Oh, that." She almost smiled. Almost. "I'd forgotten all about that."

"Really?" Art threw out astonished hands. "How could you forget something like that?"

She did not answer but drifted, her eyes going somewhere else as they stayed on the pool. Like a bolt of lightning, the timeline suddenly fell into place: Locker's knee break, Cindy running away, Art staring through the wavy glass, then the three of them up the side of the road in a rainstorm.

All within a four-month period.

"You're wrong about this place," Cindy said, crushing out the cigarette. She gave a long look around, then stood and bore down on him. "Battlefields matter." And she walked away.

Chapter 15

Thursday night

"When are you coming home?" Linda's voice, irritated, over the cell. Art rolled his eyes. Now the phone works. Now. Wind must be blowing in the right direction.

"Dunno," he said, "we're still in the middle of things."

"You have things here, too."

Yeah, he sure did. Most of them sucked the soul right out of his body. *Por ejemplo,* you, Linda. "I'll get to 'em when I get back."

"You don't even know what I'm talking about."

Art let out an expansive and quite audible sigh. He reached down beside the cot, fishing for the cigarette pack and lighter next to his shoes. Naturally, couldn't find them. "Hold on a second," he said and used the cell glow to locate both and lit one with the other and fell back on the cot and took a long, luxurious puff that he ensured she heard.

"And now you're smoking again," she said.

"Never really quit," he said.

"So you lied about that, too."

"Too?"

She was silent and Art felt warfare stirring in his blood. So you want to do this again? Ask me where I am at lunchtime, why am I getting home late, why am I never at the office or job site when you call?

Simple answer, darling. I'm with someone I like better.

"So what's the emergency?" No doubt some expensive cabinets were in danger of purchase by someone other than Linda, and I must rush home waving my credit card frantically and yelling "Stop! I'll take them!" before the 1% discount ends.

"Your son got arrested."

"Arrested." Art took in a long, disbelieving puff. "A fifteen-year-old got arrested. For what, coloring outside the lines?" He laughed at his own joke.

"Possession of stolen property and marijuana."

He blinked. "What?"

"Not so funny now, is it?"

Art sat up while she explained: the police on Arney's Mount Road stopped a vehicle stolen from Presidential Lakes last week. Driving the vehicle was a sixteen-year-old loser jackass skateboard derelict who lived down the street from Art. Rich was in the backseat, along with a couple of other Tabernacle derelict skateboard assholes. Rich didn't know the car was stolen. He also didn't know how the joint got into his front pocket.

Art smoldered. "Why was he out on a school night?"

"He was supposed to be studying at Lee's."

"So you've lost control of your son, have you?"

Now she smoldered. Art took this opportunity to grab another puff and use the nicotine to calm down before she launched into, "Maybe if his father was home instead of at some hick backwater spending all of his time and money on his worthless brother—"

"That's enough," he said quietly. "Where is Rich now?"

"They released him to me."

"Okay." That should be punishment enough. "He's not hurt?"

"No." She paused. "The cops scared him."

"Good," Art said. The anger settling into his chest was almost soothing. A long-cherished friend. "Not so bad."

She was incredulous. "Not so—! Are you insane? Your son lies about where he's going, sneaks out, and is running around smoking dope with hoodlums! And that's not so bad?"

"If I recall," Art replied, coolly, "you and I spent a few evenings playing Woodstock and suffering from the munchies."

"That was different."

"How?"

"Well, for one thing, we weren't stealing cars and going on joyrides!"

Maybe *you* weren't, darlin', but there were a few nights when Art ran around the Barrens in a vehicle of dubious ownership, and in the course of said running acquired a few pieces of property through means other than retail sales. He took a long puff. "He's just being a kid."

"Chip off the old block, right?"

"Listen." His smolder now a full-blown fire. "This is not the fucking end of the world. He did something stupid. He got caught. End of story."

"It's not the end of the story! He has a court date! And he's gonna get thrown off the football team!"

"Well, good!" Art shouted, "You hated him playing anyway!"

She started to cry, "So it's all my fault?"

Art shook his head. "I didn't say that." He hadn't. He didn't believe that. But it sounded as though he did.

"Well, that's great, just great," she sobbed, "Your son is drowning, and all you're going to do is sit down there with your brother. Maybe have a beer and a laugh over it, huh?"

"No, I'm not." Not a beer or a laugh, especially with Butch. He paused for a second. "I'll be home Monday."

"What?"

He recalculated. "Tuesday."

"What time?"

"Now how the hell do I know that? It's a two-day drive."

"Okay." Art heard the calm wash over her like a moon-borne tide. That's all it took?

"Okay." He hung up.

He finished the cigarette, stood, and used the cell phone to find his way to the hickory tree for a weasel-draining. It's midnight, the phone told him. He looked up. A quarter moon poised there as he released the Kraken. Moon-borne tide, indeed.

He shook it out ("more than three times, you playin' with it! Har! Har! Har!") and giggled. Maybe he *should* play with it and considered but, nah, let's go back to bed. He gazed at the moon once more and took in a deep breath... and something stirred in his chest. Uh-oh. The stone had formed again, bumping against his lungs. Great. Must be the 1000% humidity out here. Certainly wasn't the cigarette. No, not at all.

Dizziness swept through him, and he reeled and gasped and fell against the piss tree, barely missing what he'd just moistened. What the hell? Did he suddenly turn ninety years old or something? Using his hand as a pivot point, he spun away from the piss side and sat down heavily on the opposite side. The stone bumped harder, downright banging against his chest. "Okay," he said, "No more cigarettes. I promise."

The stone regarded him with disbelief, then slowly, very

slowly, receded. Art took in some cautionary deep breaths, probing for it, but it was back in its cage. Good. Wished he had a cigarette.

He smiled at that and looked around to get oriented but couldn't see a blasted thing. The skinny moon wasn't helping. Best he could figure, he was facing the west woods. He squinted and tried to identify a landmark but no and he'd probably have to cell phone his way back to the tent... What's that? An odd line, a black shadow, about four feet tall against the bluer shadow of the night. Looked like a circle. No, a wall.

The pool wall.

It was the pool, back from the grave, back in its old location between the washhouse and the shed. That's impossible, but Art heard its pump humming and water splashing through the filter.

"No. Fucking. Way!" Art hissed and shook his head like Bugs Bunny and the pool disappeared. Not plastic walls, you idiot, overgrowth. And, yeah, there was a pump running, but it was the new one in the washhouse merrily filling the tanks courtesy of Butch's generator, which also explained the sound of water. You idiot. Man, it's easy to fool yourself, ain't it? Explains all those Bigfoot sightings.

Does it explain all sightings, though, like figures through wavy glass obscured by rain and fog but swear, swear, they're doing something on the other side of the pool? Does it?

Something. Doing something on the other side of the pool.

Art pulled himself up the side of the tree and leaned heavily against it, cautiously locating the stone. Yep, still there, a wolf circling the campfire. "All right," he said, "I know. I'll be careful." He regained balance and stepped from the tree, peering at where the ghost pool had been.

The feeble light made the scene eerie. Appropriate. After all, this was a spook hunt and conjurations required the correct formula: cold light of the moon, a chant, and a virgin sacrifice... although that last might be a little difficult hyeah in LA... Lower Alabama.

Art stepped to the edge of the old pool's borders, or where he guessed they were. No evidence of it remaining, of course; the ring worn into the ground during its four or five years of existence was long gone, but he was confident this was the spot because *foist* of all, there weren't a lot of places back here to put a fifteen-

or twenty-foot ring of water-filled plastic. *Segundo* of all, in a childhood of darkness, the few bright spots were seared in memory and the summers he spent splashing around in the pool were islands of light. A few years ago, in the grip of a stupid nostalgia, he'd bought a giant-sized above-ground pool from a guy who was going bankrupt. Nice one, had a deck and everything and Art had plopped it right smack in the middle of the backyard and then spent the subsequent Jersey summers (which could be as brutal as the ones here) plopped on air mattresses smack in the middle of the water, all the cares of work and family and misspent life floating away. What more proof does one need that we peoples are water born?

And then, during a crappy autumn rain a couple of years ago, he looked out of the back window at his wavy and blurry pool and walked out there and drained the already-winterized water and dismantled the whole damn thing, stacking the sections and selling it for half of what he paid. "Whydja do that?" a pool-loving Rich had wailed. "Too expensive," Art muttered. "You think I'm made of money or something?" Art actually believed that explanation himself; that is, until now.

So, where had he seen the two figures?

Art turned to the house, dark, hulking, its outline oddly clear as the moonlight fell about it, shunning direct contact. Easy to place the kitchen window, not so easy to figure the parallax of a twelve-year-old peering out of it. But triangulation and perspective and a little imagination and he'd seen the lights and the blurry figures... right about here. Art tapped the ground with satisfaction.

Yeah, right here, this is the spot. Wonder what they were doing?

Wonder why he hadn't gone right out the kitchen door and right up to them and asked?

Well, for one thing, it was raining, and Art wasn't one to go splashing merrily about in the cold, soul-draining downpour of a typical Alabama winter, especially when he was safe and warm and dry in the kitchen and stealing food out of the cabinet and, really, why call attention to yourself? And if those three idiots wanted to flit about in a deluge with flashlights...

Wait a minute. *Three* idiots?

Three?

Art concentrated and, in so doing, the memory cleared. Rain, wavy glass, flashlights, two small figures doing something by the pool, check. And now a third figure, looming behind them.

Dad.

A mere shadow, mere profile, serving as a backdrop to whatever the two smaller figures were doing, but definitely Dad. Arms crossed, standing like a stone, but obviously directing the two smaller ones, who had to be Butch and Cindy.

That's the real reason why he didn't go out there.

No sane child living in this household willingly put himself in Dad's presence. And given all the available evidence, Art was more than convinced he was the only sane one living here. Mom and Butch and Cindy constantly accused Art of being lazy, never around when work had to be done, but it was carefully orchestrated Dad-avoidance, not shirking. A successful strategy is one that works, and over the years he'd applied those same techniques to other situations, like whenever Linda or Conrad, that twat, wanted him to do something he didn't particularly want to do. Worked well. Maybe too well.

No sane child steps into an obvious threat situation, either. Cindy and Butch weren't out there in the rain because they wanted to be, and the less Art knew what was going on, the less chance he'd get shanghaied into it. Walk away, dude.

And he'd done so. And he'd never asked. And done everything he could since to obscure the memory. Successfully, as it turns out.

Art took in a deep breath and looked at the ground and pressed it hard with his foot. What's here, a trap door? *Sproiiiing*, it falls away and Art plunges down the rabbit hole and has tea with Mad Hatters. More likely the gates of hell and gleeful pitchfork-wielding demons are waiting, happy to see him. Art shuffled his foot across the grass and kudzu and vines, leery of night snakes. Were there night snakes? Well sure, even snakes had to find a place to sleep and if you step on them – oh boy.

Art bounced up and down, feeling foolish. It's solid here, man, not hollow or yielding or a sinkhole above some underground magical cave that will, with the wave of the proper crystal or utterance of the right word, open and bring forth the magic lamp. Not even a bomb shelter, like the one they had in Oklahoma.

Storm shelter, actually. Everyone in Oklahoma had one; at

least, the smart everyones because, every ten minutes or so, black and green clouds raged across the plains throwing bolts and hail and tornadoes at the helpless natives. Jump into an underground shelter and cower like the pathetic, fragile little bags of meat they were as the heavens screamed and laughed maniacally and sent fingers of spinning death to devour them.

Art remembered one particular night the tornado siren wailed its *War of the Worlds* song and he and Mom and Butch and Dale and Cindy and Cha Cha the dog raced pell-mell down the back concrete steps and up the stone pathway as lightning fractured the sky and wind slammed at them like cement walls and Art fell. Just fell. Busted his knees against the stones, which was bad enough, but worse, the sheer terror of watching the others as they kept going to where Dad stood halfway down the shelter's steps propping up the metal storm door while waving them frantically on and Art screamed and cried come back! Mommy! Help me! She did, of course, scooping him off the rocks and bundling him into a corner of the mildewy shelter already reeking of kerosene lamp fumes, but it took him a good hour to stop shaking.

"Big baby," someone said.

Art whirled, the shock of a sneering voice from the dark inducing flight-or-fight panic and, unfortunately, the stone, rending, enervating, making him stumble with sudden dizziness. "Who's there?" he quavered.

"Who's there?" someone mocked back. "Little baby-ass scaredy-cat, little snot-nosed fuck, all fat and stupid and there's a damn tornado coming, boy!"

Art turned to ice. "Dad," he whispered.

There. On the other side of the pool, silhouetted against the black lines of the house, the silver half-light fleeing him, too. The Dark Lord and his lair, out of which flowed the slime and scream of lost souls. "That's right, you useless, fat, stupid piece of shit."

"What are you doing here?" Art asked. "How are you here?"

Dad was smoking a cigarette. Art could not see him actually doing so, but Dad always smoked a cigarette and the Dark Lord loved his perks. Dad took a long puff and angrily slapped his thigh. "This is my house, boy."

"But, you're dead."

"So?"

"I was at your funeral."

Dad laughed, "Yeah, I know, I saw ya. By yourself. Didn't bring your wife or son, huh? Thanks, boy, for seeing me off proper."

Art's panic gave way to anger. "I didn't want them to know you."

"Too bad. I seen your wife." Art felt the leer across the pool. "Good lookin'. I'da fucked her."

"As I recall," Art said, coolly, "you pretty much fucked half of America."

"America? I fucked the whole fucking world, boy! Just ask your brother!" and Dad reared back his head and howled, death and rot and the grave in it and horror ran up and down Art's spine because yes, ask Butch. Butch was the spawn of Dad and some German housemaid he'd repeatedly raped when he was stationed there. Dad made Mom adopt Butch, so Art had a ready-made brother up and available when he was born. Mom must have loved that.

Mom.

A hot core of anger turned the ice to steam. "The way you fucked Mom, huh?"

"Yeah," Dad chuckled. "Boy, the things I made her do. She'd just cry. If you'd do the same to your wife, she wouldn't be so damn uppity, you know?" Dad took a satisfied puff.

"Leave my wife out of this. Is Mom there with you?"

"Nah." Dad lit another cigarette. "She's over there with that faggot Jesus, all singing and clasping hands in the Loooooord!" Dad sang that as a gospel note.

"You asshole," Art said. "She died alone. Scared. In a charity hospital in a town she didn't even know."

Dad was smug. "Served her right. And if you were all worried, why didn't you take her in?"

Sledgehammer upside the head while the stone rammed against his lungs and he reeled. "Because," he wheezed, "Cindy was taking care of her." At least until Alzheimer's turned her from a sweet mush of spineless mom into a drooling, gibbering, screaming nightmare and Cindy delivered her up to the tender mercies of state institutional care. Like what else could she do? Ridge had died years before, leaving everything, including the house, to his sons, *his*, not hers, and Art was too busy, too busy.

"Ah, Cindy." The leer was back in Dad's voice. "Now she was

a good girl. Good daughter. She came to the funeral, too."

"Yeah." Art was shaking, "She came, only because she thought you were gonna leave her something to make up for being a lifelong asshole. You sure fooled her, didn't ya?"

"Yeah, I did!" Dad roared with laughter, "Shoulda seen her face when the lawyer read the will!"

"I did." He'd been right there when the lawyer, without changing tone after giving Butch and Art first choice of Dad's cheap, worthless life possessions (some old guns and fishing tackle, some old reel-to-reel tapes and a recorder which Butch had actually bought for Dad when he was in the service), left Cindy one dollar.

One. Dollar.

Cindy had turned white and then red. Art and Butch exchanged looks and then both cocked eyebrows at Cindy. What did you expect?

"Wasn't that a good joke, boy?" Dad was still chortling, "Like the one I pulled on my wife there, what's her name, Joaney or June or something like that. You know, the one I was married to when I died? She thought she was gettin' the vast Deats' fortune, didn't she?" and Dad almost fell down laughing.

Art was incredulous. "You don't remember your last wife's name?"

"I don't remember nun'a their names, boy!" Dad was in full-blown mirth. "They ain't worth it. Nun'em." Dad took another long puff and eyed Art balefully. "You learned that lesson, apparently."

"What are you talking about?"

"You treat your wife and son like shit, boy. I'm proud of you."

"No, I don't." Art shook as the stone throbbed in his chest. "I'm nothing like you. Nothing!"

Dad was suddenly there, hands around Art's throat, red lust in his bloodshot, maggot-lined eyes. "You are exactly like me, boy." Dad's graveyard breath washed over him and Dad's liver tongue licked the side of Art's face as his hands squeezed and squeezed and squeezed...

Art fought, wildly flailing at the iron grip on his throat, but unable to get purchase on Dad's wrists, slippery with rotted skin and humors. His fist connected with something.

"Ack!" Butch yelped.

Butch?

Art opened his eyes. Butch, starkly clear in the nothing moonlight, reeled away from him, one hand still on Art's T-shirt and the other pressed against the side of his head. So, that's what he'd hit. "Let. Go," he gasped.

"You hit me, you jerk!" Butch yelped, shaking Art.

"Let. Go. Please." Art's breath squeaked like a dog's toy; the stone had moved into his throat and closed his lungs. The 'please' must have had some magical effect because Butch released him. Art sank to his knees.

"Oh, my God!" Butch said, stunned. "Are you all right?"

Art went to all fours, wheezing into the overgrowth. Tranquilo, jefe. Calmate, paz, paz. The roaring in his ears grew exponentially with each chanted word. Light flashed around his eyes and it was not the light of a fabled tunnel showing the way to Elysian Fields but the scalding fires of hell reaching, reaching, and there was Dad, arms open, vomit and snot dripping from his face, and worms crawling all over him.

Art began to cry.

A hand on his back. "It's all right, it's all right. Take your time, get your air." Butch stroked him gently, eliciting a response from Art's blackened, stone-crusted lungs. A little point of air opened in Art's throat and he seized it, Butch helping him like he used to do when they were kids.

Ten minutes, ten hours, the world frozen in place with the quarter moon silvering and the wind stirring the hot fog of the night as things walked around the edges.

He took a big, clean, breath. Then he took another.

Butch stayed there, the hand a savior on his back. "You were sleepwalking," he said.

"Yes," Art said.

"Who were you talking to?"

Art took in another God-given salvation breath. "The devil," he said.

Chapter 16

Friday morning

This time, Art was glad for the blue jays. They proved he was still alive. No way God allowed them in the afterlife... unless this was Hell. Certainly hot enough.

He wiped his face with the blanket (what are you still doing with a blanket?) and checked his air. Lungs clear, oxygen flowing... okay, not dead, at least by current medical standards. Stuff to do, people to see, places to go.

Art rolled out of the cot, grabbed a towel and shave kit, and walked his naked self over to the washhouse.

Give the blue jays a thrill.

The generator was out of gas, so he fueled it, started it, listened for a moment to the water gurgling, and then tested the faucet attached to the washhouse. Some horribly brown crap spewed forth, followed moments later by relatively clear, evil-smelling water.

Hmm. Weren't the filters supposed to take care of that? Maybe the land held too much foulness.

He shut it off and scrambled about inside the washhouse until he found a short hose that Caleb thoughtfully left for them – thoughtful guy, that Caleb – attached it to the faucet, raised it over his head, braced, and turned the knob.

The screams were hideous.

"What? What?" Butch, off towards the cars somewhere, called out in alarm.

"AAAAAAAAAH!" Art screamed again, relishing the shock of ice-cold water against the red-hot air. People get heart attacks doing this, don't they?

"Oh," Butch said. Art peered through the waterfall cascading down his face. Butch, hands on hips, disapproval all over him. "I thought you were dying."

"I am," Art doused the shampoo off his head. "The water's killer. See for yourself." He turned the hose and thumbed the end, gratified to see an excellent stream of water smack Butch right in the chest.

"*Urk*!" Butch danced back, slapping at it like a little girl and ran out of range.

Art laughed and shut it down. First shower in a week; not that it made much difference odor-wise because he now smelled like rotten eggs and Right Guard. At least yesterday's floor crap was off him. He strolled past Butch attending to something at the camp stove. "Sheesh, put on some clothes!" Butch groused as Art paraded by. Art laughed again and did as ordered, then grabbed his truck keys and headed to the driveway.

Butch stared after him, "Are you all right?"

"Yep." Art kept going.

"You sure?"

"Yep." He beelined to his truck.

"Wait a minute!" Butch yelled, "Aren't you going to have breakfast?"

"I'll grab something at McDonald's." Art unlocked the truck and opened the passenger door, checked the plugged-in cell phone. Charged. Hope it didn't drain the battery.

Butch, behind him now. "Where are you going?"

"Lowe's." Art checked his wallet. "You're going to get another bill."

Butch grimaced. "What are you getting?"

"Electrical stuff. I'm going to get your house somewhat wired today. Did you call the power company?"

"Yeah. They said it'll be on sometime today. What do you mean by 'somewhat?'"

Art went to the back of the truck and checked his cover. Check everything. Check, check, and double-check. "I'm going to get you a working panel and a couple of lines you can use. Full wiring is going to take a contractor with a license. I don't have that license. And I don't have the time."

Butch followed him around. "What do you mean?"

"I mean, I have no time. As soon as I'm done, I'm gone."

"But—"

Art pushed Butch out the way. "I'm. Gone." He emphasized the words and started the truck. Battery's still charged, thank God.

Of course. It's a Ram. He backed to the road, pointed the front towards Enterprise and did his best to peel out but missed it. Jeez, gettin' old.

Somewhere past Bark's, he pulled onto a bit of shoulder dangerously close to a red gully and checked his phone.

Bars. Good.

"Are you home?" she asked, breathless and wanting.

"Tuesday," he responded, "More likely Wednesday."

"You comin' in?"

"Planning on it."

"Oh," and that's all she really had to say, underscored as it was with desire and joy.

He felt a hard stirring below. "I don't promise it," he hastily added, not wanting to set her up for a disappointment. No worries about Linda; he'd disappointed her as long as he could remember. "There's some issues with Rich."

"Oh?" Query tone.

"Got himself into some trouble and his mother is going batshit, so I gotta rescue him, I suppose."

"Oh."

Ach, idiot. Way to remind her that the child in need of rescue from smotherly motherly love was not hers.

Smotherly love. Know a lot about that, doncha?

Mom had smothered him. He acknowledged that. On occasions too numerous to quantify, Butch and Cindy had accused him of being Mom's favorite, something he hotly denied to their faces but secretly harbored as pleasure because it was true. Mom gave him the first lick of the cake batter, the biggest chocolate chip cookies, ensured he was exempt from (most) of the backbreaking labor projects Dad devised...

"*Butterball over there needs to get out and work!*"

"*No, Owen, it'll kill him!*"

...And he *was* a butterball, primarily due to Mom's cake batter and chocolate cookies and insistence he avoid strenuous effort.

She did so because Art was her *real* son, her true baby boy. Butch wasn't, another secret pleasure Art harbored because it meant Butch wasn't really his brother, was just some interloper foisted on the family because of the bigness of Deats' hearts. Dad was in the Army stationed in Germany flying helicopters and Mom's German housemaid had a kid and couldn't take care of it, so Mom and Dad took Butch in. Art came along a few months later, a real Deats and a real American, Butch, not some German foundling. Butch actually had to be naturalized at some point. Some of us are born with it, Butchie boy, others have to earn it. And be grateful. Foundling.

And then...

Flashback: 1969ish. May or June, because school was out. Butch, Cindy, Art in the Chrysler, Mom in the driver's seat, all of them terrified, hastily packed suitcases in the trunk because they had to flee the house and hide at one of Mom's friends because there was a terrible danger, something mortal. Art wasn't sure what, but it involved Dad and if Mom thought it was time to go, okay.

Mom looked at Art in the backseat and smiled as she explained that Butch was his brother, not some adopted waif. "You see, Art, your Dad is also Butch's Dad, so you have a real brother."

And the strangest thing of all, Art? You were the only one in the car who didn't know that. Butch already knew it. So did Cindy. They had known since the day we left Oklahoma for here.

So why had he been kept in the dark?

He'd puzzled over that the two weeks they hid from Dad in a nice house somewhere in the back of Daleville, the others terrified Dad would come roaring up any moment. They walked around the house with ginger steps, fearful eyes on the windows overlooking the driveway. Not Art. He was too busy wondering about things.

Art could not remember the name of Mom's friend, but she was a nice lady and her husband was a nice man and their boy was a friend of Butch's and the girl a friend of Cindy's but they had no extra child to be Art's friend and he was alone and bewildered and baffled far more than scared, because he did not know why they had to flee to a house of strangers. What had scary Dad done that was scarier than normal? Perhaps Art should be afraid, but there were other things presented for his consideration, like, Butch was his real brother, er, half-brother, and no longer some pitiful foundling. And Art was no longer the son. Well, only son. Er, only full son. Whatever.

And Butch was a bastard.

Literally. That had been sort of a given, but Butch's foundling status had trumped it. Turned out Butch was not a foundling but Dad's leavings, elevating the 'bastard' label to weaponry and Art could now weave its implications into torments of his big bastard big (half) brother whenever the spirit moved him, using derivations like whore's son, love child, lesser, tainted, the secret in the attic, the shame, the shame. From this point forward, whenever Art felt mean and inadequate, he had only to address Butch's sordid birth to bolster himself and chip a little bit more off Butch's pedestal.

And Butch *was* on a pedestal. He was astonishingly successful in school, far outstripping the peanut farmers at Yoman in just about all academic areas, even as he proved himself a complete spazz at things that counted, like baseball. Which, of course, spurred his academic efforts to even higher levels, because the peanut farmers peaked at some point in their various high school sports careers and then, lickety-split, back to the family business and a lifetime of wallowing in red clay and pigshit, like Locker – with a little assistance from Butch the bastard – while Butch went on to fame and glory...

Funny how things worked out.

Mom and Dad expressed great pride in Butch whenever he was singled out for an award. And he got lots of awards: called up at some assembly or another to get a letter or plaque or something for success in some meaningless activity like essay writing, or when he won the Coffee County 4-H Public Speaking Contest. He was the golden child.

Yet, it was Art who got the batter spoon and exemption from forced labor and was wrapped in the cocoon of Mom's protective warmth whenever Dad or Butch or Cindy came at him. Puzzling. Especially because Butch extended a protective cloak around Mom, trying to shield her from Dad's wrath. Trying. Whenever Mom had been pummeled or cursed for something innocuous like being on the phone too long with her girlfriends or not putting enough salt in the corn fritters, Butch was the one on the couch hugging and consoling her.

Corn fritters, uhm uhm uhm. Love me some corn fritters. Haven't had any since leaving Alabama. Should get Butch to cook some up.

Dad had a death grip on every penny in his pocket, so Mom sold Tupperware to buy things for herself like clothes and shoes and self-worth. Dad permitted this because, fifteen minutes after Mom left the house for one of her far-flung hen parties, he was out of the door, leaving Art and Cindy to their own devices: Art to TV and refrigerator raids, Cindy to mysterious cars pulling into the driveway.

Butch had no devices; he went with Mom.

Mom never asked him to go, but her relief was evident as he quietly slipped into the car with his books and writing tablets and pencils. Night rides through dark swampy Alabama were scary and she was glad of the company; guess because the Cryman could eat him first. Butch did his homework in the back kitchen of a house somewhere in the bogs of Dothan while the hens gabbled and cooed over the Good Son sacrificing sleep and TV to keep his mom safe while she earned her pittance.

But she wasn't his mom. She was Art's. And Mom didn't tell Art that he and Butch shared a father and were actually blood until long after everyone else knew. No one had told him. Not Dad. Not Cindy. Not even Butch.

Why not?

Maybe because all of them knew what he would do with the information, which was: invoke "bastard" at every opportunity to torment. Or, maybe, they didn't think it was important for him to know. He was, obviously, Mom's pampered favorite so paternity was moot.

No, it wasn't. It was damn effin' critical and it pissed him off that he, the only real son, was cut out of things like vital genealogical information. Didn't the laws of heredity decree that the eldest *legitimate* son inherit the kingdom? Hear that, Butch? The house is mine! Not that I want a haunted shack in the middle of Bumfuckee Alabama but there's a principle here. Dammit. I'm the real son. The real brother.

Cut out of things.

Like the iron bonds forged between Cindy and Butch. Not with her *real* brother, no. With the bastard. Look at those two. Absolutely inseparable.

Man, that bugged him.

On any given summer morning the two of them were off, hand in hand down the south woods trail that led to a mysterious ten-foot-tall pile of sawdust dumped by the side of the miasmic creek, Art stumbling along well behind, gasping and crying for them to wait up, but they never did. He ended up back home and the comfort of a batter spoon.

No matter how much Mom and Dad punished those two for their exclusion of the fat wheezing *real* son-and-brother, they closed ranks even tighter. He'd get up in the morning and they were already gone and he'd go waddling around the yard and woods and fields looking for them with no success, ending up back in the kitchen and the batter spoon. They'd come back later, glaring him off as they slipped into Cindy's bedroom for secret, whispered conferences he could not decipher, even with his ear pressed against the door slats. About the only time they included him was playing *Monopoly* or *Wahoo* or *Hearts* but, even then, they teamed up, bankrupting him early or driving his last marble off the board within the first five rounds. He'd cry and rage how unfair it was, but all they did was smile and exchange amused glances and then drove him off or ran for the sawdust pile or the bedroom.

Man.

It was odd and secretive and he didn't get it because they never showed closeness in places that they should, such as in school, where everybody was a brother or sister or first cousin or uncle of someone else. Heck, some of them were married to each other. Friends were relatives and it would be nothing for Cindy and Butch to hang out but, no, they ignored each other, Cindy running with the bad boys and girls, Butch with the spazzes and nerds. In their shared classroom (Cindy had failed third grade), Butch sat up front as the teacher's pet, Cindy in the back as the teacher's nemesis. Art, running with a group of crazy peanut-farmer kids, watched them from a distance. At home, they were joined at the hip, but at school they acted like strangers. Why? His friends and the rest of the older boys lusted after Cindy and ridiculed and bullied Butch, and Cindy could use her powers to end Butch's torture, but never did. Why?

He didn't know. He figured it had something to do with the inviolate hierarchies of kid society: what happens in school stays in school, what happens at home, yadda yadda. Except Cindy and Butch remained iron-bound everywhere else *but* school. For those two weeks when they hid in the stranger's house, Cindy and Butch huddled together in the backyard, Mom huddled with her best friend while Art, bewildered, stood alone in the middle of a strange living room and watched them all.

And then Dad showed up.

Tableau: Dad standing beside his pickup blocking the end of the circular driveway, Mom facing him, the two talking quietly. Butch, Cindy, and Art lined up on the porch, the host family in the doorway. Mom and Dad talked for a few moments and then she walked back and said they were all going home now and Butch and Art, go with Dad. Now.

Mom and Cindy disappeared into the house, leaving Butch and Art alone, nothing between them and Dad. He gestured and they looked at each other, the condemned prisoners, and got in the truck. Art was forced to the middle of the bench seat because he was the smallest and he squirmed to make it comfortable and his hand fell on Dad's Luger, the one he took off a dead Nazi during the Battle of the Bulge, jammed in the seatback. He pulled it out, held it up, and the condemned prisoners exchanged looks. Dad, snake-eyed, took it and said, "If y'all hadn't come home, I'da shot y'all and then myself."

Art stopped breathing.

Yes. Dad had said that.

Right after that pleasant little moment, school started and Locker's knee got smashed and Cindy ran away and Art saw figures by the pool in the winter rain. A few weeks later, they made their terrifying escape up the side of the road to New Jersey.

Include the lovely summer vacation hiding from Dad, and the timeline expands from a four-month to a six-month period.

Art blinked. Yes, from about the first of June through New Year's week. It was a critical six months. His whole life was based on those six months.

"Are you still there?" Anxiety in her voice.

"Yes," he said, disappointment in his because he knew, right then, that he wouldn't be home on Tuesday. He wasn't going home until he knew what was so important about the pool.

He might not ever go home.

Chapter 17

Friday

Installing electricity is not that hard. It's a matter of directing current to where it's needed, like diverting a creek into nearby fields. Electricity is like water, except it kills. Water can, too, but requires a lot more effort. Or carelessness. Art was not careless. He might drown one day, but he'd never be electrocuted.

He browsed Lowe's electrical aisle, selecting what he needed. Standard stuff: wire, junction box, switches, outlets, other simple materials simply made in factories all across China, easily installed by apes. Like him.

He smiled wryly. He could do Butch's whole house in about three days without breaking a sweat. Three outlets per wall, two bulb receptacles per ceiling fan, one ceiling fan per room. Heck, he'd get the attic fan running, too, but, after stepping back and smacking his hands together in satisfaction, big bull-necked deputies would smack handcuffs on him and frog-walk him off to jail because he was not a certified-by-the-great-state-of-Alabama electrician. He needed a little piece of paper before he could wire an entire house. Without that paper, he'd put grounding wires through the tops of mattresses and strip all that pesky insulation right down to the copper so the current would flow better and drape the wires across bare rugs or leave them dangling out of sockets. The first time someone turned on a light, the house would explode. That little piece of paper made all the difference.

Lots of little pieces of paper made all the difference.

Art could drive any machine, any: 18-wheeler; bulldozer; crane; whatever; and drive it well; back any and all into impossible areas; work hydraulic buckets into spots the experts said couldn't fit, et cetera, et cetera. And not only run them but fix 'em: break engines down to mere scraps of metal, shape those into functioning pieces, put it all back together and presto! Worked better. Any kind of engine, from a small hand drill to the pumps buried deep within a paint truck.

He was a twenty-level Trades Mage.

He wielded hammer and nail, boards, sheetrock, forms, cement and studs and nuts and bolts and tiles and, yes, electrical wire, as a wizard did a wand; a flourish of the hand and buildings and roadways and sidewalks came into existence, suburbs, whole cities. Whenever Conrad, that twat, overpromised something, extending his twatty ass beyond capacity, did he ask the pimply faced eighteen-year-old meth-heads who generally worked about a week before they stole something to step up, or the forty-year-old fuckhead foremen whose only gift was ass-kissing and, among whom, maybe two or three knew what the hell they were doing?

No. He asked the Mage.

Because Art knew how to do everything, simply everything, and knew how to do it with efficiency and economy and right the first time, saving Conrad's twatty ass and twatty money, and Conrad got another five years' worth of contracts to deliver loads of stone and gravel and asphalt to Ft. Dix or McGuire AFB. Conrad demonstrated his gratitude over Art's saving of his ass by giving Art a half-percent raise every ten years or so, after Art asked for it about twenty times, that is, and then only when Art sat at the desk in front of Conrad's office and quite publicly called other companies to see if they could use his services. Conrad smirked, "Okay, okay," and there'd be a fifty-cent increase in Art's next paycheck and Art said nothing until the next ten-year go-round because Conrad, that twat, knew that Art would never leave, ever, no matter how bad things got because no other company would give Art half the deference or even half the pay. Conrad could count on Art's services until the day Art dropped dead behind the wheel or behind a shovel because Art did not have little pieces of paper. Not one.

Well, he did have a CDL-A with Hazmat endorsement, but any ape could get one of those. Take a casual glance around the interstate sometime. Art did not have the more important heavy equipment pieces of paper or welding certifications or mechanic school diplomas or masonry licenses or memberships in the right unions and, definitely, no electrician's license. Immaterial that he could do the work at levels light years ahead of the vast majority of persons carrying said credentials. Proper authority had never blessed him.

Art had tried to obtain said blessing, buying books to study for the tests granting the little pieces of paper, and once enrolled in a Ryder College computer technician program because an eighteen-year-old pimply faced meth head had done so and now commanded an astronomical salary and if that shithead could do it... well. He rarely got past the first two pages of the books and dropped out of Ryder after the first class. They bored him. Truly, absolutely, bored him.

Reducing the wizardry of finger, hands, brain, arm and back to a series of words was meaningless. Not that Art didn't understand the words; he knew them better than the persons who wrote them. But the words were sterile, missing the entire arc of electrical circuit and cement pressures and carpentry angles. The books presented all of it as a checklist. It wasn't. It was poetry.

Poetry.

Art grimaced. If he ever uttered that sentiment, Conrad, that twat, and the meth-heads and accidental foremen and the rest of the slope-headed hillbillies he worked alongside would crow and chortle and point their fingers and accuse him of supreme faggotry until Art picked up a short sledge and put an end to it.

Do not cast your pearls before swine, and Art would never call the magic what it was.

Instead, he showed them what it was. How many times had Conrad, that twat, pulled in a big project, big project, man, and took Art off the route and threw him at the big project, man, and Art would swing the crane's arm and, with extreme precision, drop the iron supports he had just fashioned into the holes he had just drilled with an accuracy few of the credentialed could muster and stepped out of the cab and pushed through the meth-heads and applied the bolts and poured and smoothed the cement pad and presto! A warehouse, framed and ready for walls and plumbing and wires. The illegals stood around the pad admiring it. "*Ay! Dios Mio! Tus un pendejo raro!*"

"*Pues...*" Art would raise slow eyebrow and shoulders, "*...sin falta!*" And the illegals roared and slapped his back and babbled on; Art understood all of it and threw in a word or two to prove he did, while the meth-heads and the accidentals frowned at all the Mexspeak that Art had picked up in about a week. The illegals knew he was a poet. Their whole existence was a lyric.

And if the proper authorities awarded their little pieces of paper on the basis of ability rather than a bell-curve score, if they came to the site and watched Art the Wizard weave his magic instead of making Art come to them and fill in squares on an answer sheet in some cubicle in some dim state building in Trenton, they would shower him with pieces of paper and beg him to teach me, master. Then he'd command the astronomical salaries that the papered did. He'd tell Conrad, that twat, to pay him what he's worth or pound sand. And Conrad would pay, or someone else would. And Art could, with surety, pull from the shelves before him the proper items in the proper number and, in a matter of days, have a nice humming little house for Butch to skulk in.

He sighed. Butch had lots of little pieces of paper. Butch could glance at a test and instinctively know which box to fill. He excelled at it. And because of that, he was considered a greater success than Art; defrocked, de-robed, living in a tent next to a haunted house, yet the world regarded him as the better.

Art pulled out his cell phone, checked for bars – three. Amazing – and pressed the button.

"You must really miss me," she said.

"Every second. I wonder if you could do me a favor?" Which she would, of course. She was willing to do anything for him –

anything

– and oh no, something's stirring down there, but he shook it off (not literally. Save that for later) and told her what he wanted, and she repeated the information to make sure it was right and then okay, bye, love, and he hung up.

Now, we'll see what we'll see.

"He'p ya?" a too-cheerful voice boomed behind Art. He turned.

A little guy, too little to have a voice like that, beamed at him. All Lowe'd out with vest and buttons and a name tag, 'Jimmy,' and glasses way too thick. "Doin' some electric work?"

"Yep." Art figured the less said the better, and reached for cables and boxes and Jimmy jumped right in, picking out stuff and making suggestions and this was the language Art understood and it was fun and before he knew it, he was wheeling a brimming cart over to the checkout. Again. "Use your contractor's license for the discount!" Jimmy airily waved goodbye and moved off, searching for other coven members.

Another little piece of paper that would make all of this less expensive. But that's Butch's problem.

Another happy checkout girl but not Allison. Trish. She had the same Velma haircut and Allison-thick glasses (what's with thick glasses at Lowe's?), so maybe they were sisters. Evidence for that accumulated as Trish babbled on, Allison-like, about weather and, yes, boiled peanuts (what's with boiled peanuts and Lowe's checkout girls?), random shotgun blasts of subject matter that made Art dizzy and he glanced away to regain his bearings and saw Dave and Jimmy about three aisles down, staring at him. Jimmy didn't look happy anymore.

Happy? Shoot, Jimmy looked downright scared. Art had half an urge to yell "Boo!" but thought better of it, handed his card to bubbly little Trish, took the receipt and wrote "Pay up!" on it for later handing over to Butch, and pushed out of the door. Halfway through, he looked back. Dave and Jimmy stood with Trish, and she wasn't bubbly anymore. She looked downright scared, too.

Jesus.

Art blew out his cheeks and headed to the truck, loaded up, and expertly spun the cart away. He paused. The sun was flexing muscle, getting ready to bake Alabama into submission. Dave and Jimmy and Trish and now Allison had lined up behind the big door, arms crossed, to stare at him. No pitchforks or torches. Yet.

Art waved as he drove off.

A white work truck with oversized tool boxes bolted all over the bed and sides and sporting a little green logo that looked like a wave or something on the doors was parked in the driveway. Art pulled up behind and got out and looked it over: Covington Electric Co-op. That vaguely rang a bell and Art wondered if it was the same power company they had back in the good ole days. Voices came from the washhouse and Art beelined for it and found Butch standing in front of two guys with work helmets, everyone looking unhappy.

Of course. "Hey, fellas," Art greeted them.

One of them, a dark-haired, wrinkle-browed guy with a perpetually sour expression, soured even more and said, "Are you the guy who knows what he's doing?"

Art laughed. "Depends on who you're talkin' to. Compared to him," Art pointed at Butch, "I'm a friggin' electrical engineer."

Sour-face laughed without changing expression, no mean feat, while the other helmet, a short Hispanic with the best moustache Art had ever seen, grinned widely. Butch frowned widely, a study in contrasts.

"Ho'kay," the Hispanic said in an accent as outrageous as his moustache, "then we tell you what we try to tell him," thumb jam at the still-frowning Butch "that we can't hook you up without a meter."

"*Dios mio*," Art rolled his eyes expressively, "*este pendejo esta fregado.*" Which broke up Pancho Villa no end. Art stood there grinning as Sour-face grinned in response and Butch turned red, getting the gist of it from the reaction. "Anyways." Art stepped in before something more unfortunate was said. "What do you mean there's no meter?"

Pancho gestured around the house and Art followed him, Sour and Butch in trail and, yeah, sumbitch, there was an outline on the wall of where a meter used to be. Idiot, he smacked himself mentally, why didn't you check that? "They pretty much got everything, didn't they?"

Sour raised quizzical eyebrows. "They?"

"The same guys who stripped out all the piping and wires inside the house." Art put his hands on his hips and calculated what he needed to do now. Or, more accurately, calculated how much more this was going to cost Butch.

Sour and Pancho looked at each other. "You mean," – 'meank'– Pancho pronounced it, "there's no wiring in the house?"

Another mental smack of the forehead. Why don't you just tell the entire Alabama electrical community that the house is unsafe? "Well," he said, "there is, but it needs a bit of work."

"Really." Sour's eyes narrowed. "How much work?"

Butch was looking quite concerned by this time, so Art threw out 'you know' hands. Sour made a disgusted sound and Pancho looked sorrowful. "We can't hook you up," Pancho said with an apology in his voice, "Not until you pass inspection."

"Yeah, okay." Art bowed to the inevitable. "I take it you're the guys to do the certifying?"

"No," Sour said, "you'll have to get one of the authorized

electricians to do it. Through the county." He pulled a card out of his shirt pocket. "Here's the number." He offered the card to Art, but Art pointed at Butch. Sour turned his hand in that direction and Butch took the card and looked at it like it was a lit stick of dynamite.

"Can you at least install the meter?" Art asked.

Sour and Pancho looked at each other and shrugged. "Sure," Pancho said and the two of them went back to their truck and Art followed with Butch lagging behind. Pancho and Sour took their stuff out of the bins and eyed Art as he went around to the back of the Ram and unloaded, but they didn't say anything. Art appreciated that and piled all the Lowe's stuff in the kitchen, on them newly installed floors. Damn I do good work. Butch positioned himself at the apex of the screen porch and washhouse to keep track of both activities but had no idea what he was watching and gave up and walked inside the house where Art was uncoiling wire. "So what's all this mean?"

"I'll give you the Cliff Notes," Art said while measuring how much wire he needed for the first run, "You're going to call that number and arrange for an electrician, who will come out here and see that I've established one junction box and wired up the den." He nodded in that direction. "The electrician will be a bit miffed because part of the job is already done, but you're going to contract with him to do the rest of the house, including two 220-circuits so you can run big appliances and central air conditioning —"

"I'm not getting central air."

"—and even a couple of ghost circuits for the high-powered satellite internet systems and underground bunkers you're planning to add later on so the electrician won't feel like he got cheated out of a good-paying job and fail you every single time he comes out here." Art stood up, glaring at him. "You know, so you can live here? In a house? With electricity?"

"What?" Butch's mouth went into an 'o'. "You mean, this is a racket?"

"He can be taught!" Art did his best Robin Williams Genie and made to slap Butch on top of the head, but he'd moved back out of range.

"Well, that's just wrong."

"Wrong?" Art saw red. "Wrong, huh? Let me tell you what's

'wrong.' " Art made quotes with his fingers. "Wrong is thinking you can buy a derelict house and call up your brother and tell him to leave his wife and son and job and whatever and come on down and make the place into an HGTV Giveaway Prize in, oh, say, three days, and oh say, for about $1.98." He poked an iron finger in Butch's chest. "What kind of an idiot are you, anyway?"

"I'm not an idiot." Butch pushed Art's finger away violently and Art became wary. Do not rouse the beast. "I knew this wasn't going to be easy, I know. Just..." he hesitated. "Seems wrong to gouge me like that."

Art snorted. "Think of it as an investment. In case you decide to do something later." One beat. "Like install a pool."

Butch frowned, then looked out of the kitchen window in exactly the right direction. "I'd never do that," he said, flatly.

Art raised an emphatic finger. "Why not? You've got a perfect place already marked."

"What?"

Art pointed his emphatic finger out of the window. "You know, where the old pool used to be?"

Butch looked at him with a strange expression: confusion, annoyance. And fear.

Art tried to derive explanations from that, but there were none. Okay. Let's be straight up. "What happened out there?" he asked.

"Huh?" Butch was genuinely puzzled.

"At the pool." Art threw the same emphatic finger out of the window again. "What happened there?"

If he could look even more puzzled, Butch was certainly giving it an effort. "What are you talking about?"

"Back when we were living here. Something happened at the pool. What?"

Butch was a study in utter confusion. "Nothing happened at the pool. What are you talking about?"

Steam rose in Art's boilers. "I saw you guys." He jabbed the iron finger into Butch's chest at each word. "You, Dad, Cindy, all of you, out there in the rain doing something."

"Huh?" Baffled. "When was this?"

Either the guy was the greatest actor in history, or genuinely had no idea what Art was talking about. "Forget it. Call that number." Art turned to the wire.

"Forget it? You're the one who brought it up, so tell me what you're talking about."

"I said forget it." Art measured along the wall.

"No." Butch crossed his arms. "I want to know what you saw."

Hello? Art stopped, straightened up and examined him. "Why don't you tell me what I saw?"

Butch threw up exasperated hands. "How the HELL should I know? I'm not a fucking mind reader!"

"Language!" Art did his best Butch imitation and smirked. Butch went beet red, the Hulk staring out of his eyes and Art took an alarmed step back, but all Butch did was glare, spin on his heels and stalk out of the door. Art *whew*ed in some relief and watched him stomp down the porch steps and across the yard... straight to the old pool location. Butch stopped, right at the exact spot where Art had seen him all those years ago in the rain and stared down at the ground, his face expressionless. He snapped his head up and looked at Art, wheeled and stomped away, fury on his face.

And that fear.

"Sonofabitch," Art said, softly.

Chapter 18

Later Friday

Somewhere around three o'clock, Art's phone buzzed his pocket as he installed the last switch in the first – and, no doubt, only – circuit panel, so this was a good time to take a break, anyway. He pulled out the phone, surprised it worked – wind must be blowin' right – and looked at the caller, then grinned as he glanced around to ensure Butch wasn't nearby. Of course. There was work being done. "Knew it was you. I felt a throbbing in my jeans."

"Oh, I like it when you talk dirty," she giggled, "Put it back in your pocket and I'll speed dial you about a hundred times."

Art laughed. "Okay. Then give me time to smoke a cigarette and call back a hundred more." Now reminded, Art fished for a cigarette.

"Ha!" Her laugh was like crystal rain. "I don't think I've got enough minutes for that." Her voice went sly. "So, wanna hear what I found?"

"That good, huh?"

"Looks like it." He heard her do some computer stuff. "The church made an announcement that Pastor Deats was no longer shepherding the flock—"

"Wait. It really says that?"

"Word for word."

"Jesus." Art flicked the lighter. "Holy Rollers. Go on."

"Okay, and that any questions be directed to the fathers. Then there's some blah blah about some old fart taking over until a new pastor could be found."

"But no mention of the reason," Art concluded for her.

"Have faith, sugar," she continued, "I got a list of church members and ran through them and found this *ooooone* woman's page."

"People have pages?"

"You need to catch up, honey. I have one."

"You do?" A stir of unease flitted through him. "Why?"

"So I can keep my peeps up on what I'm doing without having to waste my minutes calling and telling them. Or writing letters."

"Peeps?"

She laughed. "Oh, dear, you are a dinosaur."

Unease heightened. "So what do you tell your... peeps?"

"Oh, I tell them every position we use, how many times I came, how many times I made you come. The usual."

Art felt a deep red flush start from the top of his head and run to his feet, whether from terror or pleasure, he wasn't sure. "Uh..."

She burst into laughter. "Oh, I can just imagine your expression. Relax, honey, you know I ain't stupid."

"True," he said with obvious relief, but he made a mental note to check out her page. How do you do that? Should he ask?

Now who's stupid?

"So what about this woman's page?"

"Let's just say it's enlightening."

The way she said it told Art everything. "You're kidding."

"You don't even know what I found," she chided.

"I can guess."

"Oh, no. No, you can't. It's not what you're thinking."

"What am I thinking?"

"You're thinking what a great gal I am, and how much your life is brightened by my presence."

"I'm always thinking that."

"Better be, sugar," she purred, and Art's heart skipped a beat. Definitely checking out her page. "Anyway, you're thinking this is just some standard ole fornication going on here."

Momentarily confused, Art wondered if that was a comment on their current situation because it *was* pretty standard, wasn't it? She was the girlfriend he snuck around with, a great gal, but he would never leave his wife who did not understand him because there was a child involved, and it would end like all Lifetime movies did: the wronged wife walks out head held high, mortified but now liberated because the lie that was her life has been exposed while the great gal, also mortified because of her complicity in breaking the wife, her sister (sometimes, depending on the movie, an actual sister), walks off in the opposite direction vowing to never, ever believe the lies of some man ever again, both leaving Art in the doorway, craven, pleading, wishing someone would understand him. Pretty standard for Dad, anyway, almost a weekly occurrence, but Art hadn't reached that scene yet. Yet.

Blood will tell, won't it?

But she wasn't talking about Art and her; Art's guilt had made that connection. She was referring to Pastor Butch, so let's ignore the guilt for the moment, shall we? "If it's not standard run-of-the-mill boring old adultery, what is it?"

"The woman has a daughter."

Oh no. "How old?"

"Teenager, maybe sixteen, can't tell 'cause she doesn't have her own page which is kinda odd because kids make pages, not old farts. Guess Momma took it down."

"You're not an old fart."

"No, I'm a kid, you dirty old man."

Blood will tell.

"Anyways, Momma rails along about wolves in sheep's clothing going after the innocent lambs like her daughter, and is telling everyone to stay away from the church."

"Is this legit?"

"Dunno, sugar." He could visualize her sexy shrug. "She might be trying to shake down the church and nothing actually happened. But she is making a case for herself."

"Anyone else seen it?"

"Not really." He heard her clicking some keys. "Just some locals. It's a tiny church, an independent one, maybe used to be Southern Baptist but sort of went their own way. Some of the comments look like they're from members, and just about all of them calling the mother and daughter a couple of whores. Maybe she's done this before."

"Wait. People can put comments on a page?"

"If you let them."

"Do you?"

"All the time, sugar. You should see how many of my girlfriends think you're a stud."

"Uh..."

Peals of laughter. "Ohmigod, you are soooo easy!"

Art thought of a few lewd responses but this wasn't banter,

this was serious. "It must be legit. Otherwise, the church would have backed him."

"Dunno, hon. Everyone's getting skittish these days. They may have simply solved a potential problem."

How nice of her to give the benefit of the doubt. And maybe it *was* a shakedown, a fortuitous one because, by the dice throw of the gods, the church woman had found a good target in Butch. Where there's smoke...

Flashback: Fifteen, twenty years ago, Art had gotten a bug to go see old homesteads and estranged relatives in Texas and heck, let's go. Linda might have been with him, freshly married and all as they were. He was tooling through Arkansas, where Butch's second or third or something like that parish or priory or whatever the hell those people called it was and heck, let's go see the bastard.

Art had a hard time finding Butch's one-room house behind a nondescript church but eventually did and pounded on the door and a girl answered. Girl. Right word. Fourteen, at best, all willowy and wispy and blondish and with the biggest shit-eatin' grin saying Butch wasn't here, but he might be back later and would Art like to come in? An invitation that gave Art the willies so he beat feet, because he'd seen this movie. How many times had he found similar girls, some much younger, in Dad's various post-divorce houses? When Dad's third (or fourth) wife after Mom (which made the third or fourth wife after Mom the fifth or sixth one overall, right?) divorced him, like all his wives did (except Joaney or June, whoever had won the death lottery), Butch told Art that Dad had been going after her granddaughters.

Young girls were a problem for the Deats men, weren't they?

"You all right?" Genuine concern in her voice.

"Yes." He wasn't. "Is that all it says?"

"Pretty much." Pause. "Did your brother say anything?"

"He said enough." Art considered. "It's probably true."

"Oh, boy." Concern, not glee. "What are you going to do?"

"Do?" Good question. "Finish up this project and come home."

"Shouldn't you be on your way by now?" The plaintiveness in her voice warmed him all the way down.

"Not quite yet."

"But you will be back on Wednesday?"

"Here's hoping," he said, with no hope.

"Oh." She read it. "Come back as soon as you can, sugar," and she hung up.

"I will," he said to the dial tone. It's that 'soon as you can' which is problematic.

Art spooned another bowl of chili. "I'm really starting to like your cooking."

"Thanks," Butch said, monotone, distant, staring into the woods while he mechanically ate his bowlful.

"No, seriously, I am." Art noisily crumbled Saltines over the top. "I mean, I'm a pretty straight-up meat-and-potatoes kinda guy, but you've opened me to a whole new world of kew-zeen."

Butch *tsk*ed in annoyance but said nothing. "I'm not kidding. Linda tries all this new crap but all I want is my pot roast and taters," he said that last with the best Piney accent he could muster. "But, you. You're a gore-met." And he slurped the spoon with gusto.

Butch sighed, still focused on the woods and the fading sundown. Art followed his gaze but saw nothing other than the outline of pine trees and Spanish moss, lurid in the red light. Poisonous.

"So you're leaving tomorrow," Butch said. Not a question.

"Depends." Art scraped out the last bit of the chili with some Butch-made cornbread. Uhm, uhm, uhm.

"On what?"

"What you can tell me about the pool."

Butch's face, bloody in the light, was made more so by a flush. Art watched his expression turn to stone, every line a stark black dash against it. "I can't tell you anything about the pool," Butch, finally, muttered. "I don't even know what you mean."

"Sure you do." Art pitched the Styrofoam bowl on the ground, and noted with satisfaction Butch's subsequent displeasure. "You know exactly what I mean."

"I haven't got a clue."

"Think hard."

Butch stood up, irritated, almost losing his chili on the ground

125

which is a major violation. Waste not, want not. He turned his blood-red and now furious face to Art. "What is your problem with the pool?"

"What's yours?"

Butch threw out exasperated hands. "I don't have a problem with the pool! Never did. There was nothing unusual about the pool! Nothing! It was a standard cheap plastic above-ground pool. Dad put it up, we jumped in. End of story!" and he glared.

Art regarded him calmly. "So what were you guys doing out there in the rain?"

Butch made an 'are you crazy?' head bob. "I don't even know what you're TALKING about!" Helpless hand bob.

"Yeah, you do. You know exactly what I'm talking about." Art stood, combat surging in his veins. He pointed at the old pool location. "The pool scares you to death. Why?"

"What?" Butch shook an incredulous head. "The pool? Ha!" Dismissive gesture, and then he stepped towards the house. "Not the pool," he whispered, "not at all. This place." He flipped jittery hands at it. "This place scares me. To death."

Art couldn't help a snort of ridicule. "And yet, you bought it. And you're fixing it up. What the hell are you doing, Butch?"

"I don't know."

"Why did you buy this junk heap, Butch?"

"I don't know."

Art seized Butch's shoulders from behind. "Then, leave it! Just leave it. Let it rot, Butch. Just let it all die." Art shook him a bit. "Please."

Butch threw him off, the stirrings of a green monster and Art took a defensive step away. Butch gave him an over-the-shoulder glare, still red, but fading with the last of the sun's gasp. "I can't." He was mealy-spine again. "Just can't."

"Why. The fuck. Not?"

Butch went still, then said, "Because of the ghosts."

Art recoiled. "What ghosts, Butch? What's haunting this place?"

A pause, sad, lost. "Us."

Chapter 19

Saturday morning

No blue jays, which was fine. Art was awake, anyway. He'd lain in the cot all night listening to ghost sounds. No, not rattling chains and the moans and groans of storybook haints, but the calls of familiar ghosts. Now that he knew their names, it wasn't hard to hear them:

Shrieks of "No, Daddy, no!" and the singing of the belt or bullwhip; Dad's yells of rage as he meted out the severe justice that any violation of his secret rules necessitated, those arbitrary, ever-changing rules formulated on the fly. The shrieks of pain and terror and the staccato intakes of sobby breath to hush the secret nighttime crying because oh Lord, don't let Daddy hear you, oh Lord no.

But those weren't ghosts. Those were memories. And memories were with you everywhere, no matter the efforts made to suppress or forget them. They don't inhabit a building. They don't move the planchette of a ouija board or close an open door or snuff a candle with an icy puff of wind. No. They're neither seen nor heard; they're relived: a whiff of Aqua Velva and there's Dad shaving and glaring at Art sideways as he tries to slip past the bathroom door without getting caught but no luck. Art had a bottle of Aqua Velva in the shaving kit, ergo, instant memory; Art lights a cigarette, smoke ghosting on the breeze, and there's Dad in the middle of the garden ripping off his belt, Raleigh at attack angle because Art had pulled a turnip instead of a weed.

Linda crying. Like Mom.

These were small triggers, common, unavoidable (except the bottle of Aqua Velva. Should throw that away. Keep the cigarettes, though). But the house, good God, the house, Butch. Every memory you want to forget is lurking in every corner of every room. You simply have to look out of the back windshield of your crap Ford right now and choose from a smörgåsbord of memories, Butch, all bad, all evil. If you move into the house proper, they'll leap out of every closet and hammer you into the ground. Every step you take, a memory will rise from the floorboard and gibber and moan and seize you. Not ghosts, Butch. Memory.

Why are you doing this?

Art slapped exasperated hands to his face. Why, Butch? Because it is all so unnecessary. You can't do anything about ghosts, but you can do something about memory. You can throw your camping gear into the back of the Ford and fishtail your ass out of here. You can throw a torch through a skull-eyed window just before you fishtail you ass out of here. Leave the memories behind, Butch. Get over it.

Get over it.

Art's eyes popped wide and he opened his hands and stared through them at the canvas over him. Just get over it.

Really. Do so. Everyone has a sucky childhood, everyone, even the guys who had the golden parents and the golden life where everything went exactly the way they wanted. Sure, theirs was a bare blip on the sucky scale, like they got a Jaggy-are instead of a Maserati for their birthday, but suckiness is in the eye of the beholder. The jock who spent his high school years sans Maserati can be in as much psychic pain as you.

So. Get. Over. It. Do.

Art wondered what it would feel like to have no underlying sense of outrage dogging his every thought, coloring his every view. Instead of evaluating any new situation with a pre-programmed reaction, like spotting some random smiling asshole in a bar and instantly concluding the guy was some faggot in need of an urgent beat-down, he could regard the guy as simply some harmless random smiling asshole. Until the asshole proved he was some faggot in need of a beat-down, of course, but going into it with that as a starting premise would end. He might find he even liked people. A few of them, anyway.

And what would it be like to see Linda as a woman who loved him instead of one intent on robbing him of every asset and preventing him from having fun, who regarded his income as hers, giving her carte blanche to buy anything she wanted, from shoes to handbags, while railing at him for the twenty-five cents he spent on a half bag of Cheetos? Maybe she *wasn't* a harpy destroying his life; maybe she was his woman. And maybe Rich wasn't an alien sans work ethic, sporting a grand sense of entitlement based solely on his ability to breathe, but was just a kid, just being a kid, testing the limits of behavior, discovering the consequences.

And maybe no one owed him anything. Not one thing. The circumstances of childhood did not translate into redress, into justice demanding compensation. He'd always believed the guys with less sucky childhoods must share some of their good fortune, by force, if necessary, so he'd never had a twinge of guilt when pocketing an extra cigarette pack or Hershey bar while slipping out of the store. But, that's wrong. His grievances did not validate it. The sense of injustice he carried was, in itself, possibly, maybe, unjustified.

Art willed himself to get over it.

And waited.

And waited.

And did not feel lighter. On the contrary, he was as burdened as ever. Because he was still owed.

Owed.

A normal childhood, at least. When Dad and Mom entered into the contractual obligations that his conception entailed, there were expectations that he'd be reared under average parenting theories, be taught things a child needed to be taught – such as manners – disciplined when necessary, encouraged as necessary, and allowed to find his way in this world in a normal, law-abiding manner, not terrorized, brutalized, beaten into mental submission solely to satisfy the power lusts of one person. Had this normality occurred, he'd be happy, in a happy home right now with a supported and safe woman proud of him, and an enthusiastic child with a future. Instead, Art lay in a tent listening to ghosts crying in a nearby haunted house.

Art sat up and peered through the tent flap. It was a morning world, a mourning world, filled with promise for others but dismal reminders of his shortcomings, failures, one day older and closer to death. Don't call me, Saint Peter, I am the damned.

Art stepped outside, found his favorite pee tree, did his business, then turned and regarded the house. Its empty eye sockets glowered at him. Perhaps he should work on the windows next. Kinda pointless to put in floors if the rain and mists breezed in through the skull eyes and ruined them. Art wondered why someone took the windows. They were old casement types, barely worth the scrap price. Maybe the scavengers were freeing spirits.

Or letting them in.

Art settled on the old pool location. He walked over, got his bearings from the kitchen skull eye again and moved and shifted again and... right here. Easier to find the spot now. He scrutinized the ground, squatted, probed the area with a finger. What's here?

He laid a palm on the ground. Whatever you are, reach up, grasp a thumb, tell me the secret. Give me a key. I can unlock an entire childhood with it, reveal mysteries, understand what and how and why. And then...

He could get over it.

Art waited but nothing stirred, no moldy fingers reached up, no ancient eyes opened as a strong, sure voice muttered truths long hidden. And it never will. You want to see what's down there, bub, then you're gonna have to go all Indiana Jones. With a shovel.

Art stood and looked towards the camp. A shovel. He spun in that direction. Let's find the dragon's treasure.

Cindy's car eased to a stop in front of the tent. She got out, pointedly ignoring Art as he approached, and faced a utility truck pulling in behind her. It was white and clean and had a boom on the back and looked professional and efficient, as did the two guys sporting yellow hardhats exiting the cab. Art read the logo on the driver's door: Wiregrass Electric Co-op, sporting the same wavy-line drawing as Sour and Pancho's Covington Electric Co-op. The two stood obediently before her. Cindy regarded them for a moment, wordless. They nodded obeisance and trooped up the porch steps and into the house. Also wordlessly.

Art walked over. "Friends of yours?"

She turned flat yellow eyes at him. "Something like that."

Art reached into his pocket and pulled out the cigarette pack, shook out two and gave one to Cindy. He lit them both and savored a long, wonderful draw. "Just exactly how many construction workers do you know around here?"

Slight smile. "A few."

"Hmm." Art eyed the house from which emanated shuffling sounds and talk, prep for duty. "I thought this was Covington Co-op territory."

She shrugged. "I don't know anyone over there."

"Ah." He took another puff. "This is a personal favor."

"Something like that."

"So you're planning to move back in, too."

It was as if he'd slapped her. "What?"

"You're so wired here, might as well leave New Jersey and settle in."

"I'm wired there, too." A pause. "And I would never, ever move back here."

"Why not?"

She did not answer, and Art swore he saw a flicker of her eyes towards the pool, but she was suddenly back on him, a frenzied light in her eyes that made him take a step back. "Because I never would." She whispered it fiercely.

Art wanted to ask a more specific question, like, Cindy, does your reluctance to move back to a place with which you obviously still have very strong and ongoing ties have anything to do with the pool? but the door of the nondescript Ford slammed and a sleepy-voiced Butch called, "What's going on?"

Art said nothing, waiting for Butch's slow brains to evaluate the situation and formulate a conclusion. "Oh," Butch said, shuffling up, "They're here already."

"Nothing gets past you," Art observed and Cindy giggled appreciation. Butch glowered at them both then craned his neck towards the house. "How long will it take?"

Cindy shrugged and Art eyed him. "Why, you getting tired of sleeping in the car?"

Butch turned a bleary face at him then wheeled and lumbered back to the campsite, probably to make a breakfast of Eggs Benedict or vichyssoise or something. "Did he call you?" Art asked Cindy.

She finished the cigarette, dropping it to the ground and crushing it under her shoe. "About what?"

"About needing an electrician."

She said nothing, looked at the house then pushed past Art towards the camp. Must want vichyssoise or something. Art watched her go before he went into the house.

The two Co-op guys were measuring the baseboards, taking notes and calling numbers to each other. "Mornin'!" Art boomed out, jovially.

They both stared at him. Could have been twins: early forties, short dark hair, dark eyes, white shirts with pocket protectors, black work slacks and shoes, the only differentiation being the name tags "Bud" and "Cal," respectively. Thank God for that or they'd mistake each other's lockers. "So." Art took a large drag and luxuriously puffed out the smoke. "What, exactly, are you guys here to do?"

Bud and Cal furrowed brows at the same time and looked at each other, a move so comical Art struggled not to laugh. They then looked back at Art but said nothing. "It's not a hard question," he pointed out.

They stood for a beat or two then both turned back to their jobs. Art watched them for a moment. "So." He took another drag. "How do you know Cindy?"

They stayed on task. "Was it in the Biblical sense?" No reaction to that, either. Art waited an appropriate interval then walked outside.

Butch was doing something cheffy at the camp stove and Art pulled the extra fold-out chair next to Cindy. "Tweedledee and Tweedledum want to thank you for the threesome last night, and are hoping you will come in right now and hum them."

Butch whirled and stared at him, aghast, but all Cindy did was laugh and pull the cigarette case out of Art's shirt pocket and fish two out. She lit them and gave one to Art, who put it in his mouth next to the one he hadn't quite finished. He lip-lifted both cigarettes and crossed his eyes and Cindy giggled, shook her head, and glared Butch back to his cooking.

"Wa'cha making?" Art asked around the cigarettes.

Butch did not turn around. "Omelets."

"Cheese in mine. No onions. Or peppers. Or any other faggot seasoning you might have." Art threw the almost-done cigarette on the ground and started work on the new one.

Butch did not turn around but his ears reddened. Cindy looked at Art, amused. "You're something, you know?" she said.

Art settled in. "That I am."

"Yeah, something." Cindy also settled. "Got your wife, got your son, got a house and job, and a honey on the side."

She could have stroked him with a sledgehammer. "What?"

"You heard me." She eyed him, snake-lidded.

"What the hell are you talking about?" said with rising panic.

"Don't act all innocent." She blew out a long cloud. "Everybody knows. Including Linda."

The sudden shortness of breath, the rush of weakness, the feeling of lost control was like another asthma attack, except no amount of inhalant would relieve this.

Butch had turned around and was full on him. "You're having an affair?"

Art ignored him. "Where in the HELL do you get that from?" he snarled at her.

Cindy smirked. "Like you said, I'm wired."

The hot charcoal in his lungs burned again, suffocating, and spots formed in front of his eyes. His throat closed.

"You're cheating on Linda?" Butch, incredulous, the spatula a sword in his hand, outrage in his eyes.

"Pot. Calling. Kettle. Black," Art gasped, then fell out of the chair.

He had difficulty figuring out what was going on. He was on the ground, that he knew, and an anxious and frantic Butch hovered over him and slapped at him and cried, saying... something... Art unable to hear it because of the roar in his ears.

Just outside his vision, Cindy still smoked her cigarette, stone hard, regarding him. That'll teach him to tease her.

Butch's hands on his chest and throat... not helping, not helping at all. Art made a feeble pass to get Butch off him, but all it did was encourage the idiot. Blackness around the edges now and the roaring got louder.

"Tranquilo, jefe. Calmate, paz, paz." Slow. Breathe. Get the bands around your chest to loosen. But they didn't loosen. They tightened. The darkness spun.

Rest now. Rest.

Chapter 20

Sunday evening

Man, death was cool. Not in the sense of Woodstock or hip-hop music, but temperature. A nice breeze flowed over him, nice sheets around him, a fluffy pillow, far off announcements, heels clacking on linoleum, and, yeah, yeah, he wasn't dead but in a hospital.

He opened his eyes. Linda sat in the visitor's chair, knitting. "What are you doing here?" he asked. Or, thought he did. Even to him, it sounded like a frog croak.

She looked up, her eyes a cipher. Appraising, searching, yes, but not a lot of concern in them. "How do you feel?" she asked, which might be mistaken for concern but the eyes said not.

Can you blame her?

"I'm sorry," he whispered.

She cocked her head. "What?"

"I'm sorry," he whispered again, overwhelmed by something he could not identify and he burst out crying.

A lot of things happened after that. Buzzes, calls, dozens of frantic heels slapped on linoleum and white coats leaned over him and then he was warm and asleep in a magical place. A picnic by the sea with mermaids summarized it and Art opened his eyes again because that was just plain silly. Rich sprawled in the chair, half asleep. "Where's your mom?" he asked, clearly enough this time.

Rich blinked awake. "She went home."

"Why didn't you?"

"Dad," he sobbed, tears flowing. Lot of that going on in this room. Art braced for more buzzes and bells and white coats but, nothing. Good. Art didn't want to go back to the picnic. He reached out an IV-d hand and took Rich's non-IV-d one. "It's okay," he said. "It's okay."

Rich got up and came back with a Doctor Smithfield, or something like that and a fat Nurse Bethany, or something like that. "Severe asthma attack," Dr. Smithfield-or-something-like-that said.

Really, doc?

"We're going to keep you on..." Dr. Smithfield mouthed words that sounded like "medicine and observation" and "a few days" and "you were lucky."

Matter of opinion, Doc, matter of opinion.

"So why didn't you go home with your mother?" Art asked Rich, once all the professionals had left the room.

"She said you would take me home." Which was true. He was done here. Done. Stick an IV in me, done.

"You're missing school," Art pointed out rather pointlessly, and Rich just shrugged. Which Art understood – in this giant mess of chaos and craziness called life, school was a thing to do but not to worry about. That was Art's take anyway, forged by his experience of getting by without necessary pieces of paper. But it bothered him greatly that it was Rich's, too, no doubt inherited (or taught), the difference being that Art getting by without papers was due to an insane work ethic that Rich showed no evidence of possessing. If Rich wanted to at least equal Art's level of getting by, then school and necessary papers were necessary for him. "You should have flew back with your mother."

Rich's face darkened. "She didn't want me to."

So, a ploy. Force Art to come home because, heaven forfend, Rich could not stay in a makeshift camp pitched over garage rubble, and Art could not afford a motel room in Enterprise to keep Rich in the level of comfort to which he was accustomed, therefore, back to Jersey forthwith. And there'd be the side benefit of Art giving Rich that man-to-man Straighten-Up-and-Fly-Right talk during the three days' ride home.

Amazing how stupid women can be, isn't it?

First, Art had no problem ensconcing Rich in the garage rubble camp, but not in the tent: right outside, right under a tree with one thin blanket to protect him from the ticks and mosquitos. Give him a taste of what life is like without those necessary pieces of paper. Heck, make him get up at oh-dark-thirty and march around the yard with a mop handle on his shoulder for a taste of Army life since that's where you're heading, bucko. And there was no way a man-to-man talk would have any effect. Experience was the only teacher. Women didn't get that; they believed a well-placed word was sufficient, 35,000 years of human existence to the contrary.

Second, Art still didn't know about the pool.

"Well, we're not going home," Art said and examined the IV. How much would it hurt to pull that out?

"Are we going to Aunt Cindy's?"

"What?" Art furrowed at him. "No. She's here. And why would we go there?"

"She's here?" Now Rich furrowed.

"Yes. You guys didn't know that?"

"No."

"Okay." Art was suddenly very confused, "So, why would we go to Aunt Cindy's?"

"Because Mom said she doesn't want us coming back home."

For a second, Art feared another asthma attack. "Oh," was all he could say because now he understood. By "home," Linda meant New Jersey. She didn't want them to come back to New Jersey. She wanted Art to stay at his new home in Alabama. And keep Rich with him.

Rich looked on the verge of tears again. "What's going on, Dad?"

"Nothing." Art waved his non-IV-d hand. "Just women stuff." But it was a lot more than that, a lot more. Art knew, with certainty, that he had just lost everything. Everything. Somewhere, off in the distance, he heard Dad snickering. "Help me up."

"You're not supposed to get up."

"Help me up, anyway."

"Dad, the doctor said—"

"Screw the doctor," Art snapped and pulled at the sheets and the railing and apparently made too much noise because all the professionals rushed in and yelled at Art and he yelled back and then he felt warm and magical again and, really, were they allowed to do that? Didn't he have some kind of rights or something? And, as he headed back to the mermaid picnic, he saw Rich's face. Lost. So lost.

He smiled at him. It's okay, Rich. You'll get used to it.

Monday afternoon

"You really should stay a couple of more days." Dr. Smithfield disapproved, as did Bethany.

"I'm fine, Doc," Art said as Rich helped him put on a shirt.

"You should stay," Butch echoed the doc.

Art looked at him. "I'm fine."

"The recurrence of childhood asthma is a serious thing, Mr. Deats." Doc was in full lecture mode. "It's usually brought on by a change of environment, cigarette smoke, stressors."

"Wow, Doc, three out of three." He shrugged the shirt into position, inadvertently (or maybe not) pushing Rich back. The kid looked at him, helpless. And still lost.

"Maybe you'll cut out the cigarettes now," Butch said, righteous demeanor welded in place.

Art glanced at Cindy, who leaned on the door but eyeballed the hallway very much as if she wanted a cigarette. "Not bloody likely."

Butch and the doc and Nurse Bethany fumed at him. Cindy smiled.

"I'm putting you on theophylline once a day," Doc said, "and you'll need to carry an inhaler with you at all times, should you get a recurrence."

"Yeah, Doc, whatever." Art fumbled around the stand for anything he may have brought with him: wallet, coins, his life. And his cell phone. Art picked it up. Dead. Appropriate.

"Mr. Deats." Doc adopted his lecture voice again. "This is serious. You can develop COPD."

"Isn't that what Ridge died of?" Art called out to Cindy, whose eyes remained fixed down the hall but nodded.

Doc looked at him blankly. "Ridge?"

"One of my stepfathers," Art said, shoving things into his pocket, "So, don't worry, Doc."

"We only had one stepfather." Butch, reproachful.

True. Unlike Dad, Mom had remarried just once, to stone-faced, emotionless, disapproving Ridge, immediately expanding the Deats' circle of relations by Ridge's four or five other sons gotten off three or four previous wives. Ridge treated Mom like he treated the previous three or four, as a maid, which, unlike the previous three or four, made Mom happy. What made her unhappy was Ridge dying and his sons kicking Mom to the curb where Cindy and Butch and yours truly regarded her with mild annoyance. A lonely death in some charity bed followed shortly after.

...And if you were all worried, why didn't you take her in?

Something throbbed in Art's chest. "Got that inhaler, Doc?"

Three of them pressed into his hand, giving Art enough time to calmate, paz paz, and easily dissipate the stone because this was heartbreak, not lung break. "Thanks, guys," he said and pocketed all three.

Rich leaned him into the wheelchair and the phalanx arrayed itself around the chariot and followed it down the hall and into an elevator and down a ramp and out of the door, where the morning air slapped him upside the head and he fingered a breather as he gasped but no, not lung break. Just Alabama. Doctor Smithfield threw bags on his lap and walked away shaking his head. "Where are we?" Art asked.

"Enterprise Medical Center," Butch said as Cindy headed over to the parking lot to retrieve her car.

"I didn't know Enterprise rated a hospital." Art searched his pocket for a cigarette. Nothing. Of course. Hospital Nazis got them.

"It's always been here," Butch said, "We just never used it. We went to Ft. Rucker." Butch gazed in another direction. Art followed and saw a cemetery located next door. He laughed. "That's appropriate."

Rich looked at the cemetery and then at Art, puzzled. Art waited, but no clarity washed over the boy's expression and he sighed inwardly. A fine sense of irony was not an inherited trait, apparently. Nor could it be taught.

Cindy pulled up and they all got in, rather comfortably, even enough room in the trunk for Rich's suitcases. Three of them. Art wondered if, while packing his stuff under Linda's supervision, Rich might have questioned the need to bring so much. Probably not. A fine sense of trouble was not an inherited trait, either. Had to be developed.

Art watched southern Enterprise go by. Old houses, most in

need of roofs or siding, relieved by the occasional new construction standing out like a tuxedo in Goodwill. Chain-link fences contained glowering Pitbulls in weed-ravaged yards, glowering old black men on the porches. Art didn't know if the Pitbulls were there to keep people out or in. The dreary air of defeat hung over everything. Art appreciated that.

"I didn't know you were here," Rich said to Cindy.

"Didn't tell you I was," she answered without even glancing back.

"I know, I mean..." Rich blinked helplessly at her then at Art. "Mel and Roark didn't tell me." Cindy's two sons, as unlike each other as fire and water, two different fathers resulting in, consecutively, one layabout and one hard worker who owned a cleaning business and kept as much distance from the Deats as possible. Especially his mother. Roark's father had bailed as soon as he discovered how batshit crazy Cindy truly was; proof that Roark had inherited his dad's common sense. What was that guy's name, again? Art shook his head. Couldn't remember. Couldn't remember Mel's dad, either, only that he died in prison. As Mel probably would.

"Didn't tell them, either," Cindy said, flatly, which was an excellent summary of her parenting skills. Art, annoyed, patted Rich on the knee. "Don't worry about it," he said.

"What are we going to do, Dad?" Rich quavered.

"Don't worry about that, either." Which was a pretty good summary of his own parenting skills.

They made their dreary way to the house and all got out, except Cindy, who ensured (barely) that suitcases and people had unloaded before she backed out in a dust cloud and took off. Only Rich watched her go. Butch and Art stood tableau on the driveway, facing the wrecked garage and the camp, the noon sun beating it all into submission.

"House got power?" Art eventually asked.

"Yes," Butch said.

Art did not press for details. "Got air conditioning?"

"Fans."

"Okay," he said and walked inside. Rich followed hesitantly, his shock obvious as he dropped the suitcases in the kitchen. "Good God!" he said.

Art laughed. "Watch it. This hyeah is the family ranch."

"Dad, it's a... hole!"

"Shoulda seen it before we fixed it." He turned. "And, get comfortable. It's your hole now."

Tuesday morning

Art had slept well. He'd moved the cot into the den, trading a canvas tent for one made of wood-and-brick-facade since the windows were still gaps. Butch had mysteriously acquired a big electric fan, propped it in one of the gaps and set it to 5, which was a marked improvement over the Vornado. Art could now rest in relative comfort and quiet. Butch had moved out of the car and into the tent, running a cord through the window to power his own big fan. Everyone got an upgrade.

Except Rich.

On the floor, bleary-eyed and frowning, lost and blinking in the dawn light at the blanket wrapped around his feet, he scratched at the five thousand or so mosquito bites on his arms. Or flea bites, whatever.

"Stop," Art said, "they'll get infected."

"But they itch." Rich redoubled his effort.

"Deal with it." Art stood back from the fanless window gap he'd been leaning out of, taking in the view of the shed and overgrowth and poisonous trees. Lovely.

"I gotta use the bathroom," Rich said.

Art pointed out the window. "Go claim a tree."

"But... I gotta do number two."

"Then go claim a stump."

"Dad..."

"All right, all right." Art moved off the window and went to a bag and took out a toilet roll and threw it to Rich, who missed. Well, there goes that NFL contract.

Art headed to the porch as Rich made sleepy way to his feet and stumbled after, catching a flip-flop on an uneven edge and almost pitching straight out of the door. "Ouch!" he yelped. Art ignored that and snagged a shovel propped against the shed as he passed by, Rich behind him like a confused elephant. "Make sure you put this back in the same place." He shook the shovel at a puzzled Rich. Gonna come in handy for the pool. Heck, maybe he should have at it right now but Butch was around here somewhere and, besides, number two.

At the wood's edge, he handed the shovel to Rich and pointed into the growth. "Find yourself a suitable spot. Dig a hole. Crap in it. Then, bury it. And don't do it in a place either me or your uncle will step in." He followed that with a glare.

Rich owled at him, then the shovel, then back at Art with growing astonishment. "You're kidding, right?"

Art said nothing, simply pushed past Rich and headed back to the camp. Butch was already up preparing a pan for Cornish hens in *foie gras*, probably. "Where's Rich?" Butch asked.

"Figuring out the new toilet protocols."

Butch frowned and cast a sorrowful look at the woods. He tended his cooking as Art fished his charged phone out of the Ram and then plopped in a camp chair, followed Butch's Julia Child dance for a moment then flipped the phone open. Ten voicemails. Nine more than he usually got over a similar four-day period. He checked for bars.

Waddya know, two. Must be a solar flare or something.

He dialed and listened.

Most were from Linda, detailing her progress from New Jersey to airport and Atlanta and Dothan and car rental and where in the hell is Enterprise, anyway?

Good question.

She expressed concerns over his health in messages three and seven, blaming the house and Butch for it.

Good observation.

The last one from her was the ninth message, made as she'd pulled up to the hospital and hoping to God he would answer so she could find out what room he was in.

The tenth wasn't from Linda. It was from the other woman in his life, tearful and shocked. Linda had just called and bitched her out.

"Crap," Art said softly, eliciting raised eyebrows from chef de la campsite over there. In between Linda calling her a whore, slut, whore, something that sounded like slut again, you catch the drift, Linda mentioned to her that Art was in the hospital. Art checked the date. Two days ago.

"Crap," he said.

Butch looked at him disapprovingly. "Shouldn't you go check on Rich?" At that moment Rich, red-faced, stumbled into view clutching shovel and half-used roll. He glowered at Art. "I gotta clean up."

Art pointed at the washhouse. "Hose is on the side. Right next to where the shovel goes." Gentle reminder.

Rich, incredulous, stepped to where he could see and stared at the hose. He shook his head slowly, then moved in and out of view and concern as he retrieved new clothes and underwear from inside the house and towel and dish soap from Butch and turned on the water and couldn't believe how cold it was. New shower protocols.

"Maybe we should work on the bathroom next," Butch observed.

"Uhm," Art grunted, forgoing the "whaddya mean we, paleface?" opening. "Breakfast almost ready?"

"Yep! And you're really going to en—"

"Fine," Art cut him off. "Make sure Rich gets plenty." He walked to the end of the driveway, measuring bars, and frowned at how they dipped and disappeared then came back then, no, gone. Freakin' tease. He finally got a steady, if weak, signal across the road on the shoulder next to the old bull pasture. He dialed her cell.

After what felt like about twenty rings, she answered, sleepy, "Hello?"

"Oh, God, I am so sorry about all of this."

He heard a tear-drawn breath. "I know."

"Look." Art fished around in his shirt pocket but he hadn't reloaded it with Raleighs, dammit. "It's all fucked up right now, but, it'll be okay. It will. I'll make it up to you."

"I know." She was still tear-breathed. "It's just... I didn't want to be that woman, you know?"

I didn't want to be the abandoned son of an asshole and a doormat mom or end up working construction to support a fishwife and her retarded son, but here I am, he thought furiously, then shook that away. "You're not," he said softly. "You're my woman."

"I'm not."

"You will be. After the divorce."

She started to cry. "I didn't want that, I didn't want that to happen. It was all fun, you were fun, and it was safe and now, now —"

"It's still safe." Art was irritated. Jesus, woman! "When the dust settles, you'll see. We'll be together. Everything will be fine."

"Conrad fired you."

Art looked around to see if the old bull, dead these thirty years, had just run him over. "What?"

"Linda called him. He fired me, too." And she hung up.

"Dammit!" Art yanked the phone away to redial but the bars were gone. He spent the next thirty seconds cursing with amazing creativity every cell phone ever invented. A redneck peanut-farmer motherfucking piece of dirt-rolled shit drove by in his tampon-powered fuck truck, goggling at him with astonishment and Art threw him a raging finger and would have thrown a raging cell phone but the old fuckheaded sheep fucker sped away.

Art looked back at the house. Butch and Rich stood in the driveway, both stared at him with the same open-mouthed astonishment the old mule-dick farmer had. "Fuck you too!" Art roared and wheeled, facing the overgrown, abandoned pasture, chest heaving.

Tranquilo, jefe.

He breathed deep and long. Slow down, expel, fill, inflate, take in the cyanide air, the death air, the end of all life-and-hope that was Alabama. We came here and died. We left Oklahoma where life was fun and good and wholesome because Dad was always gone doing Army helicopter business of some kind or another and it was just us kids and Mom and the neighborhood and fun and tag and bikes and school chums and trick-or-treat at Halloween and turkey and pumpkin pie at Thanksgiving and the best presents at Christmas – a Superman costume and Roy Rogers six-shooters and "GI Joe, GI Joe, action man from head to toe on the land and the sea and the air" – to come here. That one summer, when Dad and Butch disappeared and they were supposed to be all divorced and Art was confused and wary but felt it was a good thing, overall, and then Dad and Butch came back and packed them all up and they came... here.

Art surveyed the bull pasture, his breath calming. Overgrown and desolate, no bull or cows or anything anymore; off to the right the wreck of a trailer where a weird guy and his wife and baby once lived. Butch told him the guy killed puppies and Art made sure, the whole time they were growing up, to give the place a wide berth. Beyond the trailer was the wreck of a farmhouse where the parents or grandparents or cousins or godfathers, whatever, of the guy in the trailer lived. They owned the pasture and the bull, and when Art trespassed he always crossed the field at a dead run and then scrambled up the opposing ridge, terrified the bull was on his heels but it never was, and then sit up there, quiet, hidden, safe, as Dad and Mom battled and screamed over something. Quite the vantage point. He'd see Butch run away from the house with a book in his hand making for the creek and Cindy slip out of the front door and wait by the side of the road for some redneck's truck and get in and disappear and Art knew that if he went back to the house right now he'd get a beating for no other reason than the opportunity, so hunker, blend into the underbrush, disappear.

Disappear. Like they all did when they moved to Alabama.

Maybe he should go back to Oklahoma.

Art took in a deep breath, smelled the decay and rot baked into the Alabama earth. He re-crossed the road and walked into the camp. Butch was still busy at the grill. Rich sat in one of the chairs, looking with some trepidation at a plate of Butch's concoction. Art couldn't blame him. The only thing recognizable was an egg or two. "Hurry up and eat, then brush your teeth," Art ordered.

Rich looked up. "Why?"

"You're going to school."

Chapter 21

Tuesday

"Do you have records from the previous school?" Msssssss
Cewlot (pronounced 'Culotte,' another example of an
unfortunately-named person employed by the public schools)
regarded Art like a biology lab specimen. Art regarded her in kind:
an old lady with pince-nez perched in front of squinty eyes, gray
hair in a bun, and an overwhelming air of disapproval, like every
other school administrator Art had ever met. There must be a
factory somewhere.

"No," Art said, "This is rather sudden."

Rich, wearing the expression of a soldier approaching Omaha
Beach, stared out of the skinny window set in New Brockton
School's main office door, which gave a sliver view of the
hallway. Every time a kid loomed past the sliver, Rich flinched
like a German artillery shell had exploded off the bow.

"Well." Ms. Cewlot huffed. She did not like that response. Not
one bit. "That will make it difficult for us to set up a schedule."
She blinked accusingly at Art. How dare he make it difficult to set
up a schedule!

"Can't you have his old school fax you a set? You do have
faxes, right?" Art couldn't keep the snark out of his voice.

Ms. Cewlot's frown deepened, if that was possible. She did
not like easy solutions, either. Not one bit. Lose some of her
power that way. "It's not that simple, Mr. Deats. We also need
proof of Alabama vaccinations and residency."

"There are vaccinations against Alabama? Who knew?" Art
playfully smacked Rich on the shoulder, who remained intent on
the sliver.

"I believe you know to what I'm referring," Ms. Cewlot said,
frostily.

"I believe," Art mimicked her tone, "that all those

vaccinations are listed on his school records. I further believe that the state of science in New Jersey is a little more advanced than it is here, so he will have vaccinations for diseases from which you still suffer. You know, the black plague, dropsy?" Art was thoroughly enjoying himself.

"That attitude is not helpful, Mr. Deats." Frosty had turned to glacial.

Art was more than tempted to fish a cigarette out, light it and blow a smoke ring in her face while asking, "What do you think of my attitude now?" But he didn't. He stared at her stonily. "Is this a public school?"

"Yes, Mr. Deats."

"Well." Art gestured at Rich. "This is a public student. So why don't you go ahead and send a pigeon or a telegram up to New Jersey and get his records and stop giving me a hard time. Okay?" Art put a little menace in his voice.

She examined him, dislike so evident Art thought her eyes might explode. "We'll make a request," she said, "We still need, though, proof of your residency." Here, she sported a 'gotcha' smile.

"I'm living with my brother." Art tapped the form on her desk. "Here's the address."

"We'll need proof."

"Tell ya what, lady, I'll bring you some kind of proof that my brother is living there," – another form tap – "sometime in the next few years. In the interim, consider Rich a homeless student. You do enroll homeless students, doncha?" For no real particular reason, Art had become familiar with enrollment policies when Rich started school, and was fairly certain all school districts everywhere followed the same script. More or less.

Judging by Msssssss. Cewlot's souring beyond-already-sour face, bingo.

She scowled at Art, glanced down at the forms, then sighed. "We'll set... Rich... up with a basic schedule." She looked at Rich like a German defender sitting in a beach bunker, licking her chops.

"Fine," Art said, knowing when not to crow, and nudged Rich, who blinked at him. "Did you hear that?"

"What?" Rich blinked some more.

"You're getting a basic schedule. Shouldn't be a problem."

"Oh." He returned to his sliver surveillance, flinching as a couple of big linebacker looking guys glided past and glared at him.

"How do you keep the middle-schoolers separate from the high schoolers?" Art asked, which was a silly question. If he remembered correctly, there was no separation. High schoolers and elementary kids mixed all over the place when he attended. But these were different times.

Ms. Cewlot gave a tight smile. "The middle school is on different floors and has different schedules. They do not eat with the high school classes nor share PEs. It works rather well." The sadistic gleam in her eye said otherwise.

Art threw Rich a sympathetic look. Gonna have to toughen up there, bucko. "How come he can't go to the middle school over on the other side of town?" Art absently fingered a cigarette in his shirt pocket, which prompted a Cewlot frown.

"There are two middle schools in town, actually." Ms. Cewlot liked correcting people, Art noted. "But those are for city residents only. Are you city residents, then?" Ms. Cewlot also liked to beg obvious answers, as a way of putting down inquiries.

Art almost said, "Stupid question," because she knew they weren't, the address was plainly visible on the paperwork, but decided not to. Rich was in enough trouble. "What bus does he ride?"

"I could not say, Mr. Deats." She looked at the address forms. "Where is rural route three?"

"Don't you know?"

"This isn't the post office, Mr. Deats. Buses are assigned to roads, not rural routes." She blinked at him. "Do you know the name of the road on which you... live?"

The pause was a dig at his homeless ploy, Art knew, and it was all he could do to keep his temper. "Damascus Road." He waited, giving her a chance to say something like "Damascus Road is a very long road, Mr. Deats," but she didn't rise to it, so he clarified. "Just south of Yoman Road."

Her brows furrowed. "Just south?"

Art nodded.

Her expression changed as though she'd had a vision. "That place," she said, softly, and looked at Rich with pity.

"Yeah, that place." Art's chest soured a bit and he had to tell it to calm down. "The haunted one."

"What?" Rich spun around at that and stared at him, worried.

"By me." Art jammed a thumb at himself, which confused Rich even more, but not Ms. Cewlot. She now looked at Art with pity.

Art stood. "I gotta go," he said to Rich's panicked expression. "The nice lady here," Art jammed a sarcastic thumb at Ms. Cewlot, "will take care of you. Don't miss the bus."

He walked out and glanced back. Rich stood at the sliver, shocked, lost.

Like I said, get used to it, kid.

Still Tuesday

Art surveyed the choices on display in Lowe's replacement window aisle. The overpriced factory models cast come-hither glances, tempting Art with their Madison Avenue sleekness and expense. If original conditions prevailed, he would gleefully buy them. The idea of Butch paying high prices for a substandard product gave Art little twinges of joy. But it was Art's credit card in play here, Butch's "I'm good for it" about as reliable as a meth head's promissory note. Besides, Art was now living in the house, so better quality at lower cost was a priority.

Living in the house.

A chill slammed him like a Cadillac iceberg and little spots swam in front of his eyes. Living in the house.

Oh. My. God.

Never, in any combination of nightmare and worst-case scenario, had he ever considered that. It was not even an inkling of an option, no matter how bad things got or could get. Yet here he was. How did this happen?

Because the house was a monster.

A long-tentacled eternal monster, brooding and hateful in its swampy lair, tracking him over the decades with eyes bloody and vengeful, biding its time and then, *slash*! a malodorous, dripping claw deep in his chest, suckers locked to his skin and dragging him back, screaming, into its maw. Grind and gnash and swallow him over decades until it shat him out the other end, old, broken, stripped of soul and life, dissolved by old ghosts, doomed to wander the yard for eternity.

What had he done to deserve this?

Simple. He'd become Dad.

Or was Dad all along.

Six of one, half dozen of another. Whether he devolved into Dad slowly over time or Dad suddenly emerged through some triggering event, was immaterial. He was Dad. In every fiber of his being and belief.

Take marriage. Dad and previous generations of his Texas forbears had taught Art that marriage was a joke and a game, something done whenever they got horny or changed jobs or bought a car, whatever. Art supposed that the Texas people were like Catholics; as long as some legal entity absolved their sins, then everything was permitted. Want to obtain carnal knowledge of some hot babe? Marry her after the first date... hell, DURING the first date. Want to justify fucking around on the hot babe with another hot babe? Get a divorce then marry the second hot babe, on and on, world without end, amen.

Marriage was the veneer covering the multitude of sins. As long as form was observed, all the other crap was okay. The Texans gushed and cooed over each other's pending and completed nuptials, then gushed and cooed when those recent partners were put away for new ones. Art had long ago given up figuring out which uncle was married to what aunt because it was a revolving door of aunts and uncles. No shock was ever expressed by any Texas relative about this dizzying partner swap unless marriage was forgone and the couple simply decided to remove all pretenses and live together. Then, the woman was a whore and the man was a shiftless no-count. But, if they got married the next day, all was well.

Conditioned by this, Art married Linda. He did not want to. He did not ever want to get married. Based on his observations, only one person benefitted in marriage (hint: it wasn't the husband). Marriage was nothing but downside for men. A man's debts doubled, usually for stuff men would not buy, like crystal glasses and washing machines. And the benefitting spouse purchased so many crystal and washing machine-related items that funds were no longer available for important stuff like motorcycles and mag wheels. The man gave up his apartment or cot in a pal's basement for a 2600-square foot permanent maintenance project called a house. True friends were discarded for church acquaintances and in-laws; fun eschewed... nay, redefined into things like visiting fabric stores, poetry readings. Taking walks. Wine tasting.

Kill me now.

It was a trap. A trick. Women exhibited their best behavior before marriage because they had to convince the mark that they were fun and loved sex and mud racing and wrestling as much as he did; then the preacher put that all to rest. The imperatives of civilization and social cohesion took precedence, and mud wrestling and staying out all night morphed into the forms. We must observe the forms. Church, walks, wine tasting.

Then kids came along. Might as well shoot yourself.

And yet, knowing all this, Art married. Perhaps he had admired Linda's best behavior. Perhaps her fake enthusiasms for mud wrestling and staying out all night had tickled him, even though he knew it was a thumb on the scale.

But, really, in all truth, he did so because it was the done thing.

Something everyone did at some point in their lives, that is, sometimes over and over, like Dad and the rest of the Texans, and Art did so with the Texas understanding of marriage's permanence: have and to hold until something better do us part. And he had immediately engaged in the Dad-taught husbandly behavior: blaming Linda for all of his frustrations, screaming at her for spending their money on stuff she wanted instead of on stuff he wanted, thereby creating insurmountable debt that forced him to work for Conrad, that twat, her pregnancy trapping him in even more debt and driving away all of his friends as she turned frigid seemingly overnight.

So, drink a lot, call her names, put her down, refuse to give her money, treat Rich like crap, and fuck around.

Dad would be proud.

Art leaned against a display, the spots now full-blown paisley amoebas sliding across his eyes as his chest filled with burning coals. Dad was chained to the house, condemned to rattling and moaning up and down its moldy walls and malignant yards forever and ever unless he could find a substitute. Art had offered himself and the chains dropped from a cackling Dad and snaked across the rotten floors (well, not anymore. He'd fixed 'em.) and wrapped around his legs, holding fast. Art groped at his pocket, seeking the breather, hoping it was full of cyanide.

"Sir, are you all right?" A concerned voice over his shoulder. Art glanced back, the amoebas parting enough he could make out a fat girl in a Lowe's vest, name tag 'Betty,' leaning in at him.

"No," Art said and blinked away the amoebas and pulled out the breather and *pfhht*, the coals in his chest cooled. Oo, that's nice. "But," he continued to the somewhat startled Betty, "I do need some windows. Ten of them, this brand." Art gestured at the cheaper-but-better. "With these measurements," Art handed her a previously scribbled note, "to that address. And, yes, that's the haunted house and don't give me a hard time about delivery." He walked away.

"Sir?" Betty called after him and Art turned, ready for combat. "Do you want UV coating?"

Art half-smiled. "Sure," he said, squaring on the bathroom aisle.

He picked out a standard tub/shower/sink, a couple of cabinets, waterproof sheetrock, some cheap-but-quality tile and all the other little things that made a difference. He should contact a service to drain the septic field before he set things up, but both things could be done simultaneously. Heck, simply mention it to Cindy and *presto*! One of her many boyfriends would show up with a truck and *presto*! Nice clean sewage system.

Art moved onto plumbing next because the guys who stole the windows probably absconded with the bathroom piping, too. Then over to lumber to get more floor hangers in case he needed to shore things here and there. By the time he was done, he had three carts at the contractor register, much to the annoyance of a couple of hayseeds behind him. "Yew bultin' a haus or sumpin?" the more articulate of the two asked.

"Or sumpin'," Art agreed.

"Hoo yew werkin' fer?"

"CIA," Art responded and then tallied the damage, not even wincing at how close to his card limit the total hovered. And here he was, without a job. Must have valium in that breather.

The hayseeds stewed over Art's response as Betty came up and consulted with 'Rhonda,' the cashier, adding the windows and now Art was mere cents away from card confiscation. He wondered if Alabama taxes would put him over. Or the delivery charge.

"I'm not sure we can deliver."

Dave. He'd sidled up, apparently keeping an eye on Art from a distance the whole time. With cameras, probably.

"Sure you can," Art said, "You already did once. And I've just bought enough to guarantee you store of the year, so I think you can continue a past practice."

"It's outside our area," Dave said, flatly. Betty's furrowed brows proved that wasn't true.

"No, it's not," Art said. "It's outside your non-haunted house area." Which made no sense except to persons aware of prior conversations. Like Dave.

"Hainted?" The articulate hayseed, not privy to previous discussions but very interested nonetheless, blinked at Art, the CIA agent.

Art looked at him. "Yep. The Deats' place."

Both hayseeds paled and took two comically coordinated steps back. Art flung scary fingers at them – "Boogie boogie boogie!" – driving them even more comically back, and then turned to Dave. "Boogie," he said.

Dave flushed, angry eyes saying there was no way in hell, but then Art invoked the magic words: "Do we need to call your manager?"

Cross to a vampire, that.

Dave's lips tightened but he made a magical pass over the register and *presto*! Delivery!

"Thanks, Dave!" Art said brightly to his retreating back.

"Do you need help loading your truck?" Betty, worried.

"Sure," Art said. He turned, "Boogie!" one more time at Hayseed #1, and then he and Betty pushed carts out of the door.

Logistics. Get truck, move crap in truck around, play Tetris with the materials until everything was in at least transportable condition. "You're good at this," Art said to Betty.

"Thanks." She smiled, which made her peroxide-blonde-overweight-self somewhat attractive. "Just my job."

"You in trouble with Dave?" Art asked as he pulled another bungee cord over the load. Can't have enough bungee cords.

"Nah." Dismissive, she helped him lock the cord, stepped

back and put a warning hand on his shoulder. "You be careful at that house. There's something not right there."

"Don't I know it." Art slipped a five-dollar bill into her frock. "Have some Mickey D's on me."

"Thanks!" she smiled. "But I'm serious. There's ghosts there."

"Three of them," Art agreed, then stopped. "Now, four." And he drove away.

Later Tuesday

Work. Work, work, work. Good for the soul. Mind-numbing, thought-killing, a proof against brooding and moroseness. Art stepped back from the bathroom entrance, wiping his brow with a big red handkerchief.

Work makes everything okay. There is nothing but the work. It is the Balm of Gilead. Make yourself downright cheerful by dint of severe physical labor, the endorphin rush shuts off all thoughts except those emanating from the crotch. Nyah ha ha.

He surveyed his handiwork. Not bad, not bad at all. Everything was connected, a task hastened by the pleasing discovery that all the original piping was still in place.

Stunning, that. More stunning: the existing pipes were in rather good shape.

He was convinced the window strippers had gone after them, but no, probably because it was old and galvanized and not worth the effort to tear out. Good enough to still use, though. Mayhaps he should have checked that before buying all that extra expensive copper piping?

Yeah, should have, like he should have checked for the meter. Didn't matter. You're still going to pay for it all, Butch. One day. Maybe.

Ah well.

Upshot, they now had a functional shower that no one could use. Ditto for the sink and the toilet, installed and with running water but no septic yet, so, pretty to look at but don't touch. No doubt he would have to install a door next and keep the key because there were people around hyeah stupid enough to try to use the bathroom.

Yes, I'm looking at you, Butch.

He did look at Butch, behind him and coated head to foot in sheetrock dust. About the only thing the guy was good for was taping and sanding, so Art had given him a five-minute tutorial and set him loose on the short hallway. Art surveyed Butch's handiwork.

Hmm. Not bad, not bad at all. 'Course it was hard for even a klutz like Butch to screw taping up, but give the guy some credit. "Looks good," Art said.

"It does," Butch agreed, referring more to his own handiwork than Art's.

Sigh. An artist is never appreciated in his own time.

"So we've got hot water now?" Butch asked, trying to wipe sheetrock dust out of his eyes.

"Nope!" Art was almost gleeful as he imagined Butch cleaning up under the outside hose. "No heater. You should think about one of those on-demand kinds that hang on the wall. Not that it would make any difference 'cause nothing's hooked up yet."

Butch frowned at him. "I thought you were installing everything."

Art stepped back and threw a ringmaster's flourish at the bathroom. "Ta daa!"

Butch furrowed, a look made more comical by the pancake makeup. "But... everything's in."

"Think of it as a stripper: gorgeous but don't touch. 'Cause we ain't got the septic yet."

A disturbance down the hall made Art peer over Butch's shoulder at Cindy wrestling her way through the screen door. He raised his voice. "You know, a septic system? Maybe one your local boyfriends could install? Hint hint hint?" She flicked an eye at him but made no comment.

Butch frowned then shrugged an 'oh well.' "Cold water showers are better than nothing, I guess." He stepped expectantly towards the bathroom.

"Eehhhh!" Art made a buzzer sound. "Wrong answer, Sheetrock Breath. Not using this shower at all, with either hot or cold water because, as just stated, we have no septic. In other words, we still don't have a connected drain. And we still have to put up the tile, and even after that, no touchee for twenty-four hours."

"But..." Butch looked thoroughly baffled now. Easy to baffle the plumbing-ignorant. "There's water, right?"

"Certainly. The well pump's working great."

"So..." The bafflement continued. "That means the shower's working."

"Sure is. Works great. As does the sink." Art hooked his thumbs into his T-shirt and beamed at Butch. "Art tested, Art approved. Got everything draining out the crawlspace into the side yard as we speak." He drew an expressive hand across the bathroom. "So if you want to spend a few years in jail, be my guest."

"Huh?"

"You can't just dump drain water in the yard. And until we get a working septic... hint hint hint," – three simultaneous eyebrow raises at Cindy, who rolled her eyes – "that's what you'll be doing."

"Oh," Butch said, clearly disappointed, and Art smiled, re-imagining the hose shower.

"And, yes, forget the toilet," Art added, then gave Butch a dewy-eyed look. "So, honey, how about dinner?"

Butch snorted and turned about and pushed past Cindy who smiled appreciation. Art cocked his head at her to emphasize the earlier references to a boyfriend-installed septic system, but all Cindy did was give him a cryptic look and follow Butch out of the door.

Okay, that's enough mischief.

Art surveyed the area one more time, then strolled out to the porch. Cigarette time. He grabbed the pack, shook out a Raleigh, patted the breather in his pocket, and lit up. Ah. Thank God for theophylline. It cleared enough passages to make smoking possible.

A school bus pulled up to the bottom of the driveway. At least, seemed like a school bus: flashing lights strobed through the junipers and the telltale valve knock of a badly maintained engine sounded up the gravel. But nothing else. No kids shouting, singing, murdering each other, you know, the typical savagery of pre-teens and above. He watched as the lights turned off and the bus pulled down the road and fully into view once it cleared the junipers. Pre-teens and teens were plastered against the windows, staring, pointing, but silent.

Of course. The haunted house.

Rich came up the drive as the bus went out of sight, humping an obviously heavy backpack and stomping like an elephant.

"On the porch," Art called. Rich looked up, the bright red-and-black shiner broadcasting from his right eye like an airplane beacon. "What happened?" Art asked, as if he didn't already know.

"I fell," Rich said, his expression sphinxlike.

"Uh-huh." Art took a long drag. "The stairs look as bad?"

"A couple of them do." Still the inscrutable expression.

"Good." Art took a satisfied drag. "S'pose I'll be getting a phone call from the principal."

"Don't think so." Rich dropped the backpack, which hit the ground like a wrecking ball. For good measure, he kicked it, then stepped onto the porch and pushed past Art, almost belligerently. Art coolly took his measure. Rich was a big kid, growing into muscle and whipcords, potential linebacker, but still a kid. Treachery and experience overcome youth and strength every time, Rich, so you best be careful.

"Where you going?" Art put a bit of edge to his voice.

"Bathroom." Edge in Rich's over-the-shoulder response.

"Eehhhh!" Buzzer noise. Art liked that. "Wrong answer, Toilet Breath. The bathroom doesn't work."

"What?" Rich whirled, edge now morphed into full-blown belligerence. "What have you been doing all day?"

"Installing the bathroom."

"So why isn't it working?"

"Because I'm not done installing the bathroom." Art was thoroughly enjoying himself.

"Great. Just great. This is great." Rich kicked at one of the kitchen's mildew- stained walls. Art should tell him to stop but they had to come down, anyway. "I can't even have a bathroom. I can't even have a bedroom. I hate that school. I hate the kids. I hate this place!" Another kick. "I want to go home!"

"You are home," Art was, surprisingly, mild and unconcerned.

"No, I'm not!" Rich clenched both his fists at Art. "This isn't my home. New Jersey is my home! My friends are there." He paused. "And Mom." Rich's eyes, one normal and the other blackened, filled with tears.

"That was then, this is now."

Rich's teeth clenched to match his fists. "I'm! Going! HOME!" and he marched straight at Art.

Art, still mild, took a long drag, blessed theophylline once again, and then held up a palm. "Then let me tell you how to do it."

Rich stopped, confused and surprised because this wasn't the combative reaction he expected. He looked at Art warily. "What?"

"I have experience along these lines," Art waved the cigarette. "Getting from here to New Jersey, I mean."

"I can't drive yet," Rich spat.

"I couldn't, either, when I left here. In fact, I was about your age." He took another drag. "So, this is what you do. First of all, wait for a rainy day. The sloppier the better. That makes running up the side of the road much more fun, because holding your suitcase or, in your situation, backpack, up over your head to keep the wet off is a hoot. It also gives the peanut farmers driving by something to gape at.

"Make for the store at the top of the hill and you call a taxi. Yes, yes." Art held up a restraining palm to stop Rich's protest. "I know, you don't have any money. Well, you could do what we did and steal Dad's silver dollar collection, but that's not available, so lift some money out of my wallet or, better yet, take a credit card. And don't forget my cell phone. Maybe if you get enough of a signal you can use it to call for a taxi, instead of trying to get whoever's running the store up there to let you use their phone, like we did. But that might be difficult because it doesn't look like anyone's running a store there anymore, much less living there. Either way, you'll have to call a taxi. Somehow." Art took another drag.

"So, after a couple of hours hiding somewhere in the store buying candy to keep the store owner from throwing you out, while at the same time keeping a fearful eye out for Dad, er, me, coming up there and dragging you back home because the taxi's coming all the way from Enterprise," Art made an expansive cigarette gesture, "when it finally gets there, take it all the way to the Greyhound station in Dothan. Dee-Oh-Tee-Aitch-Ay-En, remember that. There, you get on the first thing smoking to New Jersey. Should be, oh, three days and about thirty different stops. Now, because you don't have the advantage of two others watching your back, you'll have to stay awake because you don't meet the nicest people at bus stations. Especially these days." Art grinned at Rich's sudden blanch, then took another drag.

"Soooo, then you call your mom from whatever bus station you end up at. Marlton, Philadelphia, whatever. If she decides to come get you, then you enroll in a school where you have a weird accent no one understands and you get beaten up every day until you join forces with a bunch of redneck greasers, and then you'll turn out all right. Just like I did." Art spread his arms in a 'ta-da' gesture.

Subdued, Rich said, "That's what happened to you?"

"That's what happened."

"Well." From subdued to belligerent in fractions of a second. God bless teenagers. "That won't happen to me. I'm already in school up there."

"Not anymore."

"I will be."

Art examined what was left of the Raleigh. "Heading out, then?"

"You mean, you'll let me go?"

"Be my guest." Art made another ta-da gesture out of the door. Was the day for them, he supposed

Rich set his jaw and took a couple of determined steps but faltered when Art made no move. "I'm going!" he announced.

Art shrugged. "Okay. Don't slam the screen door. I just fixed it."

Rich glared at him. "You're an asshole, just like Mom said."

Art raised an eyebrow. "Very brave talk and I'm going to give you a pass for showing some stones. And for fighting back at school. Just this once. You ever talk to me like that again, you'll spend a couple of months in traction." Art took the last of a very long drag from the dying butt.

Rich's jaw worked, but he said, "Fine," and stormed out, heading for the woods. He didn't slam the screen, either. Art watched him go. He felt, suddenly, as though he was on a bus heading for Philadelphia.

Chapter 22

Wednesday morning. Early.

The bus came at 0530. Art made bleary way to his feet around 0510 and got Rich up and partially dressed and incompletely fed and across the road waiting for the bus by 0529. Forget a shower. Rich had to be threatened with a gun before he took one under the best of conditions, let alone under a hose. At least he brushed his teeth, sort of. The bus arrived moments later, so, all in all, a successful operation. The bus denizens remained silent as it pulled up, due more to the hour than the ghosts.

Art waved cheerily as the bus trundled off and the driver, some old peanut farmer, gave him a surly look. Sporting a Cheshire cat grin Art lit a Raleigh, testing the condition of his lungs with a quick smokeless inhale before drawing.

Yep, still enough lobe for additional carcinogens.

Sunrise underscored the ridge across the road, throwing blood-light everywhere, bringing the bull pasture into blood-light focus. Appropriate, since it was a place of much blood-curdling terror, what with a bad-tempered bull roaming about. And a place of fun. Sanctuary. Climb the opposing ridge and sit up there quiet, hidden, safe.

Wonder if it still is.

Art crossed the road and put a wary finger on the remaining barbed-wire strand running between the leaning, gray, weathered posts, but there was no zap of electricity so he ducked under and pushed through without snagging his T-shirt, an amazing feat given his bulk and age. The pasture fell away here and he wobbled a bit on his toes, regaining balance. The place was overgrown with sneezeweed and cocklebur and horsenettle and mustards and pokes and other noxious crap, some of it taller than him. Art frowned. Be a bitch getting through this, but sanctuary was always difficult.

Art stepped on the weed base, crushing it, then stepped on the next batch and thus forced a path through, just like good ole Dad had taught him when they were out hunting...

...Boy, you walk like a goddamn ape!

No need to be quiet here, Dad. The bull was long gone and telling nearby snakes he was on the move was a good idea. But, be careful; a reeeally deep ditch, now hidden by the overgrowth, ran across the base of the ridge and Art might crush his way right off its edge. Weeks later, they'd find his worm-eaten carcass.

He cautiously broke through a canebrake and hit a little decline and stopped.

Should be getting close.

He toed the little decline. Wait a minute...

Art peered back the way he came. He was about three-quarters of the way across the field which should put him on the lip of the reeeally deep ditch... he toed again.

This was the real deep ditch? This?

Art remembered it as a place of early death. He and Butch and Cindy and the two nephews of the people who owned the bull took cardboard sheets they'd torn from boxes up the ridge and came flying down the slick-as-ice foot-thick pine needles carpeting the slope at about 137 miles per hour. Better sure as hell roll off before the cardboard cleared the ditch lip and slammed into the opposite wall, smashing them into jelly.

Good times, good times.

Art stamped around and confirmed that, yes, this pathetic little dip in the ground was the Ditch of Death. The Slight Drainage Rill of Death, now. Amazing how a few decades will casually erase the terrible.

Or enhance it.

The ridge rose steeply above him and Art measured the angle. Wow, no wonder they had so much velocity by the time they reached the ditch.

He stepped across the Rill of Death and slogged up the pine ridge. Very little brush here under the shade, the centuries-old pine-needle carpet suppressing any growth. Just a pokeberry bush here and there and Art took a minute to check them out, humming *Poke Salad Annie* under his breath. Probably too late in the season to eat them – they turned poisonous at some point.

The carpet was still slick as ice and it was tough going at this angle and the stone grumbled in his chest. Couple that with this morning's Raleigh, and maybe this was a bridge too far.

Art stopped and slapped at the breather in his pocket then leaned against the trunk of a nearby pine and slid down it to a sitting position. Tranquilo, jefe. The stone muttered at him but went away and Art looked around. He was about halfway up the ridge with a good view of the pasture and the road and the haunted house. Nice spot. Probably one he'd selected many times during those halcyon days of escape and evasion from the crisis of the moment.

Quiet, hidden, safe.

He peered at the house. Butch's POS Ford and Art's truck, but no movement.

Guess breakfast will be late, right Butch?

The morning sun had not turned the air to lava yet and Art took in a cautiously long breath.

Smell that? Grasses and weeds, nature's perfume, with pine sap cleansing the air like a freshener hanging from the sun's rearview mirror. Back in the good ole days, there'd also be a tinge of cow dung and alfalfa.

Art remembered sitting here and watching the big black bull and a couple of its wives strolling along down there, warded by the ditch. That bull was a mean 'un and came after Art whenever the opportunity presented. But the ditch was a moat back then and kept the bull at bay, kept Art safe.

Safe.

To be safe. To enjoy a feeling that all flanks are protected, contingencies in place, caches easily reached and all threats distant, even innocuous. Art wondered if he had ever felt safe in his life.

Why, yes. Up here in the pine ridge sanctuary.

He smiled. That was true. Up here, the bull couldn't get me.

Neither could Dad, standing down there at the edge of the driveway screaming, "Boy! You better get your ass home now!" irritated and angry, murder in his stance, but Dad couldn't see Art hidden in the pines and had no confirmation his message had been received so really couldn't say anything when Art, judging the proper moment, slipped into the yard from the side woods, having reached them by a furtive climb down the ridge and a skirt of the farmer's house, and then a quick dash through the storm drain running under the highway, then along the creek and up the trash trail they used to bring burned household garbage to the dump site in the woods and, here I am. Where you been, boy? Out hunting squirrels, Dad, which is an acceptable use of his time and, yes, he'd get slapped because he didn't bring any home, but that was infinitely better than getting a beating for Wasting Time Sitting in Safety on the ridge.

Maybe he'll Waste Time Sitting in Safety up here and watch Butch and Cindy – and later, Rich – stand at the edge of the driveway screaming, "Boy! You better get your ass home now!" This time, though, he wasn't going to sneak back across the road and act all innocent about where he'd been.

Maybe this time, I'll just stay here.

"Hello," someone said.

Art whirled, smacking his face against the supporting tree as his legs whipped out from under him and he slid down the slope. Grabbing at the ground, he got enough purchase to stop his descent and looked up. A boy sat against a pine stand one level above his, chewing on a straw and looking at Art like he was crazy.

"You scared me half to death!" Art announced, unnecessarily.

The boy grinned. "Didn't mean to. Thought ya seen me."

"I didn't." Art pulled himself back around and stood against the tree; calmate, jefe. "Good job of hiding. What are you, a ninja?"

"Wasn't hiding." The boy pitched the straw away. "Sat right here and watched you come all the way up." The boy cocked his head. "What's a ninja?"

Art flicked a disbelieving eyebrow. "You're kidding, right?"

"About what?"

"About ninjas. Everyone knows what they are."

"Well, I don't." The boy pressed his lips and looked off.

Art scrutinized him. Maybe ten years old, skinny, light hair, what the old folks call 'tow-headed,' wearing a stained T-shirt under a worn set of Farmer John's, one of the suspender brads undone, and an old pair of... Keds. Keds? Art frowned. Did they even make those anymore?

"You live here?" Art asked. The kid nodded.

Hmm. Art looked around, trying to spot the old farmer's house hidden by the woods. Didn't realize the place was occupied. "So I guess I'm trespassing, then."

The kid shrugged and picked at some needles and Art took that as permission to be here. "So what's your name?" Art asked as he settled on the side of the tree facing the kid.

"Owen." The kid stayed focused on the pine needles in his fingers.

"Is it?" Art's shields went up. "That was my Dad's name. It's a bit unusual. Came from some far distant ancestor in the old country, in his case." He paused. "Where did yours come from?"

The boy looked up. "I'm named after my father."

A coldness crept up from the ground, noticeable, and Art checked if some water had suddenly broken through the pine-needle carpet, but no. He scrutinized the kid. Named after your father, huh? So, what, you're another long-lost bastard half-brother, one of the hundreds to thousands Art suspected were scattered about the world, Butch serving as confirmation? Couldn't be; this kid was too young. Unless Dad had risen from his grave, shambled across the South and put his zombie dick in some local slattern. Lord knows he'd be motivated. "What's your last name?" Art asked.

"Don't have one."

Art narrowed. "Everyone has a last name."

The kid narrowed back. "I don't."

Something was off here. Off. Goose pimples worked down Art's spine and he tensed, shields at maximum power. There was a shift in the air, a menace, like a creature about to spring. "Why aren't you in school?"

"I don't go to school." The boy's stare became hard, dangerous. Angry. "I don't do anything." And he was gone.

Gone.

Art gasped, then leaped to his feet, looking wildly around. Nothing. Kid was there one second, beaming murder at him, then wasn't. "Where the HELL are you?" he yelled, echoes coming back from all directions. "How'd you DO that?"

Silence.

No birds, no locusts, no normal woodsy sounds. Utter silence.

Dread filled Art, something unspecific, and under it was a sense of mourning, of loss and emptiness; bereft, abandoned. Art thrashed at it...

...and woke up.

He was almost at the top of the ridge itself, just one step short of the crest and its descent to the Cryman's Hole and he'd been sleepwalking. Again. Just like when he was a kid. Just like the asthma, something long gone, long dead, had reawakened in the presence of the house.

Reawakened.

He whirled, the dread still in him, the sense of something old and terrible and wanting, ugly and hungry, coming for him.

The Cryman.

Art dropped to the ground, his left leg straight out and his right one figure-foured underneath it and pushed into a crazy slide down the ridge, right foot a rudder as he weaved through trees and stumps and picked up speed every three feet and, by the time he was at the Rill of Death, he was doing about 137 miles per hour, much faster than anything the Cryman could do, and he skipped to his feet like an Olympic gymnast while still in mid-slide – amazing how agile terror will make you – and across the Rill and crashed through his previous break and at the fence and agile through and across the road and up the driveway, the stone a boulder in his lungs now, the terror a goblin on his back, and he fumbled for the breather. Press. Life-giving chemicals, life-giving air, slapping the stone back into place, dizzying in its relief.

"Jesus!" Butch stood before him, so astonished he forgot his preacher values, Art guessed. "You all right? You look like you saw a ghost!"

Art sighed, the pleasure of the open lungs almost as good as sex. "I think I did," he wheezed.

Chapter 23

Wednesday, noon

A truck came up the drive as Art grabbed the last box of bathroom tile off the Ram. Took a second to identify it and Art laughed as Caleb dismounted, pushing back a John Deere ball cap while pushing out his customary belch, the two mutants at his back. "Let me guess. You got a call from Cindy."

"Shore did!" Caleb laughed back. The two mutants didn't laugh, didn't even smile but hovered at Caleb's shoulder, glaring hatred at the world, eyes even more red if that were possible. Must be cooking some primo meth.

Art put the box down on the steps. "First wells and now septic systems. Caleb, you are a true Renaissance man." And he gave a mock salute.

"Yeah," Caleb said, looking around the yard with no clue about the Renaissance. "It ain't my specialty, but I'm licensed. Gorman here," Caleb jabbed a thumb at the shorter of the mutants, "is like a septic wizard."

Gorman? Art blinked at the raging, crazy-eyed meth head. Your parents named you Gorman? Well, that certainly explained things. "Okay," he said, keeping a straight face.

Gorman glared at Art with nothing short of evisceration. Uh-oh. He must have read Art's amusement. Great. The last thing Art needed was a knock-down drag-out with a meth-fueled hillbilly. Gorman held the slaughter gaze for a moment longer then, wordlessly, looked at Caleb. Art breathed an inward sigh of relief and said, "I've got the pipe located so I can give you the tank's direction." I'm being helpful. Don't kill me, Gourmand. Gore-Met. Gormy Goo.

Caleb waved that away. "No need. I stopped by the county and looked at the old plans."

Art raised surprised brows. "You did? When did Cindy call

you?"

"Yesterday." He craned his neck at the box of tiles. "You doing the bathroom?"

Art patted them affectionately. "Yep. Just about done. My brother's helping. Or, at least he thinks he is."

Caleb chuckled appreciatively. The two mutants glared at the house as if they wanted to storm it and kill Butch. Be my guest, Art thought and stepped quietly out of the way but the creatures stayed put.

"So I take it you ain't run nothin' through the system yet," Caleb said.

"Nope," Art said, "I wanted to make sure a gen-u-wine septic guy blessed it first. Don't want to run afoul of the local authorities." He smirked at the little joke.

"Well, okay then!" Caleb grinned big and slapped Art big on the back and led the mutants past the washhouse, looking in for a second to express satisfaction at the humming pump, then stationed himself at the back corner. "Should be-eee..." drawing the word in time with each toe-to-heel step he made towards the rear portion of the collapsed tool shed, "...here!" And he bounced up and down, looking pleased as he examined the ground. "Hmm," he said.

"What?" Art had watched the whole performance with great pleasure. A fellow wizard at work.

"No dipping here. That means either I misread the plans completely..." Caleb *tsk*ed at such an impossibility, "or the lid is still intact."

"Well, heck, that'd be great. And miraculous," Art said.

Caleb bounced a little bit more and then looked at the mutants. "Go get the shovels," he said.

Fifteen minutes later, they had the lid exposed. "How 'bout that?" Caleb was even more pleased.

Yep, intact. How 'bout that?

Another twenty minutes and they had the lid off and Art held his breath, not only for the anticipated odor, but the anticipated hardcake layer of crap that, no doubt, lined the bottom of the tank, which meant a leak and the need for system replacement and the buckets of money that would entail (Butch) and the additional week or so until they had a flush toilet. But no. Peering over the edge, he saw the four of them peering back, reflected in black water.

"How 'bout that?" Caleb was even more pleased. "Right below the vent level. Like it was all brand new or something."

"That's... impossible," was all Art could say.

"Nah, not really." Caleb stepped out of the fumes and into the clear air as he gestured for the mutants to cover up the blasted thing. "Made them real good back then. We'll do a die test, of course, but you're probably all right."

"So we can hook up the house and start using it?"

Caleb nodded. "'Pear's so. Your biomass is probably deader than a doornail, but a couple of good flushes and she'll be right as rain!" He beamed.

"I just don't see how this is possible," Art insisted.

"Well, how long's it been abandoned?"

Good question. Dad sold the house sometime back in the eighties, and then a nutcase POW/MIA guy bought it and ran a crazy anti-government newsletter out of here before going bankrupt. A few years of tussling back and forth between prospective owners and the bank resulted in an auction with no bids – ghosts, doncha know – so it sat unloved and unbothered under nominal caretaker status until Butch bought it. At least, that's how Butch explained the history.

Art shrugged. "Dunno. Maybe ten years?"

"That ain't so bad, actually," Caleb said. "If it was twenty years or so, then, yeah, you'd expect collapse. Should get another ten out of it. That is, if you guys don't shit too much," and he smirked.

Art rolled his eyes but couldn't help a quick smile. Yeah, Caleb, Butch is so full of crap, he'd probably fill it up in a week. Har har har!

"Let's go check the drain field," Caleb said and followed the direction of the vent with Art and the two mutants trailing. Caleb stopped about halfway to the woods and did his bouncy test, still looking satisfied, and walked what looked to be a perimeter, no doubt memorized from the plans. Art noted how his path grazed the old pool line.

"Ain't spongy or nothin'," Caleb announced. "Don't see any pooling, neither." He sniffed, "Don't smell nothin', 'cept maybe you," and he pointed a comedian's finger at the Unnamed Mutant, who, along with Gorman, glared at Caleb, but in appreciation.

Caleb looked at Art. "Dye test will give you a final, but I think you're gonna be fine."

"Want to dig a test hole?" Art asked.

Caleb shrugged. "Yeah, what the hell, we're here." He tapped a foot on the ground. Unnamed Mutant approached with a shovel held like a weapon—

"What are you doing?"

All four looked up. Butch, covered in sheetrock dust, accentuated here and there with tile grout, pretty hilarious, except he had one fist clenched to the point of exploding, while the other gripped a tile scraper like a dagger. Unease stirred Art, but apparently not Caleb.

"We're setting you up with indoor plumbing." Caleb grinned big again and nodded at Unnamed Mutant, who moved into position.

Butch stepped in the way. "What are you doing?" he asked again, an undertone of violence now in his voice.

Unnamed blinked at him, surprised there was anything like violence in wussy boy, but Art's unease escalated. He knew there was. A lot of violence, actually. "Take it easy," Art said.

Butch rounded on him, eyes boiling with what could have been murder but looked more like panic. "WHAT ARE YOU DOING?" he screamed at Art.

"Jesus, man!" Art stepped back, alarmed. "We're just digging a test hole. What's the matter with you?"

"No digging." Butch's hard and raspy breathing made that somewhat unintelligible, but the rage underneath it was clear and dangerous and the rest of them, even Gorman, also stepped back, alarmed.

"What? We have to dig a test hole. It's what you do!" Art figured logic and expertise would win the day.

It didn't.

Butch spun on Unnamed and yanked the shovel out of his hands then hurled it over the top of the washhouse where the sound of clanging metal told Art it had landed square on the front of his truck.

"What the hell?" was on Art's outraged lips but never got a chance for expression because Butch's face, wracked by spasms and rage, morphed into a mask of sheer murder – Bruce Banner in mid-transformation – and he grabbed Unnamed by the lapels, yanked him off his feet and threw him to the ground in front of Caleb.

"What the hell?" Caleb threw Art's words right at Butch, apparently convinced an incredulous tone would settle things.

It didn't.

As Unnamed flopped about at Caleb's feet trying to get his breath, Gorman, his eyes fired with meth-infused hate, screamed, "Yew muthafucker!" stepped up and swung a meth-powered fist at the side of Butch's head. *Smack!*

Anybody else would have been knocked silly, but the Hulk withstood artillery shells.

Butch, unfazed, took in Gorman for about a half-second and then dropped a hammer hand right on top of Gorman's skull, driving the mutant three feet into the ground... well, if Stan Lee were writing the scene. In real life, Gorman collapsed like a pile of upset bricks. Butch stepped over him and stomped towards Caleb, who goggled in utter disbelief. Art didn't goggle, but leaped aside, because Butch was about to go all Locker on their asses.

"Stop it!"

Like a bucket of cold water across rutting dogs, Butch seized mid-stride. He stumbled back, confused, unsure of what had just happened and where he was. Cindy, blazing with volcanic, determined anger, walked straight over to Butch and slapped him hard across the face, twice, three times, the last one raising a good welt across his cheek. "Stop it!" she screamed through each slap. "You stop it right now!"

A shamefaced Bruce Banner stood there, eyes teary from the slaps, but he said nothing, did nothing. Cindy gave Butch one last slap then rounded on Art. "No digging!" she yelled. Then, more gently to Caleb: "No digging."

Gorman, still wanting to kill someone, stood up and lurched at a now easily killed Butch but took in Cindy's death face and decided otherwise. He picked up a still-gasping Unnamed and walked him around the washhouse and out of sight.

Caleb, in shock, gaped at each of them, then finally got angry. "Fix it yourself," he said to Art and followed the mutants around and out of sight. Doors slammed, truck started, rush of tires over gravel and they were gone.

Art stepped in front of Butch. "What the FUCK is wrong with you?"

Silent, eyes downcast, Butch had fallen into himself, hollow, the red slap-marks a beacon across his cheeks. Art could probably punch him dead in the nose and Butch wouldn't respond. He was the anti-Locker now, standard Uriah Heep.

"Leave him alone," Cindy said, looking towards the woods.

"Leave him alone?" Art sputtered. "He needs his goddamn ass kicked. Or his goddamn ass arrested!" Art craned his neck around the washhouse, expecting a Coffee County sheriff's car to roar up the driveway.

"No one's going to arrest him." Cindy kept up her scrutiny of the wood line and Art followed her gaze to a flicker of movement along the weeds. Swear it was a kid wearing Farmer Johns. "What in the fuck is going on?" he asked her, quietly.

She didn't respond, scrutinized the woods a moment more, then took Butch gently by the elbow and led him towards the washhouse. "No digging," she emphasized over her shoulder, and the two of them disappeared around the corner.

Art watched them go, then studied the ground. He dropped to his knees and probed the wiregrass and nettles but felt nothing, saw nothing. "What's down here?" he called after, but they were long gone.

Chapter 24

Wednesday evening

"Dad, what are we gonna do?"

"Finish our dinner," Art said. Which they were having inside. Inside! Not squatting around a camp fire like a bunch of Cossacks. Still had to swat at mosquitos enjoying their own dinner at Art and Rich's expense but at least they had electric light and a fan to cool the room from 120 degrees to 110 and were using chairs and a table like civilized people.

Okay, camp chairs and table, but still.

"I don't mean that." Rich's tone was petulant, guaranteed to raise hackles but... appropriate, Art had to admit, given that the kid's world had recently shattered. Art recalled his own petulance when the same thing had happened to him.

"I know what you mean. And, I don't know," Art answered with a surprising amount of gentleness. Man, it's like he was getting empathic or something.

Rich reacted with a petulant, self-absorbed I'm-the-only-one-in-the-universe-everything-is-about-me-punkass eye-roll and pouty-lip exclamation of, "God, Dad!" and instinctively Art's hackles rose but, he had to admit, Rich's sass was understandable and fitting. Up to a point. "We gotta do something!"

"I know." That they had to do something, that is. What, he had no idea.

"Well, what are we going to do, then?"

"This argument is getting circular. Eat your spaghetti." Art sucked down a spoonful of Chef Boyardee from the Chinet bowl. Dinner of champions, courtesy of Art, who'd heated the can outside over the charcoal fire because, well, no working kitchen appliances. Was kinda dangerous carrying the can from the fire to the kitchen with a pair of pliers, bubbling Boyardee threatening to spill everywhere, but living on the edge, that was him. Even the way he made dinner. Art had heard somewhere that cooking food inside its can was deadly, forms botulism or something, a notion refuted by generations of hobos cooking out of cans without deleterious effects... other than hoboism. Hmm, was it the can-cooking or the hoboism that came first? A question for the philosophers. He'd have asked Chef Butch-ardee about it but Butch remained in his tent where Cindy had banished him before she drove off. So, go with the hobo evidence.

Rich snorted and took a forkful, eyeing Art balefully (but silently, thank God). The question, though, remained, smelly and obvious like a turd on a Chinet plate: what WERE they going to do?

Option number one: stay here. Things were humming along quite nicely. They had a working bathroom; Art had thrown caution to the wind after Caleb's report and hooked everything up, although it would be a day before they could use the shower. Tiles have to cure, doncha know. And once they all took a shower and a civilized shit, then this place wouldn't be so bad. Sure, amenities like TV and walls and kitchen appliances were absent, but it was livable, in an early 20th Century kind of way.

With Cindy's help, Art could find a job around here someplace. Rich would get used to New Brockton. After a few years, New Jersey would fade into an unpleasant memory. As would Linda.

But ghosts in Farmer Johns stalked the woods and something evil was buried by the pool: a sarcophagus waiting for Art to dig up and drag from its clay prison then dash its stone cover to the ground freeing Amenhotep to wander the Alabama woods in search of his lover (Cindy, no doubt). And then there was the Hulk, cowering over there in his tent.

So, no.

Two, go back to New Jersey? Actually the better option since he had a built-in girlfriend waiting up there, even if she was now equally jobless, a situation remedied rather quickly because skill sets were skill sets and, even in this crappy economy, they'd both get snapped up by someone, probably one of Conrad's enemies, although at a lower wage. Rich would be happy; he'd get to smoke dope with his pals again. But there was a messy divorce looming and the longer Art avoided a place with servable papers, the longer he got to keep his stuff.

So, no.

So, what?

Art took in the kitchen, then looked across at the den. The only things making this place unlivable were the ghosts and the owner.

So why not get rid of both?

He blinked. Get rid of the ghosts. Get rid of Butch. Maybe in one fell swoop.

Art swallowed his last sporkful and stood, knee-backing the chair out of the way, and peered outside, timing the view between the thick plastic strips and mosquitos flapping in and out of the kitchen window opening. When were those replacement windows getting here, anyway? Might have to give Dave-at-Lowe's an irritated call.

Okay, now, imagine it's a rainy night and that you are three feet shorter (and thinner) and imagine the placement of shadowy figures blurring in the dark... there, got it, again. Jeez, should have dropped a flag the last time he marked it but then Butch would know what he was up to and might object. Strenuously. The Hulk was banished, though, so now was as good a time as any. He stepped around a frowning Rich. "What are you doing, Dad?"

"Checking something," Art said as he braced himself against the wrecked sink.

"Checking what?" Rich was suddenly beside him, kid concern, peering through the same flapping plastic. "Is somebody out there?"

"No, it's fine." Art waved him away. "Finish your dinner. And your homework."

"I don't have any homework," Rich groused in an obvious lie. "What are you looking at?"

"A possible way out of our current troubles." Okay, location fixed once again, about ninety percent of it anyway, enough to take an educated stab. Er, dig. Now, find a shovel and get to it. Art shifted towards the door.

"Who's that kid?" Rich asked.

"Huh?" Startled, Art turned to him.

Rich pointed through the flapping plastic. "That kid." He shook his finger in emphasis.

Art stared hard along the line of Rich's point. "I don't see anyone," he said.

"Right there!" Rich jabbed an exasperated finger. "Some farmer's kid! Wearing overalls. Jeez, Dad, are you blind?"

Overalls? You mean, Farmer John's? Art goggled. How in the blue-blazing hell was Rich able to see a figment of Art's sleepwalking dream, but he can't of course, he can't, which meant... Art whirled and was out of the door and down the steps and across the yard before Rich could get, "Where you going?" completely out.

Art rushed across the back of the lot, stumbling here and there in the failing light but focused on the wood line. There was an odd shadow there and he beelined straight for it. As he approached, the shadow shifted and faded back into the trees. "Oh, no, you don't!" Art called and plunged into the growth.

Amazing how quickly he was swallowed up. He lost view of the house in seconds and disoriented, screeched to a halt in some noxious-smelling weed patch. Surprised to find the stone flopping around his chest, Art pawed for the breather. Good, in the pocket. Now, let's see to this.

Scrutinizing the terrain, he noted a lighter area cutting through the overgrowth to his left. Animal track of some kind. Art placed an uncertain foot on the top of it and found it smoother and flatter and more inviting than trying to force his way through the chokecherries and kudzu, so he followed it, hesitant, worried about sleeping snakes. Or worse, wide-awake ones. Before he got too far along, though, he zeroed on the remnants of sunset and did the usual calculations to figure out where north was and kept his right shoulder pointed that way as he went along. Easy to get lost in these woods, even this close to the house.

The path was almost a straight line, which was really odd for an animal track. It should meander without rhyme or reason and then quickly disappear into brush, but no, it continued. So, a human track. And still being used. Enough to keep it open, anyway. Art frowned. Someone's been keeping an eye on the place, have they?

Now why is that?

Art noted that the path dropped in the direction of the creek. Made sense. The flatland down there was about the only good course through this tangle. How many times had Art used it as a natural highway to go to and from the pasture? Heck, how many times had Art accessed the creek itself, which had attractions all along it like random pools of green water that made interesting splashes when he threw big rocks in them and snakes (asleep and otherwise) and other noxious creatures crawling around and most importantly of all...

...the sawdust pile.

The trail suddenly emptied at the foot of it. The Pile of Mystery, so called because neither he nor Butch nor Cindy could figure out why it was here. There was absolutely no reason for it. No sawmill within ten miles; at least, no wreckage of one, and no evidence of any kind of lumbering going on. T'weren't any tracks of giant trucks coming down here to dump the stuff, either, so how in the hell? And how does it remain? Because it looked just as tall and fresh as it did when Art chased Butch and Cindy down here in a frustrated effort to get them to play with him.

Play with me.

Art stopped, listening. Whatever shadow he pursued had led him here, so there was a good chance the shadow was still around, probably in ambush. Had to be whoever was keeping the trail open, and since Art could not think of one legitimate reason for so doing, was not a pleasant fellow. Fellow, as in a ten-year-old hick kid who called himself Owen. Or Owen's larger and more dangerous relatives. Should have brought a weapon, a pipe wrench or a club of some kind. Better, a shotgun.

All of the swamp creatures that chirped and cawed and screeched at each other had stopped, further evidence that someone else was stomping around out here. Usually, nature couldn't care less if fat little Art puffed along trying to find Butch and Cindy. Nature usually got downright malevolent, sending swarms of chiggers and black flies and every other stinging thing his way as he stumbled along, crying and mad and scared as the two of them ran ahead, laughing and jeering and predicting his imminent devouring by swamp creatures.

Not this time.

"Who's here?" he called out, letting the ambush know it was uncovered. Nothing moved, though, and the silence continued. Art stepped around the pile and scrutinized the gloom, waiting for the movement of a bush or a splash along the creek to give away a position. But there was only stillness.

Art stared at the pile. Man, what was the deal with this thing? As a kid, he didn't question its existence, instead, regarded it as a gift. It was a lot of fun climbing up the sides, sinking to his knees with each step and then throwing himself off the top and tumbling his spongy way down. He usually did that alone and with the intention of leveling the pile to the ground so Butch and Cindy could never, ever play on it again. But it withstood his every effort; indeed, responded to him with even greater support and almost audible cries to keep it up! Keep going, kid! As though the pile knew the joys of childhood, thrived on it, even.

"Good ole pile," Art said and patted it affectionately.

Shuffling on the other side made Art jump and he ran around to see what it was. Branches on some of the overgrowth running up to the pile waved as though someone had rushed through and Art stepped up to see. Nothing, at least nothing man-sized or even child-sized, moved, so must have been a squirrel or a weasel or Amenhotep. The light failing, Art turned to go. There was no kid out here, despite what Rich had seen. There might be ghosts, though.

Something crinkled under Art's foot. Foil. He bent down to pick it up. A crushed cigarette pack, rather old, about a year old. He unfolded it.

Camel Lights: Cindy's brand.

Chapter 25

Thursday morning

As Art gave cheery waves to the pissed-off driver gunning a school bus loaded with surly teenagers (including Rich) up the road as fast as a crappily maintained, underpowered engine could, a big box truck with half-walls and lots of long cardboard packages precariously strapped to them trundled over the hill and headed straight for the driveway, almost upending as it made the tight turn. Art stepped back as the Lowe's logo brushed past him and the packages – obviously the windows – rattled dangerously.

'Bout time. He drew a cigarette, making his customary lung check before lighting up, and followed the truck to the wreckage of the garage. A big black guy dropped out of the cab and lumbered over to the lift on the back. "Where you want 'em?" he asked. Art cigarette-pointed at the one part of the collapsed garage intact enough to provide some shelter and the black guy, aided by another equally big black guy, had the windows off and stacked in record time.

"Wanna stay for breakfast?" Art called as they scrambled back into the truck. Both of them looked at him as if he were crazy and broke all land-speed records backing up and getting the hell out of Dodge. Art wasn't sure if it was the residual tension between the races that still lay heavy on the land, or the ghosts alleged to be hyeah 'bouts.

Alleged.

Butch did not stir out of the tent during the window *sturm und drang*, and Art wondered if he were dead in there or something. "Hey!" Art called outside the flap, "You need to get moving. We got windows."

Nothing. Maybe he *was* dead. "Hey!" Art smacked a palm against the canvas. "What are you doing in there, jerking off?"

A stirring and a massive shove of the tent flap, and Art

stepped back to let the beast emerge. "Knew that'd get a rise out of you," he snickered, "No pun intended."

"You're disgusting," Butch snarled.

"And you look like shit," Art observed. Man, did he. He was still in the same clothes as yesterday, still covered with a sheen of sheetrock and grout; must have rubbed the excess into his bedroll. Yuck. And it looked like a squirrel had been at Butch's weird-ass curly hair. The welt Cindy had laid on his cheek remained prominent, accented by a day's stubble and a bleariness usually associated with insomnia. "Didn't sleep well?"

Butch said nothing as he pushed past and headed for the woods. "We have a working bathroom now!" Art called and smiled when Butch angrily waved him off.

Art examined the stacked windows turning orange in the sunrise glow. Cheaper-but-better; regrettably, not cheaper-but-*best*. Should have asked for Simontons, which, hands down, outshone all the usual suspects and cost even less, but doing so implied he was going to live here.

Was he?

That question remained unanswered, as did a few others, like who's Owen and what was he doing here last night and why was Cindy visiting the sawdust pile a year ago and what, exactly, is buried somewhere along the pool's perimeter and why does this object so terrify Butch and Cindy? Taking a shovel to the area would answer that.

But not yet. Now, there are windows.

Butch stumbled back and Art put a hand on top of the first window stack and raised an eyebrow. "I'm eating first," Butch declared and stumbled towards the camp stove.

"Shoulda got up with Rich and me," Art said, "We had a fine breakfast of cold Chef Boyardee and some bread. Which brings us to the next items on the list." Art strolled over to where Butch scrambled around lighting charcoal. "Once you and I get the windows installed, you should give long thought to getting a kitchen sink, a stove, a microwave, and a refrigerator. Maybe even a dishwasher."

Butch pointedly ignored him, slapping pans around. Art absently fished for another cigarette. Two in thirty minutes. Damn. He resumed the lecture: "Doing so would mean preparing meals in a fashion remarkably compatible with twentieth and this most recent twenty-first-century. It would lower your release of carbon particulates into the atmosphere and slow the progress of global warming. Or cooling. I forget which is going on." Art threw a significant look at the smoking charcoal.

"Shut up," Butch said and did some arcane things above the charcoal that caused it to flare. Had to hand it to him, the guy could start a fire. Butch suddenly reached out and yanked the just-lit cigarette out of Art's lips and threw it in the coals. "And that's enough of those, too."

"Dude, not cool," Art said, but maybe Butch had a point. The stone was rattling around his chest again and he thought about a squeeze of breather. Had he taken his theophylline this morning? Yesterday morning? Who knows?

Who cares?

Butch had pans of eggs and bacon sizzling in moments and Art salivated. Cold canned spaghetti paled in comparison, and he swayed in and out of the smoke. "Mmm." He smacked his lips. "Yew sho nuff knows youse cookin', massa."

Butch actually smiled. "Grab a plate. There's plenty."

So Art did and they both sat in camp chairs (Jeez, how many did Butch bring?) and ate and, yeah, it was good and coffee boiled and Art had to admit, this was pretty nice. He stopped himself from reaching for a cigarette and took a cup of coffee instead. "Thanks, I needed that," he said.

"I can't believe you ate the whole thing," Butch replied.

"Tastes great. Less filling," Art burped.

"You bet your sweet bippy."

"Sock it to me, baby," and they were off, ranging from "You rang?" in their best approximations of Lurch to "Sorry about that, Chief," in their best Don Adams, giggling at the end of it.

"We are the TV generation," Art said.

"True." Butch sat happily back into his chair.

"So, I do have to ask you one question." Art took a dramatic pause as he refilled his mug. "What the hell was that all about yesterday?"

"Nothing. So how do we do the windows?"

"Hmm, a rather clumsy evasion, that. One would think you're avoiding the question, but okay." Art sipped. "The short answer is, with lots of lifting and holding and doing exactly what I say. Which is a digression because, you know, you're lucky you're not in jail."

"We all are." Butch looked off, his eyes smoky. After a very uncomfortable moment, he said, "Maybe we should get started," and headed for the window stack.

Art watched him go. "Aren't you going to take a shower first?" he called. Butch waved an irritated hand at him and Art chortled and got up.

By noon, they had finished the kitchen, the den, and were on their way to caulking up the bathroom. "Is it always this quick?" Butch asked as he cut the tip off a cylinder.

Art brushed his hands clean. "Demolition is half the job. We had a lot of help from the guys who stole the casements."

"Oh." Butch wasn't sure if that was good or not.

Art helped him decide. "That's not an advantage. You could have lived with the casements, avoiding the new window cost. But, at least you've upgraded and now the house is worth more. Say $45,000."

Butch *tsk*ed and began a real sloppy caulk bead. Art watched but didn't interfere. Butch's house, not his, and he wouldn't have to live with it. Unless he chose Option 1. "You know," he said, surveying the not-too-sloppy new bathroom window with satisfaction, "there's a very good chance we could be done today."

Butch raised hopeful eyebrows. "Really?"

"Yeah, with a big push. Fortunately, all the living room double bow needs is some trimming and caulking. The bitch is going to be the dining room picture window. That's one heavy mother."

Butch frowned at Art's crudity but the idea of finishing the job trumped. "Well, let's do it, then. It's just hard work. Can't hurt us."

"Yeah?" Art gave him a wry look. "Wanna know how many pain pills I'm on?"

"No one told you to go into construction."

"True," Art conceded, "but there really wasn't anything else."

"Coulda done what I did. Joined the Air Force."

Art patted the breather. "Couldn't. Asthma, remember? So when you left to go on your world adventures and find God and crap, I had to stay behind." He raised significant eyebrows at Butch.

It took Butch a moment. "What? You sayin' I abandoned you or something?"

"No." Art kept the eyebrows at the significant level. "That

would be illogical. Irrational. But there I was, left alone, with no resources."

"No, you weren't. You had Mom and Ridge and Cindy."

Art laughed loud and long. "Yeah, I had them. They were just peaches." And he switched to a wounded look. A quite practiced one.

Butch went from confusion to incredulity. "What did you want me to do, give you my paychecks? Have you come live with me? Send you to school?" His look changed, cruel and harsh. Oh, he knew how Art did in school. He knew.

Art's response was equally harsh. "I didn't want you to do anything." And he spun on his heels and stomped out, wondering at the sudden tidal wave of unfairness and injustice washing over him. Talk about irrational and illogical. What, exactly, DID he want Butch to do? Or Mom? Or anyone, for that matter?

Simple. Rescue me.

The thought overwhelmed him as he made a quick right turn into Mom and Dad's old bedroom and straight to the first gaping window hole.

Rescue me. An angel in a golden chariot should have appeared at some point, grabbed him by the nape of the neck and tossed him into the back and launched across the heavens, landing by a golden river in a golden land where buxom virgins fed Art grapes forever. Or, at least, dropped a bag of money. Little chance celestial beings would get directly involved like that, so Mom should have given him a bag of money. Or Ridge. Or Dad.

Dad.

Art shook his head. Dad's idea of helping his children was not leaving permanent marks. Or shunt them to an out-of-the-way location where they could not report his crimes. Like here. Or like the trailer.

Back thirty years ago or so, when he got tired of Mom showing up once a week to stuff the freezer with Elio's Pizza (food resource of the poor) and then disappear with Ridge, when he was already tired of Cindy and her Piney boyfriend-of-the-week screwing all night in Mom's bedroom, and even more tired of Butch and his hippie asshole pals sleeping six deep in the living room all stoned on something (which made Butch's later religious conversion that much more implausible), Art took off for Alabama. Dad welcomed him like he was a long-lost son, ironically enough. He'd already sold the house by then, or was in the process of selling it or maybe it was just sitting here beginning its long rot, whatever, and managed a trailer park in Enterprise along with wife number six or seven and, about five minutes after Art showed up on his doorstep, took him deep into the park and ensconced him in his very own double-wide. Couldn't live in the house with stepmom number whatever and her kids because no room, ya know. So maybe it wasn't exactly a long-lost-son type of welcome but, hey, who cared? It made Art a high school sophomore with his own place far from the prying eyes of parents and law enforcement. Teenage royalty, and Art had a real good time.

For three months or so.

Dad visited once a week and filled the refrigerator with hot dogs and frozen French fries and beer (contributing to Art's royal status), not too different from Mom and her Elio's Pizza except with the added benefit of illegal alcohol... but, unlike Mom, also brought along a different person each time: women persons, none of whom were wife six or seven. Bit disconcerting, that, especially when Dad took them into the back of the trailer and, based on the noises, conducted himself in a rather untoward manner with women not his wife.

Like Art should care since he carried on hisself in a rather untoward manner as befitted his teenage royalty but, you know, dads shouldn't do that. The women got younger and younger each visit until Dad showed up with a girl from Art's class, on whom Art had already shown royal favor. Somewhat off-putting.

While Art appreciated beer and French fries and an isolated trailer, he pointed out that he needed other things like clothes and soap. "I'm not made of money!" was Dad's standard BS response. Art suspected that Dad's only purpose for keeping him here was to serve as counterpoint to Mom's ownership of Butch and Cindy; to that end, the beer and French fries and a trailer of his own ensured Art remained. Expecting Dad to care for him beyond that was a hope too far.

Then (surprise) Dad lost wife number six or seven and subsequently his trailer park and Dad said Art had to move in with him and wife number eight or nine in another scurvy house in Opp and one does not go from royalty to peasant easily. So he went back to New Jersey, where being a peasant was *de rigueur*.

Dad wasn't made of money, all right. More like erect penis cells. Art was more likely to get angel-tossed bags of cash than anything from dick-for-brains. As it turned out.

Still, it would have been nice to find, some point after the funeral, that Dad had a secret account or insurance policy consisting of something more than a dollar, Cindy, to soothe the wounds he'd inflicted on his children. It would have obviated Art's need to work his ass off for Conrad, that twat, and all the jerkoffs preceding Conrad, slaving to buy a house that only Linda wanted and furniture Linda wanted and the redecorating Linda wanted and the remodeling of the house to fit Linda's whim of the moment ("We need a new kitchen"), the work of which he did himself after spending all day working, and don't forget the clothes for Rich and the tutors for Rich and the toys for Rich and this and that and this and that and that.

One good thing about the pending divorce, at least he didn't have to deal with such crap anymore. Other crap, of course, would take its place, like finding a place to live and another job and another girlfriend and he would still have to do this and that and this and that and that for Rich.

Just. Doesn't. End.

Art fished about in his pocket for a cigarette. The hell with asthma because that doesn't end, either. Nothing does. He was condemned for the rest of his remaining life to work in a trade he didn't like for people he hated so he could buy crap for other people while snatching whatever satisfactions he could out of the time and money left.

Life sucks.

He drew in a long smoke-filled breath and looked out of the window hole at the pasture across the street. Nice breeze today cooling the sweat on his brow and the fire in his lungs.

So, what to do about this current suck-filled situation?

Finding another means of making money was out since he was not going back to school or doing any entry-level crap to learn some new soul-killing trade and, besides, he liked that whole work as Balm of Gilead thing, an automatic set of tasks of which he was master and in which he could get lost. The suckiness lay in the rewards for his work, not the work itself. The surplus value of his labor was stolen by others. What could he do about that?

Leave.

He stopped in mid-drag, knocked silly by the thought. Just leave. Walk outside right now and get in the truck and back down the driveway and point north and just go. Go.

Somewhere.

Back to New Jersey. Pull up to her house and say, "C'mon. Just as you are," and she gets in and they drive to Canada and get jobs in the oil fields. Or, go east to Georgia and find a farm that needs a hand, or south to Mexico and a cartel that needs a pissed-off gringo with excellent aim, or west to Wyoming or Utah or...

Oklahoma.

He finished the drag and savored the taste.

Oklahoma. Hmm. Possibility.

He did know the place. Or, used to know the place. What did he know about it anymore? Still filled with tornadoes and assholes, if any of the few snatches of news he'd seen about it these last ten years or so meant anything. But, once upon a time, it had been Magic Land.

Magic Land.

Art luxuriously slipped smoke into the air, following the cancer cloud as it tendriled and wove its way ceiling-ward. Time and distance put a golden haze around childhood, he knew, and nothing was ideal but there had been... something... about the place. Maybe it was the weather which, one second wanted to kill you and then, a second later, invited you out to play. Hot summer afternoon and he'd be running around under a cloudless sky with a bare breeze providing minimal relief and out of nowhere, *eeerrrRRRRRRRRR*!! Klaxons and warbling and oh no! Tornado sirens! And he was screaming and falling all over himself in a desperate attempt to reach the storm cellar but it was just a test and he felt foolish as everyone razzed him but had to admit, a pretty good joke. Part of the thrill of living there.

A honeysuckle hedge ran across the backyard wafting the perfume of summer. Walk outside and be lifted off his feet by the incense while something whispered 'come out, come out, because the sun is high and there's games of tag and baseball and hide-and-seek and hopscotch,' which turned into a big craze with tournaments held between neighborhoods that Cindy always won. Frisbees appeared one summer: Frisbee catching and Frisbee dodging and Frisbee baseball. Slip and Slides by Wham-O followed close on Frisbee's heels (weren't Frisbees made by

Wham-O, too?) and everyone wanted one but Dad wasn't made of money, no sir, but then Butch's friend next door... what was his name? Johnny? Tommy? ...got one and Dad tried it out and, whaddya know, the next day, they had one.

They drank hot rubber water out of nearby garden hoses and then sprayed each other with it. The nights were cloaked in ghost mists shifting in the breezes and the stars were closer and the moon bigger and in high humor and it nodded at the kids as they raced through the streets chasing bats from one light pole to another, all of them young enough to still hear the high-pitched squeaks, and they played Frankenstein and Dracula and ran and hid in alternate backyards trying not to giggle as the monsters searched for them. They made firefly lanterns out of Mason jars and huddled in moon-speckled grape arbors and whispered deathless secrets about who liked whom and who didn't like whom and then scrambled out of the vines with screams of delight to be paralyzed by "Freeze!" and you'd better, or you'd be It.

The streets were endless, the days in gold and the nights in silver imbued him with magic. He donned a moon-and-star robe and pointed hat and flourished a wand and the magic sprayed in rainbow colors and candy bolts and turned the snows of winter into cake and the ice storms into sugar frosting. Rabbits danced on the lawn at Easter and hid their giant chocolate eggs but not so well he couldn't find them, and there were May Day maypole dances in the schoolyard, and then school was over and some kid got murdered by his own mom...

He stilled. He'd forgotten about that.

A friend of Butch's. Last day of school and the kid's mom had beaten him to a pulp over something stupid – Art wasn't sure what – but knew it was trivial, an act that would barely trigger a Dad finger-flick much less a working-over with a baseball bat. Have to ask Butch what it was, but Art remembered being shocked because, man, really? Say... wasn't that the same time Butch disappeared for the summer, *poof*, him and Dad gone? And then Dad and Butch came back. And then they all came here.

That WAS the same time, wasn't it?

Art frowned and wondered if there was a connection between some kid getting a baseball-bat shampoo and all of them moving here. Well, no. Unless the batted kid was one of Dad's secret love children (like Butch) and then, hoo boy. No wonder Mom wanted a divorce back then. But no divorce materialized and they all ended up at this house.

This house.

Art cast a baleful eye. This house. This place. Mordor.

If he thought about it, Magic Land was Mordor-ish in its own right. For one thing, Art didn't have that many friends there. Most of the neighbor kids were Butch and Cindy's age, with the exception of one or two little girls who were Art's contemporaries, but c'mon, girls? What self-respecting seven-year-old boy played with girls? So he was reduced to keeping up with the bigger kids, turning himself into a wailing nuisance as Butch and Cindy sped off and he struggled to catch up, on one occasion getting his hand caught on the spikes of a tall chain fence the two of them had hopped over, screaming as he dangled from the wire twists which had driven through the back of his hand. The fuck of it, he was the one who got into trouble (and six stitches) for that, not those two for leaving him behind. He was always getting into trouble for others' actions, even when Butch tried to kill him.

Twice.

Dad had been a big bow hunter back there in Magic Land and belonged to a bow hunters' league on Ft. Sill, and took them out to the range all the time so they could shoot the kid-sized bows and arrows Dad had bought them. Real arrows, not that Nerf crap. Ah, the sixties: monkey bars made of steel built on top of rock-hard clay, BB guns and firecrackers and Jarts and a thousand other means of eviscerating or maiming pointy-headed kids. Good times, good times.

Dad had put a haystack in the backyard so they could shoot arrows anytime they felt like it. One day, Butch felt like it and Art didn't. Art wanted to climb the haystack, not shoot at it, and he was up there feeling quite pleased with himself when Butch marched up, bow and arrows in hand, and ordered him off. What? Thou thinkest thou rulest me?

Giggling, Art flattened and kept dropping his hand in front of the paper target wired to the stack.

"I'm going to shoot," Butch said.

"No, you're not," Art raspberried and played block-the-bullseye with a spread-fingered palm.

"Yes, I am!"

"No, you're not!"

Yes, he did.

Pinned Art's hand to the bullseye. Pretty good shot, Art had to admit. The fuck of it, Art got into more trouble than Butch did because he was downrange when there was an active shooter in position. Rules, ya know.

The second time was more akin to outright murder and also involved a bow and arrow. On this occasion, both Art and Butch were armed and shooting at the target when Butch said or did something to which Art took umbrage. Can't remember what, but it was egregious enough to send Art whirling about, arrows and bow flying, and stomp off screaming that he was going to tell Dad.

"No, you're not," and *thwack*! An arrow in Art's back. This time, it wasn't that good a shot because it hit Art in the quiver and not the spine or heart, sparing him paralysis and/or death... or maybe it WAS a good shot; he should ask Butch about that. Anyways, the subsequent trouble was balanced: Butch for trying to murder Art, and Art for precipitating the murder by threatening to tattle-tale on Butch which, apparently, was an equal felony.

Murgatroyd.

Maybe Oklahoma wasn't all that. But, of all the places he'd lived and were now options, it had been the most magical. So, by default...

Take about, what, ten, fifteen hours to get there? Maybe longer; did have to go through half of Texas, after all. But, by midnight tomorrow, he'd be back in Magic Land.

And what would that mean? On the upside, he wouldn't have to work on this freakin' house anymore; could leave the bills and incompleteness to Butch. Finish the place yourself, dude. Oh, good Lord, imagine klutzhead trying to wire the kitchen. The explosions would be heard for miles. Also left behind: Cindy prowling through the woods and her endless supply of hick boyfriends, and whatever is buried by the pool and ghost kids skulking in the backyard. Linda would never find him. She could wave her subpoenas and collections and lawyer decrees or whatever the hell is involved with divorce these days and scream and scream all she wanted. Tough crap, baby. He smiled at that.

On the downside...

...Rich. What would he do with Rich?

"Leave him," something cold and spidery said in his head.

The kid could stay here with Butch and maybe Cindy, if she decides to forgo New Jersey and remain here to keep a watchful eye on the Mystery Sawdust Pile and the horror-by-the-pool. The three of them might turn into a real family... yeah, the Addams Family. Rich would absorb lower Alabama's redneck culture and get hisself a fine little farm girl to bear him young'uns and they could plow the land together. American Gothic.

"He'll become you," another spidery voice said in his head.

He shuddered at that. Become him, a bitter, raging, nicotine-addicted loser, in shock, who wondered every day how he'd managed to stumble onto this inexorable path of loserdom. Except, Rich would know, clearly, the seminal event that put him on the downward spiral: his Dad had left him high and dry and at the mercy of Gomez and Morticia.

No. Can't leave him behind. Can't leave him at the mercy of others. Must snatch a brand from the fire—

"Ouch!" Art spazzed as the unattended cigarette cooked his fingertips and he flicked it out of the window. Hope it falls in some thatch and burns the whole place to the ground. Okay, so, this is what we'll do: when Rich gets home from school, march him out to the truck and take off for Magic Land because I can't abandon him, I just can't. Which Art supposed meant he loved the kid.

Love.

Pfhht.

Love did not exist. Simply didn't. It was like a UFO: everyone talked about it, even claimed they had seen it or experienced it, but actual evidence was lacking. Art had certainly seen no proof. What he thought was love had really been lust, and he had pursued women and married one of them and begun an affair with yet another because the head of his dick throbbed with passion, not his heart with the purity of longing.

Love, itself, was a mere social construct designed to turn this whole ugly, sordid, demeaning lust stuff into something civilized, pure, chivalric, imposing a series of procedures to keep us guys from doing what our throbbing dicks demanded, which was club the girls over the head and drag them to the cave for a night of nasty rutting, regardless of the girls' objections. Art had followed the rules and married and subsequently discovered that love was just a way for women to trap men into a legally binding relationship which gave them access to men's surplus value of labor and the freedom to develop an astonishing number of consecutive-night headaches, forcing him and every other husband in America into masturbation and affairs with other women, and subsequently losing their jobs and dignity because of aforementioned affairs, triggering once again the rules of love and civilization because now they had to take care of the other women they were forced to seek out in the first place because they'd initially been tricked, ad infinitum, ad nauseam.

Which wasn't love. It was guilt, the real basis for every single relationship in life. Or so Art believed.

And yet his heart cracked when he thought of leaving Rich behind.

Art's hand crept up to the cigarette pack, but he stayed it. Was his cracking heart a sign of love or was it further proof of guilt? Face it, a child was nothing more than the secondary effects of lust, one of the risks, like gonorrhea. There were legends about people who actually wanted children and married for that reason specifically, but Art put them in the same category as Bigfoot. Most everyone he knew put cart before horse and got married when bun was in oven. But, even then, society approved, albeit with sidelong glances, because the bringing of a child into the world was a good thing, the actual purpose of marriage, and as long as the forms were observed, everything was fine. Seemed, though, to be a barn-door-after-horse argument, a gilding of the lily, a purse from a sow's ear...

Man, what's with the similes? Or were they metaphors?

Clichés.

The life well-lived was a string of clichés sanctioned by those in observance. If you go to school and serve your country and as a virgin marry a virgin and bring good obedient children into the world every nine months and eschew drinking and smoking and gambling and whoring and TV and rock'n'roll, you are a good person. And if you say you love your wife and child and horses and her boyfriend, too, then you have made a civilization.

Maybe love was the civilizing of guilt.

Or maybe the only true love, the only real love that existed, was that of parent for child, no matter how unintentional the begetting of that child. And that's why his heart cracked.

"We doing this or not?" Butch, irritated, said behind him.

Art regarded the window hole before him. This thing between parent and child. "Love," he whispered.

"Huh?"

"Love to," Art said, making his voice sound as sarcastic as he could. "Let's go get another window." And he led the way out.

Chapter 26

Thursday afternoon

Rich announced his arrival home by slamming the kitchen door, dropping his books too loudly on the camp table and then clomping over to the dining room doorway. Silence followed, a strong indication he was staring at Art and Butch's backs as they struggled to maneuver the picture window into place.

"Wanna help?" Art asked the air.

A snort followed by squeaking Adidas; strong indications of a hasty retreat. Art gave an internal smirk. Can't blame 'im; who would want to do this? Art certainly didn't but, hey, ya do whatcha gotta do, even if one is thoroughly sick to death of all the gotta dos.

Time to have some fun. "Here," he said to Butch, "hold it right in this position while I go outside." Without waiting for a response, Art shifted the window's weight onto Butch and stepped back, stifling a hearty laugh as Butch went, "*Oof*!" Casually, Art strolled out of the front door and onto the long cement porch, enjoying the shade of the overhang until he judged Butch was on the verge of collapse and then wheeled to the opening and leisurely pulled the window into position. "Keep 'holt of it," Art ordered the struggling Butch as he shimmed the window until leveled. Butch kept 'holt' long after it was necessary, but Art felt no need to enlighten him. After a very unreasonable amount of time, he strolled back in. "You can let go of it now," he said.

Butch, gasping, dropped his hands and stood back, wiping his dirt-and-caulk-encrusted forehead. "Man, that was harder than the living room!"

Deliberately so, Art thought, but sympathy-shrugged. "Every window is different," he lied. "Let's take a break." He went into the kitchen, smirking internally.

Rich was at the table with books open and notebooks out and

Art stopped, surprised. "You're doing your homework?"

"Nothin' else to do around here," Rich muttered, without looking up. He had a glass of milk and some Oreos in a plate before him and Art had to admire the presentation, especially since the milk was dangerously old. No one set-to like this unless they were serious. But Rich had never been serious about homework, so Art suspected a ploy.

"Well, if you're that bored, you can help us with the last two dining room windows. Or start working on this." Art tapped the missing sink.

Butch, who'd walked in behind him, laughed. "Man, you sound just like Dad!"

Wham! Sledegehammer to the back of the head. Art almost pitched over the table. "No, I don't!" he yelped.

"Yeah, you do." Butch snatched an Oreo off the plate. "Whenever we said we were bored, he'd 'unbore' us." Butch air-quoted the word while skillfully juggling the Oreo. "Remember the boat?"

"Boat?" Rich looked up hopefully. Anything was better than Spanish conjugations, even a Butch story.

"Yeah." Butch took a chair. "A boat that Dad bought, some piece of blue crap, and he wanted to paint it yellow which meant we," Butch swept an inclusive thumb across his and Art's reeling chest, "were drafted. So every day after school and all weekend long we had to sand this boat down. It was under one of the overhangs out there," Butch pointed aimlessly towards the garage wreck, "when there *were* overhangs so didn't matter if it was hot or cold or raining, or if we were sick or had too much homework." Gesture at Rich's books. "Didn't matter. Every. Single. Day." Butch shook his head. "And, every day, Dad would come out and scream at us and hit us with the paint cans or whatever because we missed a spot because it had gotten so dark we couldn't even see the boat anymore, much less the old blue paint. Right?" and he raised an eyebrow at Art who was too shocked to respond.

"Anyways," Butch took another Oreo, "took us, what, six months to finish it?" Butch raised another inquiring eyebrow but Art was completely numb. "Something like that."

"Six months?" Rich turned to Art, incredulous. "That long?"

"Well," Butch made an expansive wave of his hands, "maybe it was just over the winter. Wanna know what happened?"

Rich was full-on attentive. "What happened?"

"Dad takes us all, Mom and us kids, off to Black Creek, which was his favorite fishing spot in Florida, and backs his brand new yellow boat, painted courtesy of us," another thumb wave, "all proud of it, right into the water with everyone standing around watching and admiring and..." Butch made a dramatic pause. "All the paint came right off. Right there in the water." Butch burst out laughing.

"What?" Rich laughed, too, more because of the contagion than the humor.

"Yeah!" Butch was in high mirth. "That cheap bastard had us slap on some old house paint he had lying around instead of putting out the cash for marine paint."

"You're kidding!" Rich was now in on the joke, his laughter genuine.

"No, I'm not. And you can guess who got blamed for it." Butch looked at Art grimly. "What's wrong with you?" he suddenly asked, alarmed over Art's paleness.

"I don't sound like Dad," Art breathed.

"What?" Butch gaped at him, as did Rich, both puzzled.

"I don't sound like Dad. Not. At. All!" he yelled and pushed past Butch, almost upending him.

"Hey!" Butch protested but Art kept going until he was in the middle of the driveway, shaking.

"What the hell?" Butch, on the screened porch, still protesting. Art reached into his pocket to find a cigarette, but his hand shook too much and the stone... the stone was pulsing, breathing, stretching talons into his lung walls and scraping at them. He clenched fists and pounded his chest.

"Oh, crap!" Butch was off the porch and had a hand behind Art's back in a second. "Where's your breather? Where's your breather?"

Weakly, Art tapped his side pocket. Large spots formed across his vision, the crows of coming death cawing and flapping in delight. The stone was molten lava burning through his chest to unleash a multi-headed alien, its jaws clamping down on his throat and trying to rip it out. The world spun and he saw Rich in the doorway, mouth open, fear contorting his face.

Something hard and plastic shoved into his mouth. "Breathe! Breathe!" it looked like the fuzzy outlines of Butch's head shouted but all Art could hear were crows cawing, loud and inexorable, and he grasped Butch's hand and found the top and pushed...

And sweet, cool air flooded through his lungs to his heart to his brain, spring air, refreshing and healing and the crows became songbirds and the lava in his chest cooled and softened and swirled into a wind-blown cushion.

He looked up at both Butch and Rich, their worried and stricken faces now crystal clear. Rocks cut into his shoulder blades. Huh? Ah. Got it. Butch must have lowered him onto the driveway after the spring breezes took over Art's body. He inhaled deeply, feeling all the chains and ropes dissolve.

"Are you all right?" Butch asked, over and over and over.

"Don't ever say that again," Art whispered.

Butch frowned. "Say what? 'Are you all right?'"

"No. That I sound like Dad."

Rich was puzzled, but not Butch. "Oh. Yeah. Okay," he said, softly, "Okay."

"What's going on?" Cindy's frown of disapproval jammed into the group, creating a triangle of stares.

"Dad had another asthma attack!" Rich excitedly brought her up to speed.

"Oh." She straightened out of Art's view. "I brought dinner," she said and Art heard the rattling of paper bags. He rolled his head until he could see an upside-down Cindy with about five KFC bags dangling from her hands. "Extra crispy?" he asked.

She nodded and Art smiled. A treat before dying.

Thursday evening

"Umm, umm, umm!" Art smacked his lips. "Finger-lickin' good!" he said and made exaggerated and deliberately gross efforts to lick the last of the chicken off his hands.

"Eww, Dad, you're disgusting!" Rich doubled over with happy revulsion as Art redoubled his efforts.

"No, he ain't," Cindy said and commenced her own finger-licking routine, but with a lewdness that made Art suddenly uncomfortable. "Don't be teaching him any more bad habits," he warned Cindy, nodding at the suddenly attentive Rich.

She dismissed that as she grabbed a napkin. "You started it."

Yeah, but I didn't turn it into porno, he almost said aloud, but discretion stayed him. Didn't feel like explaining it to Rich. Didn't feel like getting backhanded by Cindy, either.

"You're both disgusting," Butch declared from his position in front of the grill.

All this food and the guy still had to cook something? "Are those Brussel sprouts?" Art asked, pointing at a boiling pot.

"Yes. And it's 'Brussels,' not 'Brussel.'" Butch fooled with the pot. "Gotta have something healthy to offset this crap." He pointed an offended finger at the KFC bags crumpled around the campsite.

Art blew a raspberry. "Jeez, get that stick outta your ass, will ya?" causing Rich to double redoubled laughter as Cindy joined in.

"Nice talk." Butch scowled at Rich and then turned it full on Art. "Apparently, you're all right now."

"Never felt better," Art said and tossed a chicken leg past Butch and into the coals. Butch yelped and attacked it with a spatula, which made Rich laugh even harder, if that was possible.

Cindy, smiling, looked him over critically. "You ARE okay now, right?"

"I am. Thanks for your concern."

She shrugged. "Don't want you dying before the house gets fixed."

"Why?" Art raised an eyebrow. "Change your mind? Planning to move in or something?"

Her look was as murderous and burning as the earlier stone in his chest. "Not in a million years."

"Then why do you care if the house gets fixed?"

She gestured at Butch off behind the washhouse clumsily stomping the burning chicken leg. "So that idiot will have a decent place to live."

"Ah." Art nodded. "Sisterly concern, then. Quite touching, given everything that's happened."

She regarded him coolly. "What's happened?"

"Yeah, Dad," Rich piped, "What's happened?"

Art gave Rich a 'back-off' look. "You never mind. And you." He gave Cindy an innocent one. "Well... you know."

"Know what?" Still the cool regard.

"You know. What happened in Arizona." He raised significant eyebrows in Butch's direction.

Cindy's voice was deadpan, neutral. "What happened in Arizona?"

Drat. She's not going to say anything. Too smart for that, even though the glitter in her eyes told Art that she, indeed, knew exactly what had happened in Arizona.

"Yeah," Rich piped up again, "What happened?"

"Big hole opened up in the ground. They called it the Grand Canyon," Art toned while staring at the still neutral Cindy.

"Ha, ha, ha, that's so funny I almost forgot to laugh." Rich, irritated, shook his head and fished around in a bag for more chicken.

Butch, finally done extinguishing the leg, asked, "What's so funny?" as he walked up.

"Oh, nothing," Art said airily, "Other than your Brussel*sss* sprouts."

"Ha, ha, ha," Butch said and returned to stirring the pot. "They're ready, by the way. You guys want some?"

The three of them looked at him as if he were crazy. "More for me," he said and spooned green mush into a Chinet bowl then plopped with satisfaction into a chair.

They watched him for a bit, incredulous, and then Rich broke the spell when he slapped at something on his cheek. "Ow!" he said, examining the little blood smear in his hand. "Mosquito! Why aren't we eating inside?"

Art waggled a hand. "Wouldn't matter. We didn't get the last two windows done. We were rudely interrupted."

"Yeah, by your paper lungs."

"Wow, making fun of the handicapped. I'm so proud of you, son."

Rich glowered at him. "Well, it's true. And it'd be cooler in there with the fan. Just need to make some more room around the table. Have to move your bellies out of the way." Rich eye-rolled Art's gut.

Art slapped it appreciatively. "You know how much beer I had to drink to get this? It's a work of Art." And he kept his face deadpan as the rest of them groaned.

"Gee, I wonder how many times I've heard THAT one before?" Rich smacked another mosquito and rubbed the smeared remains onto his jeans. "Guess that means we're gonna get all bitten up tonight. Again." He gave Art an accusing look.

Art turned his palms over. "Oh well. So it goes, so it is, so it shall be. Unless you want to actually help. Actually. Right now. Tonight. We could have the last few windows installed by midnight. Then your Uncle Butch will have a decent place to live." And he stared at Cindy, who returned the stare, expressionless.

Rich sniffed that away. "No thanks."

Kid not wanting to do physical labor, what a surprise. Like *you* wanted to sand the boat all winter long, bucko.

"Besides," Rich added, "you might get another asthma attack or something."

"Could," Art agreed, "But we might have to do it tonight, anyway. Have to get the house livable as soon as possible. It's real important that somebody stay here 24/7 and keep an eye on this place."

Cindy's eyes glaciered. Butch, spooning another mouthful of sprout mush, cocked his head. "Why? Somebody gonna try and steal the windows?" A pause. "Again?"

Art ignored him. "Say, Cindy, got a cigarette?"

She laughed derisively. "I'm not giving you a cigarette. After your little episode this afternoon, you shouldn't smoke anymore."

"Oh, c'mon, I'll be fine. Especially if it's a girl cigarette. Camel Lights, right?"

She threw a suspicious eye at him. "Yeah. For years now. As you know. And you hate them."

"True, but I might have to go the girlie route, what with my paper lungs trying to kill me and all. I think they might be hard to find around here since it's all rednecks and farmers and other Marlboro men. In fact, I'm willing to bet you are about the only person who smokes Camel Lights in, say, the surrounding five counties."

"I doubt that."

"I don't. I think that's spot on. While servicing your various tradesmen, have you ever run into anyone else who smoked Camel Lights?" Art threw out exaggerated hands. "Around here, I mean."

She looked at him, speechless.

"Dad," Rich interrupted, "That's a weird question."

Art sat back. "Nah, not really. Think of it as math homework, say a question about the base population of possible Camel Light smokers within a given demographic."

Butch stopped spooning mush. "Huh?"

"A mental exercise. Hard for you, I know." Art indicated Butch, who glared. "But bear with me. Let's suppose that somebody who smokes Camel Lights has been keeping the old trash trail fresh and open. All the way down to the sawdust pile."

Rich was suddenly interested. "Sawdust pile?"

Butch was suddenly perplexed. "What are you talking about?"

Cindy wasn't perplexed. Her eyes bored into him.

"Because, in my humble opinion," Art continued as if no one had said anything, "someone... in this case, someone who smokes Camel Lights... would have to make a whole helluva lot of trips over a whole helluva long period of time up and down the old trash trail all the way to and from the sawdust pile to keep said trail as open and obvious as it now is. You know?" He raised eyebrows at Cindy.

"There's a sawdust pile?" Rich looked eagerly towards the woods.

"What are you talking about?" Butch repeated but he had changed from puzzled to alarmed.

Art ignored him. "Sort of like," he said directly at Cindy, "and again, this is my humble opinion, someone was keeping an eye on this place."

Art gauged Cindy's reaction. Stone-faced and wary, but a quiver at the corner of her eyes told Art it was sheer force of will that kept her from looking away. Slowly, deliberately, without breaking contact, she reached into her blouse and took out a cigarette pack, deliberately ensuring everyone saw it was Camel Lights. She shook one out and lit it, all the time staring at Art. Which, he had to admit, was quite skillful.

Art, through sheer force of will, held her gaze, but couldn't for much longer. Let's escalate. "And I think that would certainly be quite the investment of time and effort. Someone coming all the way down here to tramp up and down the old trash trail, I mean. Someone would have to disappear for about a week every other month or so from their regular life to do that, you know?" He cocked his head at Cindy like a curious puppy. "Say, Cindy, haven't you been disappearing for a week or so every other month out of New Jersey for the past, oh, what, several decades?"

Well, no, she hadn't, not on as regular a schedule as he implied, but she did inexplicably disappear from time to time. If that was nothing more than periodic drunken fuckfests, she'll deny it and then, to diffuse him, admit to being at the pile a couple of times since arriving and what of it? Art'd been down there himself. Thus ends this line of questioning.

But she said nothing.

"Where's this sawdust pile?" Rich asked.

"Whoa," Art said softly, more to himself. He was on to something bigger than he originally thought. "Hmm. This is a very interesting situation," he said in his best Jimmy Stewart, "Because it's just occurred to me that if someone who smoked Camel Lights came down here at random times through the years to walk the old trail and play in the sawdust pile like when they were kids, then they could stay in touch with old friends. Visit 'em, maintain contact, stuff like that. Because you just never know when you might need a place to crash while you're walking that old trail to keep it open. You also might never know when an old contact can do you a favor. Someone like say, Caleb?"

She never moved, never acknowledged anything he said, kept puffing on the cigarette.

"Cindy?" Butch asked, shock in his voice, his tone begging her to explain, to answer, deny Art's ridiculous assertions, but she still said nothing, merely drew in smoke and exhaled it. Luxuriously.

"Where's this trail that leads to the sawdust pile?" Rich asked.

Cindy leaned her head back and allowed another great puff of smoke to rise into the air. "What," she asked, staring at the smoke, "were you doing back at the sawdust pile?"

Rich leaned in. "So there really is a sawdust pile, huh?"

"Following somebody," Art said.

"Who?"

You, he almost answered but if she denied it, then everything stops. "Some kid."

Cindy's head snapped up, dismay on her face. "Kid? What kid?"

Art flinched, taken aback. "I don't know, some kid."

"What kid?" This from Butch; Art turned in his direction, surprised because the Chinet bowl was upside down on the ground, Butch, terror on his face, hunched forward gripping the arms of his camp chair ready to yank them off.

"I don't know!" Art said, throwing out his hands and wondering at what point his skillfully manipulated conversation had derailed. "Some farmer kid." Who walked right out of my sleepwalker dream and became flesh. "Out there in the woods." He gestured.

"I saw him, too," Rich added.

Cindy and Butch looked at each other, lightning flowing between them. Butch rocked to his feet, overturned the chair, and spun about, Cindy hot on his heels, the look on both their faces like stricken, terrified animals.

"What the hell?" Art yelled, barely throwing himself out of the way as the two of them rushed past, almost bowling over Rich and the stove in their haste. Art jumped the stove, stabilized it and watched, with astonishment, as the two idiots beelined towards the trash trail.

"Hey!" Rich yelled after, "You going to the sawdust pile? Can I come, too?" and he stepped off, gathering speed to join them.

Art grabbed a handful of Rich's shirt, yanking him back.

"Ow!" the boy called, "That hurts!" He brushed Art's hand off savagely and took an unbalanced step, almost crashing into the stove. Art held him up. "What'd you do that for?" he looked at Art accusingly.

"You can't go," Art said.

"Why not?" Rich was mad.

Art stared towards the trail. "Ghosts," he said.

Chapter 27

Thursday night

Art stood on the steps of the screened porch watching the night, a cigarette dangling from his fingers. Cooler weather right now; well, cooler than normal, almost bearable. A thunderstorm muttered in the distance... or, more likely, Rich in his sleep somewhere back in the den, no doubt dream-bitching about Art's excessive oversight of his homework.

Sorry, kid, and I sympathize. Decades ago, little Art had happily invoked bedtime as a way of escaping the nightly screaming and torture that constituted Deats' family life. Not that sleeping in the den put that much distance between combatants; it did cause Mom to lower the cone of silence, though. "Please, Owen, let the kids sleep."

Yeah, Dad. Please. Don't kill us.

A little light glowed inside Butch's tent, from a night light or something, and Cindy's car was gone, so the two of them had returned sometime while Art attended to Rich. He hadn't heard them, not even the sound of Cindy's car starting. It's like they'd dropped Mom's cone of silence. So Rich could sleep? No. So Art wouldn't confront them.

About what?

Well, c'mon, isn't it obvious? he asked the night. Both of them know who Pasture Kid – Owen – is, and both of them don't want Art to know that they know and don't want Art to know who Owen is because... well, they don't. But the kid isn't a dream. The kid isn't a ghost. Kid's real. Rich proved that. So why keep it secret?

Because Owen was more sin in a family beset with them.

But whose?

Most likely answer: Cindy. The kid is Cindy's, another in her unfortunate run of unwanted progeny from various fathers. When you pump a lot of water, there's a heightened chance of overflow, despite precautions. So she'd gotten pregnant. Maybe by Caleb. Art smirked and shook his head in disgust and then frowned.

How's that possible?

The kid was about ten years old, and ten years ago Art saw Cindy about every other week (except for those odd disappearances every other month or so) and would know if she'd been pregnant or not. She swelled to about eighteen times her normal size when she had the other kids, so no way she'd be able to hide this one. Besides, getting pregnant in one's upper forties was a formidable task, hopeful articles by frustrated feminists to the contrary. Granted, Cindy's town-pumpedness gave her more opportunity than most old gals to get knocked up; but nature tended to side with the hidden flaw, so, not bloody likely.

More likely, the kid was Butch's.

That explained the mystery better than anything. Preacher Boy couldn't have a little bastard running around, now could he? Would be detrimental to the career, so hide the bastard's little bastard in the wilds of Alabama and use your loyal big sister to keep tabs on him.

Except...

It wasn't in Butch's nature to be so cruel. Butch got upset when he saw a dead cat by the side of the road, so how in the hell would he treat his own progeny with such disregard? The kid said he didn't go to school and if there was anything Butch valued it was education so it would be really out of character for the bastard to keep his little bastard dirty, unsupervised, and ignorant. Even at the cost of his career. As Art had previously concluded, the only genuine love involved child and parent and Butch had no one else in his life, apparently not even God anymore, so there's no way.

Dad's? The kid said he was named after his father. But that was ridiculous, unless the Devil had taken a sample of Dad's unholy seed and visited it on some coyote or jackal. But then Owen would be living with some ambassador's family, not with the Cryman.

So, not Dad's. Not Butch's or Cindy's. Not Damien. Must be a ghost.

Riiiight.

Already considered and discarded that, bub. Yes, the kid was odd, seemed out of place and phase but that didn't mean ghostiness; it meant isolation. Weren't there occasional stories of kids chained up in basements and bedrooms who, when released, didn't know who the president was? Who *is* the president, anyway? Oh yeah, *that* guy. Wasn't much of a stretch that a kid kept ig'nint in the woods had heard nothing of ninjas. But cannibals along the Amazon have heard of ninjas, so what the hell? Could it be the kid was having him on?

Art considered that. Nothing was more amusing to moppets than befuddling the old farts, especially if said moppet was a chronic truant and befuddling was a survival skill. If you want to keep roaming the woods when you're supposed to be conjugating Spanish verbs, then you have to keep the occasional adult stumbling into your paradise off-balance. So, be weird. Wear Keds, not Nikes. Disappear into thin air. Have an unusual name that just happens to be the same unusual name as the befuddled old fart's Dad.

Weird, all right. Too weird.

Art frowned. He'd thought it all a sleepwalker's dream until Rich saw the kid and Cindy and Butch flipped out. Now, he didn't know. Kid's either a flesh and blood master manipulator or a collective hallucination or a ghost. Logic inclined to the most former but Owen had been so... vacant. Like he wasn't really there. Like he was lost and sad and stuck in time.

Which was ghost SOP.

So, whose ghost?

Art mused. Okay, who do I know that died at ten years old and was partial to overalls and Keds? Well... nobody. Art simply didn't know any kids who'd died around here, not when he was himself a kid, and not after. Not even a kid he didn't know at all, some local tragedy in the paper made more tragic because children were involved. A house fire. A bus accident.

A mom beating her kid to death with a baseball bat.

Butch's friend.

Art thought about that for a few seconds and then gave his opinion: "*Pffhht!*" How absurd. Bat Kid is haunting Oklahoma or his mom or dad or someplace or somebody directly related to him, not Alabama and the bull pasture.

No, if Owen was a ghost, he became one here.

Like Art, Cindy, and Butch.

Art dwelled on that. They had all been beaten with belts and fists and tree limbs and whatever was handy, maybe even a baseball bat, which you'd think he'd remember – unless he'd been hit a little too hard – up and down these grounds over about a four-year period. Time-released murder. With each blow, whether from stick or whip or back of hand, a bit of their souls leaked onto the ground.

Could enough collect over time to form the ghost of murdered childhood?

Wow, Art, that's almost poetry.

He chuckled and gazed over the yard. Yeah, there's definitely enough of their blood and skin spread across the land to gather up and sew together and blast some lightning through and it's alive, it's alive. Might make a cool movie, but, c'mon, this is silly. Owen isn't the Frankenstein of ghosts: he's something else, something that obviously scared the crap out of Butch and Cindy.

Why?

Let's find out.

Art stepped off the porch and tossed the cigarette, watching it meteor over the screen and explode on the driveway. He strode to Butch's tent, yanked the flap back and launched himself inside. "*RAHR*!" he screamed, making monster claws as he flew at Butch's cot.

"Holy shit!" Butch screamed back, lifting off his cot about three feet and almost flinging a paperback right at him, a look of pure terror on his face.

Art burst out laughing as he settled into a pile of crap next to a guttering kerosene lamp. "You should see your face," he chortled.

"You asshole!" Butch scrabbled for the paperback – some Siddharder thing by some Hesse guy – to keep from dropping it. "You think that's funny?"

"Relax," Art said, working himself into the pile. Pretty comfortable. "You should expect some good old-fashioned scares if you're camping. What's all this stuff, anyway?" Art jumped up and down on the crap.

"My stuff," Butch snapped at him, "And what are you, a ten-year-old?"

"Funny you should mention that age." Art made exaggerated examinations of his fingernails in the lamplight. "Because I am wondering about ten-year-olds. Do you know of any who died on this property?"

"What?" Butch looked at him as if he was crazy.

"Ten-year-olds. Who died. Here." Art made exaggerated points at the ground.

"I have no idea what you're talking about." Butch attended to the paperback.

"The ghost of some kid is hanging around here and I'm trying to figure out why. You and Cindy didn't kill some local yokel and bury him out there by the sawdust pile, didja?"

Butch's jaw clenched but said nothing. He did pale considerably, though.

"Struck a nerve, did I?"

Butch went from pale to beet red almost instantaneously. "How in the FUCK could you think something like that?"

"Such language," Art *tsk*ed, settling in, "And what other conclusion could I reach, given the weirdness?"

"What weirdness?"

"Oh, stop it." Art canted a dismissive hand. "You know very well."

Butch looked at him, still livid, but there was a light in his eye of a secret kept. "Nothing like that happened."

"Then what DID happen?"

Butch looked at the book for a moment, then sighed. "Frank Vaughn."

Art snapped his fingers. "That's the guy! His mom killed him, right?"

Butch nodded. "He forgot his report card and his mom took after him."

"Seems a bit of an overreaction." Art snuggled down. "You know, this is pretty nice. I just might fall asleep here. You won't forget to wake me in the morning?" And he raised an eyebrow.

Butch waved that off. "Frank was a good guy."

"Didn't know him." Art fished around in his pocket for a cigarette. Let's really piss Butch off.

"We played baseball together." Butch ignored his cigarette efforts. "He was really decent. Didn't deserve to die like that."

"Deserved a life of abuse and cruelty at his mom's hands for the next ten, twenty years instead?" Like us, Art didn't say.

"Don't be stupid," Butch warned. "He got his childhood stolen."

This, Art could not leave unsaid. "Like us?"

Butch considered and then slowly nodded. "Yes. Like us."

"Looks like Frank got the better deal." Art tried to keep the irony out of his voice.

Butch downright gasped. "Don't say things like that!"

"Why not?" Art found the cigarette and then commenced a lighter hunt. "His deal was over quick, and you remember him well. Look at us. We don't even want to talk about our childhoods. And we didn't turn out so good."

"You don't know how lost he is," Butch toned.

Art blinked. "Huh?"

"He got lost. After it happened. He was... stuck in places. Bad places."

"What are you talking about?"

"Frank." Butch made an impatient gesture. "I saw him from time to time."

"Uh... what?"

Butch shook his head. "He was so lonely."

Chills ran up and down Art's spine and he sat up straight, eyeing Butch warily. "Are you out of your freaking mind?"

Butch *tsk*ed. "They were dreams. That's all. But you have to imagine it, the moment when his mom beat him to death. The terror. The pain. The sense of... unfairness."

"Unfairness?" Art blew out a snort. "I think that would be the last thing on my mind. I'd be more like, 'My mom is beating the crap out of me and I should try and get the hell out of here.'"

Butch shrugged. "She caught him on the bed. And it *was* unfair. Especially after."

"You are truly weirding me out." Art lit the cigarette and blew a well-aimed cloud at Butch, who ignored it. Further sign of the guy's distraction. "Is that the kid, then?"

"Huh?" Butch looked up, startled, and then waved the smoke away irritably. "Who are you talking about? And don't smoke in here."

"Too late." Art took another puff. "And I'm talking about the kid you and Cindy took off after."

"Him?" Butch snorted, "No, that's not Frank. That's some local jackass."

"You know the kid?"

"Not by name. But we've seen him around messing with the place."

Art deliberately lowered the cigarette and bored into Butch. "What do you mean 'we,' paleface?"

Butch looked like he'd been slapped, and he stared at Art, stunned. Caught.

Art nodded. "So, the two of you. Not just Cindy. Nice job of acting there by the campfire, gotta say. So just how long have you and Cindy been coming back here and checking on the house?"

Butch said nothing.

"Okay." Art decided to be helpful. "Let's say it's been for some time. Here's the bigger question... *why* have you and Cindy been coming back here and checking on the house?" Art did not give him a chance to answer. "Because, ya know, I never saw this as a place to remember fondly. It's John Wayne Gacy's house. And you don't go there to relive the memories." He took a puff. "At least, normal people don't."

Butch took in a long breath and let it out slowly. "It's too hard to explain."

"You're good with words." Art pointed out. "Try."

"I... can't."

"Can't?" Art raised eyebrows. "Or won't?"

Butch said nothing.

Art nodded. "Won't, then. So let me ask the bare questions. Does whatever you and Cindy worry about have something to do with the pool?"

Butch threw up exasperated hands. "There you go with the pool again."

"Yes!" Art stabbed the cigarette at him. "There I go with the pool again. Because something happened at the pool." He eyed Butch murderously. "I saw you guys out there."

"You didn't see anything."

Art flipped the cigarette contemptuously. "Don't tell me what I saw. I saw. So tell me what I saw."

"Nothing." Butch would not meet his gaze.

Art closed his eyes and then opened them, glaring at Butch. "You and Cindy," he said, softly. "Always you two. Cutting me out all the time. Leaving me behind. I just wanted to play with you, be your friend, be included. I wanted to be part of everything you did. But you treated me like shit. All the time."

"No, we didn't."

"Oh, bullshit, you know damn well you did. You guys did

everything to keep me out of what you were up to. Well." Art found a spot on the ground and stubbed the cigarette out. "Here's your chance to make it right."

Butch stared at him for a long moment. "Nothing. Happened."

Art let out a long, exasperated breath. Fuck it. Just fuck it. "Let's go see." He rolled to his feet and was out of the tent before Butch had a chance to respond. He strode to the back shed, somehow managing to avoid roots and crap in the dark. Righteous anger made you sure-footed, he supposed. Turn left, step it out. He was marking the pool's old circumference by the time Butch came stumbling out of the dark. Guilt made you clumsy.

"What are you doing?" Butch breathed.

"Oh." Art prodded the ground with his foot. "I'm going to get a shovel and start digging around here to see what you and Cindy and Dad buried, something so damned important that you had to smack some poor stupid meth head around for it."

Art felt more than saw the shock that ran through Butch. "There's nothing buried here."

"Then you'll have no objections." Art turned and faced the house, a pale shimmer in the starlight. Here. Right here. Again. And again and again.

"You're wasting your time," Butch insisted.

"It's my time." Art stabbed his heel into the ground. "This looks like a good spot. Help me find the shovel. Should be over where you smacked the meth head. And put a dent in my hood, by the way. Which you are going to pay for." He grabbed Butch's shoulder.

Butch wrenched out of his grasp. "I'm telling you, there's nothing here."

"Then think of it as aerobics." And he pushed Butch hard, who fell back and caught his leg on something that sounded metallic. "Ah," Art said and bent down to grab the shovel out from under him, "Here it is."

Butch leaped to his feet, full-on Hulk, rage and murder pulsating off him like a supernova; even the dark could not hide it. Art took a step back, hefting the shovel like a baseball bat. "I will take your fucking head off," he warned. Would a shovel blow stop the Hulk? No. It would just make him madder.

Heat blasted from Butch and he took a step forward and Art knew the shovel head would melt when he struck but it was his only defense...

A rustle of brush and a snap of twigs. Startled, the two of them looked at the wood line behind the old chicken shed. It was too dark to see anything properly but Art got the impression of something there, a shadow within a shadow. Kid-sized.

"You!" Butch yelled and took off. Art watched, speechless, as Butch tore through the dark straight for the shadow. Zip! The shadow was gone, yards ahead of the bellowing Hulk. That didn't stop Butch from plunging on.

"Unbelievable," Art said and used his ears to follow the progress of Butch's one-man chase, the facile movements of an agile kid drowned out by mastodon Butch thrashing farther and farther away and it was all Art could do to keep from laughing. Idiot will get lost in the vampire woods. Will get eaten.

Serve him right.

Art waited a moment then hefted the shovel. Time to get to this. He spun and took a giant step towards the pool...

Wham!

Something heavy and splintery smashed across Art's forehead and he went down like a sack of anvils, the shovel spinning off somewhere. Stars, not real ones, but the cartoon version Bugs Bunny was always dealing with, buzzed around his head and eyes and white lights blinked on and off and all he could think was how much his freakin' head hurt and when he got his hands on whoever had just cold-cocked him he was going to murdalize 'em...

"Y'all rite?"

Owen.

"No, I'm not all right," Art said, trying to squeeze his brains back into his skull. "Why in the fuck did you hit me?"

"Didn' hit ye," the kid snorted, "You done walked smack into a branch."

"Bullshit." Art tried to squeeze vision back into his eyes, too, with as little success. "There isn't a tree branch low enough around here to do that. Where are you, anyway?" Because Art wanted to rip him into little tiny pieces.

"The hickory tree behind the shed just next to where you were standing has branches low enough."

"Oh." Kid had a point. And the kid was too damn short to have hit him so high on the head so, okay, chalk this one up to clumsiness. But, wait a minute... he hadn't been standing anywhere near the back of the ruined shed. He'd been in front of it, where the pool was located. You little bastard! "I repeat, where are you?"

Silence.

Goosebumps ran up and down Art's spine and he really, REALLY needed to get his vision back, so he blinked and rubbed but the white lights still flashed. He peered hard through it and ya know, he WAS behind the shed. At least, as far as he could tell in this cursed dark. Didn't remember how he got back here. 'Course, when someone slaps you with a sledgehammer, short-term memory loss is one result, along with blasted vision and Bugs Bunny stars. So where are you, ya little bastard? Art rolled to his knees, screaming lava-hot headache be damned, and squinted. There, yeah, there... maybe, silhouetted against Butch's distant camp, a dark-on-dark shadow. "Frank?" he asked.

The shadow moved and made a derisive laugh. "I ain't him," the kid said.

"You know him?"

"'Course I do." The kid was contemptuous. "That one. He ain't nothin.'"

"We're talking about Frank Vaughn, right?" Art looked at the shadow, trying to make out detail, but it was inconstant, maybe there, maybe not, nothing more than a trick of light, or maybe something trying to manifest.

The kid said nothing.

"That's the Frank you mean?" Art asked again, but still no answer and Art got annoyed. "Who are you?" he challenged.

The shadow shifted. "You know."

"If I did, I wouldn't ask," Art said and took another step.

"Ain't true. You know. You just too afraid to face it." And the shadow was gone.

Art blinked and rubbed at his eyes again because enough was enough, time to get hold of this kid and beat some answers out of him. He shifted...

...and opened his eyes.

He was on his back still, but his vision was clear and Alabama stars wheeled, sharp and clear, above him. As did the looming branches of the hickory tree. "What the hell?" he whispered and touched his head gingerly and yes, there was a lovely knot forming there. He sat up and felt a moment's dizziness and a warning lurch in his chest, but he was all right. "What the hell?" he asked again. But there were no shadows. And no answers.

Slowly, reaching up to ensure no ambush branches were readying themselves for another go at him, Art stood. Shaky, but his bearings reasserted and, yes, dark as hell out here, so it was possible to walk smack into a low-hanging limb – like the real thick one his questing hand just brushed – and knock yourself silly. And hallucinate. Funny how his visions and dreams were consistent with each other.

Art squinted at the dark, hoping to spot the shadow, but nothing. "I can face anything," he whispered to the dark. He waited for a response, but all that sounded was the breeze.

And Butch still bellowing, fainter now, out there in the woods.

Art turned towards the pool. No use looking for the shovel, although it's probably right here. Somewhere. Not worth risking another concussion. He remained quiet, unmoving. "Anything," he said.

After a moment, he figured he better find Butch before the idiot ran into his own low hanging hickory branch. He carefully made his way to Butch's tent to get a flashlight, zeroed on Butch's bellows, and headed that way.

Chapter 28

Friday morning

"What were you guys doing out there last night?" Rich asked around his Pop-Tart.

"Snipe hunting," Art said. "Hurry up. The bus is coming."

Rich gulped the last bit. "What's snipe?"

"Probably the tastiest game bird you've ever had," Butch said, fumbling with a coffee pot on the precariously balanced fire grate. "One slice of that and you'll never eat turkey again."

"Really?" Rich's brow raised and Art kept his face straight. "Why do you hunt them at night?"

"It's the only time they're out. They're hard to catch. Which is why you never see them in stores."

Rich considered that as Art and Butch exchanged innocent looks.

Art looked away to keep from smiling and sipped his coffee. Mmm mmm good. The least Butch owed him after last night's rescue, dragging him back to camp after a couple of hours stomping around trying to locate the idiot in the middle of the brambles, and then both of them trying to locate Owen, then both of them trying to figure out where north was (a helluva argument that Butch finally won when he pointed out the Big Dipper) and finally, finally falling into the tent all nettle- and blackberry-torn and they dressed each other's wounds as best they could and then fell into shock-induced coma for an hour or two before Rich's alarm, gonging like Big Ben in the morning mists, yanked them back to consciousness and what the hell, let's do breakfast.

"How do you shoot them in the dark?" Rich asked.

"You don't shoot them. You catch them." Butch did an excellent job of sounding nonchalant.

"Catch them?" Rich looked dubious. "How do you do that?"

"You need beaters and a bagger." Butch made exaggerated

movements over the eggs he was scrambling, trying to keep from laughing.

Rich blanked at him. "Huh?"

"The beaters go in the woods ahead of the bagger. They make a lot of noise, like deer. Snipe hate deer. It's pretty dangerous being a beater. Just look at your Dad's head if you want proof." Butch threw a thumb over his shoulder, which Art fielded by pointing at the nice goose egg sitting at his hairline. "Anyway, the bagger sits in the tall grass with the bag open in front of him, making the snipe call. The snipe run right into the bag, thinking it's a safe place and their buddies are in there."

"What's the snipe call?"

"Snipe-snipe-snipe." Butch responded and it was all Art could do not to bust a gut laughing.

"Whaaat?" Rich's note of incredulity hit frequencies known only to dogs. He looked at Art with suspicion. "You guys are messing with me."

"No, we're not." Art got control of himself. "It's how you do it. Wanna go out tonight and try?"

Rich looked at them both, doubt all over him but, still, intrigued. "So where's the snipe you caught last night?"

A horn honked on the road.

"The bus." Art identified. "Go."

Rich went flying out of the camp chair, almost knocking over one of the tables, snatched up the backpack on the run and was down the driveway at the speed of light. "Watch it!" Art called but he was long gone. As the bus chugged off, he sipped a bit more. "Saved by the horn."

"Uhm," Butch grunted, then, "Snipe hunt tonight."

Art shrugged, taking the last sip. "Better than a kid hunt."

Butch said nothing but Art could see his ears turning red. "I talked to him last night."

"Who?" Butch was fixed on his eggs.

"The kid."

Butch turned, spatula held like a gun. "How'd you do that? I thought you were knocked out."

"He came over to help me."

That's impossible."

"How's that impossible?"

"It's—" Butch changed his mind. "What'd he say?"

"Said we knew who he was." Art watched Butch closely.

There. A flicker of concern, which Butch tried to cover with dismissal. "If that were true, I'd go over to his house and tell his parents to keep him off the property."

Art set the cup on the ground. "What do you think the kid is doing on the property?"

"I... don't know." A very cautious reply. Very cautious.

"'Cause I can't imagine what a kid is doing here at night. It's not like there's a swing set here or something. So what would attract him?" Art put an exaggerated finger on his chin. "Hmm, let me think. Maybe... he's the one who stole all the pipes and plumbing and windows?"

Butch flicked that away. "Of course not."

"Then... what?"

"Kids like old houses."

"True. It's fun to scare yourself ghost hunting." Art pursed his lips. "Don't think he needs to come here for that, though. Can look in a mirror."

"What does that mean?"

"Nothing," Art stood up. "Just nothing. Eggs about ready?"

Butch nodded and took the pan off the stove. Moments after they were done eating, Art dropped his Chinet on the ground next to his cup and went to the house. Butch grumbled something, but Art ignored him and walked up on the porch.

Finish this. Today. Be finished with this. Today.

One way or the other, he was done. He would install the last of the windows and then that's it, stick a fork in me, D-U-N, done. He wasn't going to touch one more thing, not the kitchen, the walls, roof, furniture, cable, none of it. None. Of. It. If Butch wanted to live here, he could do the rest himself.

He and Cindy. And Owen.

Art viciously pulled a cigarette out of his pocket and lit it, spraying an angry cloud of smoke at the kitchen door in front of him. "I'm done with you," he said and resisted an urge to kick the door off its hinges. "I was done with you years ago."

Which was true. Once the shock and trauma of their hasty rain-soaked flight up the side of the road had worn off, once he had embraced the *vida* New Jersey, he'd stopped thinking of this place as home. *Au contraire*; it became Dracula's castle, the Bates Motel, the fog-bound horror house of his nightmares.

He'd never been back, not even when he was living in Dad's trailer or when he popped by in subsequent years to visit Dad and his wife of the moment. He did not need to come back. There was nothing to see here. It was an abandoned cemetery of three graves. Three ghosts sat up nightly in their overgrown plots and gazed at the wreckage and floated up and along, directionless, broken, drifting up and away but there were chains around their legs and every time they found a place on which to alight, to rest, the chains pulled taut, yanking them back. Like Butch running off to be Preacher Boy but now he was living in a tent in the cemetery's yard and Cindy was party girl and wild in the streets but here she was back at the cemetery's gates, face pressed against the bars.

And little Art right next to them, the chains of fear and failure and insufficiency binding him from head to toe and locking him to the pitted, rusted fence.

At the sound of tires on gravel, Art rolled his eyes. Party girl back, huh? Just can't peel her face off these bars. He supposed that she and Butch were going on a kid hunt somewhere down by the Pile of Mystery later today.

Enjoy yourselves. When you get back, I'll be gone.

He took another long puff and blew it at the door. Wasn't there some kind of voodoo rite using blown smoke, and spitting wine, to rid a house of evil spirits? He blew another puff at the door. Too bad he had no wine.

"Mr. Deats?"

Surprised, Art turned. A reedy man stood on the lower patio, thin blondish hair barely covering his pate; a pockmarked face, evenly spaced teeth spread in an expectant smile. Dressed in Dockers and a pale short-sleeved shirt, with penny loafers on his feet. Complete with pennies. A nondescript old Ford was in the driveway behind him.

"Yes?" Art said.

"Art Deats?" The man still looked expectant.

"Well, yeah." Art was irritated. "You here to inspect or something?"

The man smiled and nodded but made no move and Art watched him, puzzled. What do you need, buddy, an invitation? Art made an impatient gesture with his cigarette. "Well, then, come on up."

A relieved look came over the man's face, and he stepped

briskly up to the porch, opening the screen door, smiling the whole time.

"You from the Co-op?" Art asked.

The man nodded and took out an envelope, offering it to Art. Absently he grabbed it; it didn't look like a checklist or anything. More like a bill. Well, Butchie old boy, you're gonna get this one, too.

"You've been served." The man, still smiling, backed out of the door and down the porch, keeping an eye on Art the whole time.

"What?" Art asked but the guy was in his car and down the driveway in seconds flat.

Art stared at the envelope. "Oh, crap," he said. He opened it.

Original Petition for Divorce. From him, by Linda.

For cruelty.

Oh, crap.

Stunned, he barely glanced at the rest of it, which was a demand for spousal support three to four times in excess of his salary – heck, his entire lifetime earnings – and designation of him as Rich's custodial parent. A date for a preliminary meeting next month.

Cruelty.

Somewhere off in the distance, he heard Dad laughing insanely.

"Who was that?" Butch asked, coming up behind him.

Art slowly folded the petition back into the envelope and put it in his back pocket. "The angel of death," he said, "Let's get this done." He pushed through the door, leaving a bewildered Butch on the porch.

Friday, noon

They were done quickly. Butch had, by now, developed enough of the hang of it to be an actual help, and Art didn't have to yell at him. Too much. Not that he was in the mood to yell at Butch or anyone else about anything. He was too numb.

"Excellent," Butch beamed, dusting off his hands as he

critically examined the kitchen window.

"Yeah," was all Art said.

"So the house is now livable." Butch still beamed. "I mean, floors fixed, working bathroom, power, now windows. I guess that means I can move out of the tent and inside tonight."

"You still don't have a kitchen," Art said.

Butch shrugged. "I can cook outside until we do. How long will it take us to get one installed?"

"Not we, not us, you," Art said, "I'm done."

"Done?"

"Done."

"But..." Butch looked at him helplessly. "What about the kitchen?"

"What about it?"

Butch said nothing but continued the look of helplessness. Ordinarily, Art would be rather irritated by that, but he was just too numb.

Butch eventually realized that assumed helplessness wasn't moving the conversation where he wanted, so he switched to logic. "You've done all this, you might as well finish up the kitchen."

"Butch, I'm leaving."

"Leaving?" Butch was genuinely surprised. "Where you going?"

"I... don't know. But I'm not staying here."

Butch threw out 'what-for?' hands. "Why not? It's not a bad place. I mean, after all you've done to fix it up. Sure, the walls are crap but we'll get those replaced. With my help, we'll get the kitchen in, too, and this place will be real decent."

Art looked at him. "I am not staying here."

"Well, what about Rich? You just got him enrolled and it looks like he's taking to it pretty good. You gonna disrupt that?"

Another sensation quickly pushed the numbness aside: anger. "That's my business," he snapped, "Not yours. And in case you're still not getting it. Neither Rich nor I are staying here."

"So, what then?" By the way Butch waved his arms around, he was apparently feeling a degree of anger himself. "Where you going to go? Back to New Jersey? You can't do that."

"Huh?" Art narrowed at him. "Why can't I do that?"

"Because." Butch made a helpless gesture at the envelope

sticking out of Art's pocket.

"You know about this?"

"Well, yeah."

Art was incredulous. "How the fuck do you know about this? And if you knew it was coming, why didn't you warn me?"

"Everyone knew about it," Cindy said from the kitchen doorway.

Art pivoted. She stood there smoky, dangerous, and regarding him with deadly eyes. Medusa. Harpy.

Art threw his hands up. "Great. Fine. Wonderful. I'm down here doing this shit for you two, and you stab me in the back."

"You stabbed yourself," she said.

Here we go, the two of them ganging up on him again, just like when they were kids, and he was pinned, helpless, a bug struggling against the spike holding it to velvet, an object of critical examination. His face darkened. "I am not staying here," he hissed at her.

She shrugged. "Why not? Like Butch said, get the kitchen done, and it won't be that bad."

He smirked at her. "So I guess that means you're moving in, too?"

The murder came back on her like a landslide. "No," was all she said.

"Why not?" he mimicked her tone. "Once the kitchen's done, it won't be that bad. You can keep an eye on the place all you want then. Right from inside. Not the sawdust pile."

Her look escalated into Black Death and, for a moment, Art was sure she would grow claws and fangs and rend him. But, after a moment, she settled, gave him a dismissive once-over and then focused on Butch. "Come on," she said, head-gesturing out of the door.

Butch obediently followed her. Art stepped into the doorway and watched them walk towards Cindy's car. "Whar y'all gowen?" he called in his best redneck.

"Lowe's," Cindy spoke without turning. "Order a new kitchen."

"Lowe's, huh?" Art rocked back and forth, "Say hi to Dave for me."

Cindy ignored him and got in, looking impatiently at Butch who wavered between the car and the porch. "Shouldn't you take a shower first?" Art asked him.

"Get in," Cindy ordered and Butch rushed around the car to the passenger side.

"You don't even know what sizes to get," Art said to her.

"We'll figure it out." She started the car.

Art stepped down to the patio. "Be sure you hire someone to install the kitchen. Caleb, maybe. Or another one of your boyfriends. Maybe the sawdust pile kid can help. Oh, and don't forget a water heater. Cold showers get old. But, in your case, might be the ticket."

She was flat, unresponsive as she backed down the driveway. Art followed, sticking to the front of the car. "I won't be here when you get back," he called.

She was in the road. The car paused and the two of them turned to him. For a moment, caught in the windshield glare, they looked like hitmen. Then she sped off towards Enterprise.

"I WON'T," he called after, but knew they didn't hear.

He looked back at the house. "Won't," he whispered.

Friday afternoon

He packed in record time, even Rich's stuff, even some of Butch's things, like the tent and a smaller stove and extra sleeping bags and an ice chest and some food. Art had to live out of the truck for a while and needed Butch's stuff to support that. Only fair; Butch now had a house, courtesy of Art, so reciprocity required some trade of assets, whether Butch knew about it or not. But jeez, how in the heck did Butch get all this crap in that crap Ford of his? Stowing it in the Ram had turned into another game of Tetris but, lookee lookee, all done, all packed in a reasonable and pleasing manner allowing for quick unloading at rest stops and out-of-the-way picnic areas.

As soon as Rich steps off the bus, we go.

Where?

That was a good question. Back to New Jersey was the first and best option. Rich could resume his former schooling and have the Alabama taint washed from his brains. Art threatens Conrad and gets his job back and sweet talks her and gets her back and maybe even moves into her place, obviating the need for living out of the truck. And then spend the next few years fighting with, and losing to, Linda.

Might be fun.

But something cold stirred inside when he considered this prospect. Fighting with Linda turns him into a raving, slobbering beast of hate and pity and he'd eat Rich alive and butcher everyone else's souls and be this object of scorn and ridicule at work and home and play. All his friends choose sides and, given the evidence, it wouldn't be his. He'd lose his immortal soul. Like he had one to lose in the first place, but he'd like to keep whatever modicum of humanity he had left. Besides, New Jersey had only been a way station. A thirty-year way station, but one, nonetheless.

So, where?

No, no, no, not here. He wasn't going to stay here. He said he wasn't, and he wasn't.

Question remains, bud.

Art leaned against the truck gate and tilted his head back and regarded the clear blue sky. Wherever he chose to go, it would need clear blue skies stretching forever so that, when he finished a day's work at whatever crap job he ended up with, he could stand next to the backhoe or bulldozer or tractor and see all the way around the world, see trouble coming long before it reached him.

What had vistas like that? Nebraska, flat to all horizons, a gopher hole about the only thing breaking up the view, or so he had heard. Wyoming, views of far mountains that were a barrier to California...

California. Hmm.

Art took in a long breath of disturbed air and considered California. It was New Jersey on a different coast: ocean and boardwalks, lots of crazy people, and lots of beautiful babes. Lots of drugs and Commies, too, but that was everywhere these days. Fairly expensive, but he supposed that would depend on where he lived. Forget San Francisco; he wouldn't fit in. Art liked women too much. Forget LA; place was Philadelphia on meth and Art really didn't like Philadelphia all that much, except for the Eagles and occasional shows. Butch had visited Monterey once and said it was the most beautiful place he'd ever seen. Wonder if that was during the time he lived with Dale or later. Wasn't Clint Eastwood the mayor there or something? Might be worth checking out.

Art patted the truck. Five days to get there, four or five nights sleeping in the back of the beast here, figure an additional week of sleeping in Butch's tent before he found a place to live... unless he could find Dale. "Hi! Remember me? We're brother and sister! Can I live in your garage?" He chuckled. That would go over well. He didn't even know what Dale's last name was anymore, or where in California she had ended up. But, once he got a place and a job, he could go look for her.

Give him something to do.

Art pulled the petition out of his back pocket and read it again. According to this, in a few weeks, he had to be in a Mt. Holly courtroom to sit across a well-made-and-polished oak table and glower at Linda and her lawyer as they listed his sins (which could take a while) and then divvied him up.

What would happen if he didn't show?

Well, no doubt, the granting of a divorce and the seizing of assets but, really, how painful would that be? His assets were all pretty much right here in the truck, although he would sorely miss his motorcycle and trailer and big power tools.

Eh, replaceable.

Whatever was in the house and outside the house and, hell, the house itself, Linda could help herself to, although how she'd hang onto the house and all its accoutrements without his grudging salary from Conrad, that twat, he couldn't figure. Which meant she'd have a lot of incentive to find him and garnish everything, up to and including a pint of blood.

So don't be found.

Art considered that. It was a big country. Linda had small assets. There was a very good chance he could relocate to an obscure corner where Linda's limited assets could not penetrate. That would necessitate abandoning certain identifying information, like his social security number (will have to work under the table, which had an extra benefit: no tax payments) and name.

Abandon his name.

Art slowly turned and regarded the house. He had read somewhere, during the time he thought casual reading sufficient enough entertainment to waste his time on, that the ancients believed power resided in the names of things. Some of the old myths he'd skimmed involved elves or fairies or some such crap trying to discover each other's monikers so they could gain control over each other. Rumpelstiltskin. Yeah, like that.

So, if you abandon the name, its power is gone. Its curse, too.

Art cocked his head, visualizing the black power flowing out of the house like tar, an evil grasping sludge that overwhelmed him and pulled him down, screaming, into depths unplumbed for millions of years until some noxious tide threw up the discards for some future millennium to scrutinize. Abandon the name, the tide cannot find you. He cannot be held to account. He can be born anew.

Was that possible?

It depended on the old 'nature or nurture' argument. If the curse was permanently attached to his DNA, a consequence of Dad's momentary spurt of lust, gasp of satisfaction, and roll over and go to sleep, then he could change his name to Rumpelstiltskin and still be the same bitter, grousing, vindictive-eyed asshole he had been his whole life. All a name change did, then, was make it more difficult for Linda to find him. Not a bad thing in itself.

But if it was a matter of conditioning, then he could simply decide not to be an asshole.

Art fished around for a cigarette and pulled one out, lit it, all the time watching the house. Decide to be someone else, just get over it, despite the decades of training. Hadn't we already tried this exercise? Well, no, that earlier effort concerned the past; this was the future, so why not? Change his ever-present darkness for one of light. Not like one of those silly holy boys singing in a pew somewhere, or walking around knocking on doors to see if you'd heard from Jesus lately – Butch, *por ejemplo* – but a guy who simply sees the upside. Say you're living in South Dakota and working on a ranch and avoiding process servers but hey, it's a beautiful day filled with sunshine and fresh air and maybe we'll have a good crop this year, Hiram. Or the pigs will foal real good, or whatever pigs did. Right, Hiram?

Is that what Butch did, woke up one morning and decided he was no longer an asshole? Because, face it, he was a gigantic dick in high school and after, a crazy one, running around until all hours of the night with his even crazier friends, rumors of drug dealing and the attendant violence hanging about him, as well as rumors of getting some girl pregnant with a subsequent abortion, and the girl's relatives and some rival dealers and maybe some people who felt that Butch had not held up his end were all converging and that's why Butch joined the Air Force, one step ahead of warrants and dismemberment and burial in a shallow grave somewhere in the Barrens.

Which was odd: Butch wasn't the criminal type, and Art wondered if a death wish had driven him in that direction. Almost got that wish, but then off to the Air Farce. And then became a preacher boy.

Decided not to be an asshole. Like deciding to get over it.

But...

Here Butch is, in some kind of trouble that smells suspiciously like the same kind of trouble that Dad was always in, trying to restore the house with its tars and swamps and black, black curses. Perhaps Butch was now its keeper, shrouded in his moon-and-star robe, the key to the crypt hanging around his neck, one gleaming eye watching fearfully as things stirred in the depths, his familiar, Cindy, watching from the edge of the witch woods.

Not exactly a good argument for nurture.

Well, he could always try the willpower route and put on a happy face. Art regarded the cigarette. If it meant giving these up, though, forget it.

So, about resigned to things, are we?

Art let out a long slow stream of Raleigh. Yes, we are. He was on the verge of taking off for places he had never been to start a completely new life. Leaving everything behind. His world. His past. His future. And it was all his own doing. No series of dust storms rendered the homestead untillable, forcing him to pack the family into an open-back truck and head for the grapes of California. No army of Aryans marched across his homeland putting his relatives into ovens and he must flee into the night and furtive hiding, eyes turned towards the Promised Land.

No. These were self-inflicted wounds.

Art looked at the house again. All the events of his life had led, inexorably, to this point. Well, not all the events: Oklahoma didn't count; he was just a stupid kid there and his decisions were limited to things like sneaking Reddi-wip out of the fridge without getting caught. Hardly life-altering. But from the screened-in porch over thereon, every decision he had made had led him to being a fifty-year-old loser sans necessary pieces of paper, whose entire life was now reduced to what he could pack into a truck, albeit a nice one. He'd have to prove over and over again to any prospective employer that he, at an age where everything hurt, at an age where he should be running the company, not running the company's bulldozer, had the skills to do the required jobs, and prove it with a barely contained desperation spurring the boss, that twat, to offer him part-time without benefits, below minimum wage, and Art had to take it. Desperately. Gratefully.

He was now one of those pathetic old veterans on street corners, no longer useful, ridiculous old uniforms torn and faded and proof of bad decisions made from a previous position of advantage. His had been a similar decline, a slow spin from the edge of Charybdis to its life-ending center, pulled down to drown, while, admittedly, somewhat enjoying the ride.

And it all started here. Because of something Butch and Cindy, under Dad's direction, had buried next to the pool.

Art pitched the cigarette down the driveway and wheeled away from the truck and marched into the yard, past the washhouse. Yep, there's the shovel, right where he'd dropped it and, yep, there's a hickory branch low enough for him to bang into at night.

Gingerly, Art rubbed the goose egg. So much for ghosts. There are no ghosts here. There's something tangible instead, the source of all his life's evil, and all he had to do was dig it up.

And gain redemption.

He blinked. Was that true? Would the weight lift, the darkness flee, light and realization pour into his soul when his shovel struck the terrible secret of the pool, like in a Hardy Boys mystery? He wasn't really an asshole, no, not at all, but a victim tossed by invisible tides, thinking he was in control when something else had moved him this whole time, an iron mass under the ground here pulling his compass off north, his path drifting a few degrees from center until he was lost without realizing it. He'd paid the retribution for a dark deed he didn't know about.

No, he was really an asshole. But it'd be nice to find out why.

Art retrieved the shovel and made his umpteenth slow pace around the pool's perimeter, checking, again, the view against the kitchen window. Had to be right here, and, for the umpteenth time, he tapped the ground with the shovel. Right. Here.

Is it?

Things change their perspective over the years and he had been a kid and short and it had been raining and he could be wrong by feet. Even wrong by inches meant fruitless digging because he had no idea what he was looking for. Something big? Something small?

A body?

Art jammed the tip of the shovel into the ground, leaving it upright, then walked back to the house and up the porch and into the kitchen and scrunched down until he was ten and looking over the edge of the (non-existent) sink and it was dark and raining and what the heck where those guys doing out there?

It *was* raining.

Surprised, Art rose to adult height and rubbed his eyes, thinking this was more hickory-branch-induced hallucinating but no, it was actually raining. He hadn't noticed clouds building, although there had been an odd cast to the breeze, something stirring somewhere. Well, here it is. And he had left the truck open.

Muttering, he ran outside and closed the top of the bed lid, noting with renewed satisfaction how he had packed everything with more than enough clearance. The rain was light, quiet, a washing, and Art peered towards the pool. The shovel had fallen, and he walked and stood over it, the handle lying on a spot exactly on the perimeter's arc.

Right here, it said.

Art stubbed an 'X' with his heel, a task made easier by the rain, noting this heel X was next to the heel mark he'd made last night, further sign of divine favor, and picked up the shovel and leaned the blade into the X and it sank easily, almost with relief. Signs and portents.

He dug, cooled by a nice drizzle, the clay softened by it, the way made easier. He dug outwards first, about a four-foot circumference to increase the chances of hitting whatever was down here, and then excavated, taking a layer at a time so that the hole would be even all the way across. Like an archeologist looking for Amenhotep.

"Dad, what are you doing?"

Art looked up. He was about calf-deep in the hole now, pretty good going, and he wiped rain out of his eyes. Rich stood at the edge of the hole, holding his backpack over his head to keep the rain off. "Go get a shovel," he said, pointing at the washhouse. "And give me a hand."

"What?" Rich, incredulous. "It's raining!"

"You're not sugar," Art reasoned, "So you won't melt."

"But..." Rich cocked an insubordinate head. "It's raining!"

Art straightened. "Get the shovel."

Rich's jaw set and he flushed, but turned and headed towards the house. "I'm gonna put my backpack inside first before all my stuff gets soaked," he grumped over his shoulder.

"Put it in the truck instead," Art called after him

"Huh?" Rich pirouetted, suspicious. "Why?"

Asshole mode, or being-of-light mode? Art weighed both, and opted for light. "We're leaving. After we do this." He tapped the squishy hole.

"Are we going back to New Jersey?"

Such a hopeful tone. Again, crush it like an asshole, or leave a glimmer of light? "Faster you get a shovel, sooner we can go." Okay, quasi-asshole, but the light flickered there in Rich's instantly alive eyes and the kid threw the backpack into the cab and had a shovel back at the hole in what was probably world record time. At least for Rich.

"So what are we doing?" the hopeful tone remained.

Art dug an exploratory inch with his blade. "We're looking for something."

"What?"

Art paused, about to say he didn't know. After a moment he said, "Talisman."

Rich's eyebrows rose and he took the far point of the hole and, after some adjustments, the two of them were in self-supporting positions. "Don't just dig and throw dirt," Art instructed, "Take it out in layers, like I'm doing." He showed Rich the technique. "Think of it as treasure hunting, not well digging."

"Okay," Rich said and bent to it.

Art marveled at himself for a moment. Look at that, you just taught him something without screaming, without expecting him to have mastered an untried skill before he had even touched the shovel. Or screwdriver. Or boat sander.

Right, Dad?

It got darker but the rain stayed at a drizzle, still cooling, still helpful, although the clay stuck to the blades now. But it flung off easily, so even that wasn't an issue.

As though they were getting help.

Art glanced around for a shadow standing on the wood line, but nothing. He shrugged and went back to it.

He lost track of time, the clouds obscuring the sun's progress but it was still daylight; at least there was sufficient cloud glow they could see what they were doing. Rich was actually helpful and Art looked at him, bent to it, concentrating. Be a shame to disappoint the kid when this was over. Sorry, not New Jersey. Monterey. Or the Black Hills.

A set of headlights brightened the driveway. "Oh good!" Rich said, "Now Uncle Butch can help."

"It may not be good," Art said, leaning on his shovel and watching the light advance.

"Why not?"

"Because the dragon does not want his treasure stolen."

"Huh?" Rich puzzled at him but Art kept on the driveway. Lights off, engine off, car doors slamming and Butch and Cindy, drizzle-hidden, hustling up the porch. "We're over here!" Rich called out.

The two of them paused and Art saw them spasm and look at each other and they rushed over and were at the edge of the hole.

"What the HELL are you doing?" Cindy, ferocious, burning, the drizzle coming off her like steam.

"Digging a pool," Art said, watching Butch.

"Is that what we're doing?" Rich asked, "I thought we were treasure hunting."

Cindy looked at the kid, aghast, then back to Art. "Stop, right now."

"No," Art said, still watching Butch.

"You have no RIGHT!" she took a murderous step towards him, stamping the ground with an angry heel.

Art gave her a warning glance before returning to Butch. "I have every right in the world," he said.

"No, you DON'T!" and she made a grab at Rich's shovel but Art pushed his blade at her face and she reared back. Rich, astonishment turning to fear, looked between them, his head swiveling like a tennis spectator.

"Get out of the hole," Butch said quietly.

Art gripped his shovel. "No."

"Get. Out. Of. The. Hole."

"No."

The expected Hulk came raging up but Art timed it perfectly, stepping into it: *Whack!* He stroked the side of Butch's head with the flat of the shovel and Butch flew, literally flew, off his feet and about a yard away, landing on his back like a sack of wet cement. Cindy and Rich both screamed at him, but Cindy's turned to one of outrage as Art smoothly reversed the shovel on the backswing and cut her ankles out from under her with the handle, all in one motion. Another bag of wet cement.

Not bad.

"Are you CRAZY?" Rich shrieked at him and stepped back against the hole wall to increase the distance, convinced that Dad was, yes, crazy and about to blade-slap him, too, Rich's shovel swinging down in a spasmodic and uncoordinated effort at self-defense...

Thunk.

It was like a whistle in a football game. They both froze, then looked. Rich's shovel was against the side of the hole. He lifted it up and down in a sawing motion and it sounded as if he were rubbing wood, or at least something that wasn't clay or rock. Art moved forward and Rich stepped away, not scared, curious. Art squatted and used his blade to scrap at the wall. Yes, something wooden, a big box of some kind, but with metal edges. Art squinted in the drizzle. Man, this thing looked familiar...

Of course. Dad's footlocker. The one he brought back from Dubya Dubya Too.

"What is it?" Rich asked, squatting beside him.

"Pandora's box," Art said, leveraging dirt away from it, joined moments later by a wary Rich.

"Don't," Cindy said above him.

Art looked up, gripping the shovel ready for another swing but there was no need. He had never seen Cindy look so stricken, so grieved. She was crying full tears now, something he had not seen since... when? On the Greyhound winding its way across the southern landscapes, farther and farther from Alabama to the fabled lands of Jersey? Probably.

"Just don't," she said again.

"What's inside, Cindy?" he asked.

"Please."

"What is it?" Art stayed on her, stone-faced.

"Just cover it back up." Pleading.

Rich, round-eyed, looked between them, frightened. "Maybe we should, Dad," he said, staring at the half-uncovered box. No doubt, he took that Pandora comment seriously.

"Move," Art ordered, thumbing him up and out of the hole. Rich scrambled next to Cindy, looking at her and then at the prone figure of Butch, still and drizzle-soaked, behind them. "Attend to him," Art ordered and Rich hastily stepped over and knelt next to the unconscious bag of wet cement.

Art measured Cindy: she was submissive, unresponsive, and Art wondered about that. Nothing had that kind of power over her. This box must be filled with kryptonite. He grabbed a handle sticking out of the side of the box and pulled, but it broke off in his hand, taking its backing with it. Hadn't done very well buried in clay for forty-odd years, had it?

What did?

Art dug a platform under the bottom of the box and then used the shovel to fulcrum it out of the suction. It dropped at his feet, half of it still on the ledge, and he grabbed the bottom of it and walked it out of the hole and onto the lip, the box staying mostly intact through this. He stood, rubbing the clay off his hands with the drizzle, staring down at it. It suddenly got darker and Art scrutinized the lowering clouds.

A bolt of lightning about now would be perfect.

"Dad," Rich said, "I think he's dead." He gestured helplessly at Butch, who did look dead.

"He's not dead," Art said, now scrutinizing the box top. Nothing there. No Templar inscription, no Latin words of warning. No cross and garlic. "Go get my flashlight out of the truck."

Rich looked over at him, worried, but then headed off.

Cindy stood quietly, tears and drizzle raining down, defeated, deflated, not looking at the box but at him, the plea on her face. Art blinked.

"Walk away," a voice whispered in one ear. "Don't," another voice whispered from behind him and Art whirled, ready for combat, but there was no one there. "Open it," still another voice back in his ear. Or maybe it was the wind.

Walk away.

Be the light, or be the dark? Look at your sister, your raging, stricken, tough, vulnerable, fearless and broken, sister. This box broke her forty years ago and now, now, you break her again. If you open it. If you don't, if you re-bury it, you save her. Be the light. Save her.

But then I am lost. Butch, lying dead over there, is lost. We don the moon-and-star robes and wear the key and guard the crypt for the rest of our lives, sit vigil on a box sealed with silver and hawthorn, the thing inside scratching at the lid. We wander the vampire woods and ghost-plagued ridge casting fearful glances at the sunken mound where nothing grows, the sound of bony fingers drifting on the miasmic wind and we chase away the jackals and vultures and huddle around a midnight candle and read incantations and burn parchments... and we rot. We rot.

Or...

We meet the wagon at the crossroads and drive off the Magyars and dash the coffin of earth and damnation to the ground and the lid shatters and the thing, the undead, slavering thing inside rolls into the sunlight and it burns, burns, the holy light exposing it, cleansing it.

Freeing us, Cindy.

Breaking the chains, Cindy.

Those chains pulled taut, link by link, as Butch floundered around the country and the world seeking redemption and Art floundered blind and stupid through roadside ditches fog-bound and bewildered and they both sat up in their overgrown cemetery plots and they were both. Back. Here. Like you, Cindy, stalking the trail, skirting the woods and peering fearfully at a sunken mound to see if a bony hand gripped its edge and Cindy, to break the chain. Throw the box to the ground. Let the red-eyed leech inside burn.

Rich came up, handed him the flashlight and then stepped back, staring at the box with trepidation. Maybe he heard bony fingers. Art glanced at Cindy, who remained in full plead, and then he dropped the shovel and reached to where the front hasp should be. An old Stanley padlock, still intact, surprise. He grabbed the shovel and one punch with the blade and the lock was no more. He dug his fingers under the lid and yanked. Half of it came apart in his grip and fell back in the hole, but it was open.

Art braced for a demon's claw reaching up and eviscerating

him, or a Jack-in-the-box, making this one of the most long-term elaborate pranks in history, but only a rise of clay and mustiness. He looked up and braced, expecting that revelatory bolt of lightning, but it was just sad mournful drizzle. He snapped on the light.

Plastic. A lot of it, almost filling the container and Art bobbed his way past the reflected light to make it out. Looked like drop sheets, the kind used to cover the floor during a paint job and yes, there were streaks of yellow paint all through it...

Oh man. The plastic drop sheets he and Butch had used when they were sanding and painting the boat. "Great," he muttered.

"What is it?" Rich moved closer but Art waved him back irritably. Dad didn't go to all this trouble just to hide big sheets of plastic. Working your kids to exhaustion and numbness wasn't considered abuse back then (and maybe not even now), so there was no need to hide the evidence. No, the plastic covered something else, something so terrible that, even back in the good ole days, it was a crime.

Art squatted next to the box and brought the flashlight against the plastic, eliminating the reflection and illuminating the interior. Yes. There. A bedsheet in the middle of the plastic, stained by old fluids. The sheet conformed perfectly to the shape of a body. A small body. A child.

"Oh, no," Rich whispered in horror and scrambled away, ready to flee should the sheet and plastic stir and the hellspawn within come tearing out, eyes red and savage, seeking blood.

But Art knew it wouldn't. It was not a devil.

It was a fallen angel.

He looked up. Cindy stood bare, judged, the drizzle unable to wash away the sin. All of her power gone, because Art had discovered her name.

"Whose?" he asked, but it was a stupid question. He already knew.

"Mine," she toned.

"And?" But he knew the answer to that, too, knew it all along, just like the ghost child, whose genesis was here in plastic and sheet and clay, had told him, long-repressed memories and denials now flooding his mind: Mom, so distant, so beaten; furtive night movements and sounds unexplained; Cindy crying for no reason at certain times of the day; Cindy running away right after Butch rearranged Locker's knee; Cindy getting all of them to flee up the side of the road in a rain so very similar to this one.

"Dad's," she said.

"Ready?"

Rich said nothing, merely nodded, a motion registering on Art's peripheral vision, sufficient enough that he didn't need to snarl a Dad remark along the lines of, "You better answer me, boy!"

Creature of light. Be a creature of light.

Because, God knows, Rich had seen enough creatures of darkness these last few days.

The kid was still incapable of speech. Art understood that. He was reeling, too. This was how the survivors of Hiroshima felt. Without the burns, of course.

Somehow, he and Cindy had gotten the still unconscious Butch to the Enterprise Hospital and, somehow, managed to get him admitted without too much suspicion, even though "fell off the roof" didn't match his injuries. "Looks like he got hit with a shovel," the ER doc said and Art was amazed he'd read the physical evidence so clearly. How do murderers think they're ever going to get away with it?

Art gazed at the night-shrouded filled-in hole. Because, they do.

Cindy had elected to stay by Butch's side, less out of sisterly concern than the need to brief him when he awoke. If he awoke. The doc wasn't so sure. Which would be a huge shame, not only for the manslaughter charge Art faced but because Butch was as much a victim of all this as anyone.

In between dodging the doctor and his increasingly suspicious questions, Cindy told Art the story, in dribs and drabs:

Dad had been at her for years.

Mom knew. Said nothing. Did nothing.

Cindy got pregnant.

When she began to show, Locker said that unfortunate thing and got his knee snapped. She and Shorty, having similar Dad problems, ran away, heading towards an Atlanta back-alley abortionist they'd heard about when the staties caught up with them. She said nothing; this was Alabama. Sometime the following October, she gave premature birth. Butch helped.

Art, for the life of him, could not figure out where he had been when that happened because it was in the upstairs garage room and that was his bedroom and he should have been there, too. But, he could not remember anything like that. Could not remember Cindy feverish and wrapped in sheets for a week after, while Butch attended her and the preemie and Dad kept going to work and Mom kept making dinner, and the whole thing was just a blank.

But, at some point, Dad decided the preemie was too risky and he smothered it and made the two of them help bury it.

And all Art had was a flitting image seen through a wavy, rain-drenched pane.

How is that possible?

Art took in a long, deep breath and stared in the direction of the former hole. There is no way any of this could happen without him having some idea of it, even though he was just an idiot kid and naive and stupid and obtuse and things sailed right over his head. He should remember things like Cindy missing school because she was fighting off an infection.

And a preemie screaming to be fed. Until Dad decided to stop it.

"I would have heard," Art muttered to the windshield.

Rich looked at him. "What?"

Well, the kid is capable of speech again, thank God. "Nothing," Art said, even though Rich deserved to be part of his internal dialogue because he had been part of the aftermath. Had helped get Butch into Cindy's car. Had remained silent in the ER. And had helped re-bury the locker in the rain-soaked dark when he and Art came back in Cindy's car. How Cindy was getting back, Art didn't know and didn't care. She shouldn't come back here. No one should. There's only monsters here.

Like me, Art thought.

Because he *was* a monster. He heard the baby's cries, had to have, but, like Mom, chose not to hear. Or remember. He walked around those three months with his mouth and eyes and ears closed, numb, shaking, avoiding everyone and everything because to call it out was to call out the blood, the murder, the horror of it, and risk your own rain-soaked appointment with a shallow hole dug under the pool.

That's why Mom had left. Not to visit her sick grandparents; to silence the screams of her grandchild/stepdaughter (half-daughter)? And that's why the rest of them ran away, too, because Dad would eventually put them in holes if they didn't. And that's why Art had been an asshole his whole life.

He was an accomplice to murder. Child murder. Fratricide, or... what was the word for sister murder? Sorority-cide?

Oh, not in any way that would get him convicted. No. He could make a very convincing defense based on his age and stupidity and distressing inability to remember anything. But he was guilty just the same, because he knew. Although he could not cite one single detail, he knew.

"I knew," he said.

Rich still looked at him, still silent. "I knew," Art told him and the air and God, "even though I didn't. I knew enough. And I've been punished for it all this time." He paused, turning in the seat and gazing at the house. "The house," he toned, "the house."

It was a tomb, a reliquary. A crypt. The crypt keepers, Butch and Cindy, had attended it all these years, washing the bones. They had wandered about New Jersey and, in Butch's case, the world, trying to live but murderers deserve no life and they were shifted onto side tracks and abandoned, every once in a while walking up this driveway to look for redemption but there was none.

And the chains had finally dragged Butch back to sit vigil.

No one should sit vigil on Moloch's altar.

Art got out of the truck, Rich watching him, fearful, but he waved a reassuring hand. It will be all right. He lifted the bed lid and fished around with the flashlight and found what he needed and closed it and walked up the porch and inside and, a few moments later, back down the porch and put everything back in the bed and slid into the truck. He started it and put it in reverse and drifted to the end of the driveway, almost half in the road, where he could see the house, and stopped. And looked.

Black on black, the House of Usher against the night, and saw motion, a wafting up near the far eave.

Smoke. Waddya know, a leak. Shoulda fixed that, and he almost laughed. It would take about an hour before the place was completely engulfed, but he'd be long gone. He doubted anyone else would see it. Or call the fire department, if they did.

After all, it was a haunted house.

Art peered hard at a flicker of motion in the rearview mirror, but it was too dark. He could swear, though, just swear, that some kid was up in the pines on the ridge waving at him. He suppressed an urge to wave back.

Instead, he backed into the road, the truck pointed towards Enterprise without his intention. So, that way.

"Where are we going?" Rich asked.

Art considered. "Magic Land," he said, and put it in drive.

ABOUT THE AUTHOR

D. Krauss currently resides in the Shenandoah Valley. He's been a cottonpicker, a sod buster, a surgical orderly, the guy who paints the little white line down the middle of the road, a weatherman, a gun-totin' door-kickin' lawman, a layabout, and a bus driver, in that order.

Website:
http://www.dustyskull.com

Goodreads:
https://bit.ly/3bkPDCm

YouTube: Old Guy Reviews Books
https://bit.ly/3y3KHLY

MeWe: dkrauss

OTHER BOOKS BY D. KRAUSS

The Frank Vaughn Trilogy
Frank Vaughn, Killed by His Mom
Southern Gothic
Looking for Don

The Partholon Trilogy
Partholon
Tu'An
Col'm

The Ship Trilogy
The Ship to Look for Good
The Ship Looking for God
The Ship Finding God

Story Collections
The Moonlight in Genevieve's Eyes
and other Strange Stories
The Last Man in the World Explains All
and other strange tales

www.ingramcontent.com/pod-product-compliance
Lightning Source LLC
Chambersburg PA
CBHW050308110726
47899CB00007B/2156